PRAISE FOR *REGRETTING YOU*

"Betr... ...pages turning in th... ...Hoover at her very ... ...starred review

"A poignant, addictive read."

—*People Magazine*

"There is plenty of trademark Hoover emotion and surprises in this engrossing read . . . This twisting novel will instigate excellent book discussions about regrets and second chances."

—*Booklist*

"The emotions run high, the conversations run deep, and the relationships ebb and flow with grace."

—*Kirkus Reviews*

"A fantastically raw story about love, grief, and family."

—HelloGiggles

"Colleen Hoover's new novel delivers moments that are heartbreaking and heartfelt . . . a stirring mother-daughter story full of hope, loss, and great love."

—*Woman's World*

PRAISE FOR COLLEEN HOOVER

"What a glorious and touching read, a forever keeper. The kind of book that gets handed down."

—*USA Today* on *It Ends with Us*

"*Confess*, by Colleen Hoover, is a beautiful and devastating story that will make you feel so much."

—*Guardian*

"*It Ends with Us* tackles [a] difficult subject . . . with romantic tenderness and emotional heft. The relationships are portrayed with compassion and honesty, and the author's note at the end that explains Hoover's personal connection to the subject matter is a must-read. Packed with riveting drama and painful truths, this book powerfully illustrates the devastation of abuse—and the strength of the survivors."

—*Kirkus*, starred review

"Hoover joins the ranks of such luminaries as Jennifer Weiner and Jojo Moyes, with a dash of Gillian Flynn. Sure to please a plethora of readers."

—*Library Journal*, starred review, for *November 9*

"Hoover builds a terrific new-adult world here with two people growing in their careers and discovering mature love."

—*Booklist*, starred review, for *Ugly Love*

Layla

OTHER TITLES BY COLLEEN HOOVER

Heart Bones
Regretting You
Verity
All Your Perfects
Without Merit
Too Late
It Ends with Us
November 9
Confess
Ugly Love
Hopeless
Losing Hope
Finding Cinderella: A Novella

MAYBE SOMEDAY SERIES

Maybe Someday
Maybe Not: A Novella
Maybe Now

SLAMMED SERIES

Slammed
Point of Retreat
This Girl

Layla

COLLEEN HOOVER

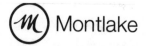 Montlake

Published by Montlake, Seattle

www.apub.com

Amazon, the Amazon logo, and Montlake are trademarks of Amazon.com, Inc., or its affiliates.

ISBN-13: 9781542000178
ISBN-10: 1542000173

Cover design by David Drummond

Printed in the United States of America

For Beckham. When I die, you'll be the first person I haunt. You are so much fun to scare.

The supernatural is the natural not yet understood.

—Elbert Hubbard

THE INTERVIEW

I placed two layers of duct tape over Layla's mouth before I came downstairs, but I can still hear her muffled screams as the detective takes a seat at the table.

He has the kind of old recorder you'd see in a movie from the eighties. It's about ten inches long and six inches wide with a big red circle on the left button. He presses it down with the play button and slides the recorder to the center of the table. The wheels on the cassette begin to rotate.

"Please state your name," he says.

I clear my throat. "Leeds Gabriel."

The battery compartment is held together with old duct tape running up the sides of the machine. I find it kind of humorous. This severely outdated machine is going to record every word I'm about to say, and that's somehow going to help?

At this point, I've all but given up. There's no light at the end of this tunnel. I'm not even sure there's an *end* to this tunnel.

How can I have hope for a way out of this when things have gotten so out of control? I'm speaking to a detective I met online while my girlfriend is upstairs, losing her damn mind.

As if she knows I'm thinking about her, the noise picks up again. The wooden headboard pounds against the wall upstairs, creating an eerie echo in this huge empty house.

"So," the man says. "Where do you want to start?" He seems like he'll be able to work through the noise, but I'm not sure I can. Knowing Layla is suffering because of my actions is not something I can easily ignore. Every sound coming from upstairs makes me flinch. "Why don't we start with how the two of you met," the man suggests.

I'm hesitant to respond to questions that I know won't lead to answers, but at this point, I'd rather hear my own voice than Layla's muffled screams. "We met here last summer. This used to be a bed and breakfast. I was the bass player in the band that played her sister's wedding."

The man doesn't respond. He leans back in his chair, staring at me quietly. I don't know what else to say. Am I supposed to elaborate on that? "How does meeting Layla relate to what's happening inside this house?"

He shakes his head as he leans forward, folding his arms across the table. "Maybe it doesn't. But that's why I'm here, Leeds. Anything could be a clue. I need you to go back to the first day you were here. What was Layla wearing? Why were you both here? What was the first thing she said to you? Did either of you notice anything out of the ordinary about the house that night? The more information you can give me, the better. No detail is too small."

I rest my elbows on the table and slide my palms over my ears to drown out the sounds Layla is making upstairs. I can't take hearing her upset like this. I love her so much, but I don't know that I can go back and talk about *why* I love her so much when I'm putting her through this.

I try not to think about how perfect things were in the beginning. When I do that, it solidifies the fact that I'm more than likely at fault for how it has all come to an end.

I close my eyes and think back to the first night I met her. Back when life was easier. When ignorance really was bliss.

"She was a terrible dancer," I say to the man. "It's the first thing I noticed about her . . ."

CHAPTER ONE

She's a terrible dancer.

It's the first thing I notice about her while I'm on the stage, playing to a dwindling crowd. Long arms she seems to have no idea how to control. She's barefoot, moving around in the grass, deliberately stomping her feet without any of the delicacy the song expects. She jerks her head wildly, and her unruly black curls sling back to front like she's jamming out to a heavy metal song.

What makes it funny is that this is a modern country band. A modern *bland* country band. An entire set of songs that is excruciating to listen to and is even more painful to play.

It's Garrett's Band.

That's literally what it's called. *Garrett's Band*. It's the best Garrett could come up with.

I'm the unofficial fourth member—the last one to join the band. I play bass. Not the kind of stand-up bass people respect. I play electric bass. The underrated, invisible instrument that's usually held by the invisible member of the band—the one that fades into the background of each song. I don't mind fading into the background, though. Maybe that's why I prefer electric bass over anything else.

After I studied music at Belmont, my goal was to be a singer-songwriter, but I don't help Garrett write these songs. He doesn't want the help. We don't have the same appreciation for music, so I just write songs for myself and hoard them for a future day when I'll be confident enough to release a solo album.

The band has gotten more popular over the last few years, and even though we're in more demand, which results in better pay, my rate as the bass player hasn't increased. I've thought about bringing it up to the rest of the band, but I'm not sure it's worth it, and they need the money more than I do. Not to mention, if I approach them, they might actually offer me an official spot in the band, and to be honest, I hate this music so much I'm embarrassed I'm even standing up here.

Every show eats away at my soul. A nibble here, a nibble there. I'm afraid if I keep doing this much longer, there won't be anything left of me but a body.

I'm honestly not sure what keeps me here. I never intended for this to be a permanent thing when I joined, but for whatever reason, I can't seem to get my ass in gear to step out on my own. My father died when I was eighteen, and as a result of his death, money has never been an issue. He left my mother and me a sizeable life insurance policy, along with an internet installation company that runs itself and employees who prefer I don't step in and change up years of practices that have been successful. Instead, my mother and I stay at a distance and live off the income.

It's definitely something I'm grateful for, but it's not something I'm proud of. If people knew how little was required of me in this life, I wouldn't be respected. Maybe that's why I've stayed with the band. It's a lot of travel, a lot of work, a lot of late nights. But the self-torture makes me feel I at least deserve a portion of what sits in my bank account.

I stand in my designated spot on the stage and watch the girl as I play, wondering if she's drunk or high, or if there's a chance she's out there dancing the way she is to poke fun at just how much this band sucks. Whatever the reason for her flailing around like a dehydrated fish, I'm thankful for it. It's the most entertaining thing to happen during a show in a while. I even catch myself smiling at one point—something

I haven't done in God knows how long. And to think I was dreading coming here.

Maybe it's the atmosphere—the privacy of the venue mixed with the aftermath of a wedding. Maybe it's the fact that no one is paying us any attention and 90 percent of the wedding party has left. Maybe it's the grass in the girl's hair and the green stains all over her dress from the three times she's taken a tumble during this song. Or maybe it's the six-month dry spell I've forced myself to endure since breaking up with my ex.

Maybe it's a combination of all those things that is making this girl my entire focus tonight. It's not surprising because even with makeup smeared down her cheeks and a couple of her curls matted to her forehead from sweat, she's the prettiest girl out here. Which makes it even stranger that no one is paying her any attention. The few remaining guests are gathered around the pool with the newly married couple while we play our last song for the night.

My terrible dancer is the only one still listening when we finally finish and then start packing up.

I hear the girl screaming *encore* as I walk to the back of the stage and put my guitar in the case. I close it in a hurry, hoping to hell I can find her once we get all the instruments loaded into the van.

The four of us have booked two rooms here at the bed and breakfast for the night. It's an eleven-hour drive back to Nashville, and none of us wanted to hit that at midnight.

The groom approaches Garrett as he's closing the doors to the van and invites us all over for a drink. Normally, I'd decline, but I'm kind of hoping the bad dancer stuck around. She was entertaining. And I liked the fact that she never mouthed a single lyric. I don't know that I could be attracted to a girl who actually likes Garrett's music.

I find her in the pool, floating on her back, still wearing the cream-colored bridesmaid dress with the grass stains all over it.

She's the only one in the pool, so after I grab a beer, I walk over to the deep end, kick off my shoes, and stick my legs in the water, jeans and all.

The ripples from the disturbance at my end of the pool eventually reach her, but she doesn't look up to see who has joined her in the water. She just keeps staring up at the sky, as quiet and still as a log floating on top of the water. Such a contrast to the ridiculous display she put on earlier.

After a few minutes of me watching her, the water envelops her entire body, and she's gone. When her hands push up and part the water and her head breaks through the surface, she's looking right at me, as if she knew I was here all along.

She keeps herself afloat with small movements of her feet and waves of her arms on top of the water. She slowly closes the gap between us until she's directly in front of my legs, staring up at me. The moon is behind me, her eyes reflecting its glow like two tiny light bulbs.

From the stage, I thought she was pretty. But from one foot in front of her, I see she's the most beautiful thing I've ever seen. Puffy pink lips, a delicate jawline I'm hoping I might get to run my hand across at some point. Her eyes are as green as the grass that surrounds the pool. I want to slide into the water with her, but my cell phone is in my pocket, and there's a half-full can of beer in my hand.

"Do you ever watch those YouTube videos of people dying inside?" she asks.

I have no idea why she asks that question, but anything could have come out of her mouth just now and it would have moved through me with the same strength those words just did. Her voice is wispy and light, like it floats effortlessly out of her throat.

"No," I respond.

She's a little out of breath as she works to keep herself afloat. "They're compilations of embarrassing things that happen to people. The camera always zooms in on people's faces at the worst moment.

Their expressions make it look like they're dying inside." She wipes water from her eyes with both hands. "That's what you looked like up there tonight. Like you were dying inside."

I don't even remember her looking up at the stage, much less eyeing me long enough to accurately assess how it feels every time I'm forced to play those shitty songs onstage.

"I'm already dead inside. Died the first night I started playing for the band."

"I thought so. Did you like my dancing? I was trying to cheer you up."

I nod and take a sip of the beer. "It worked."

She grins and slinks underwater for a few seconds. When she comes back up again, she wipes all her hair out of her face and says, "You got a girlfriend?"

"No."

"Boyfriend?"

"No."

"Wife?"

I shake my head.

"Do you have friends, at least?"

"Not really," I admit.

"Siblings?"

"Only child."

"Shit. You're lonely."

Another accurate assessment. Although in my case, lonely is a choice.

"Who is the most important person in your life?" she asks. "Parents don't count."

"Right now?"

She nods. "Yes. Right now. Who is the most important person in your life?"

I reflect on her question for a moment and realize there's no one I'd take a bullet for other than my mom. I'm indifferent toward the guys in the band. They're more like coworkers I have nothing in common with. And since parents don't count, this girl is literally the only person on my mind right now.

"I guess you," I say.

She tilts her head, narrowing her eyes. "That's kinda sad." She lifts her feet and kicks the wall between my legs, pushing away from me. "I better make this a good night for you, then." Her smile is flirtatious. An invite.

I accept her invite by placing my phone on the concrete next to the now-empty beer. I take off my shirt and watch her eye me as I slip the rest of the way into the pool.

We're at the same level now, and dammit if she didn't just get prettier somehow.

We swim around each other in a slow circle, careful not to touch, even though it's obvious we both want to.

"Who are you?" she asks.

"The bass player."

She laughs at that, and her laughter is the opposite of her wispy voice. It's deliberate and abrupt, and I might even like it more than her voice. "What's your *name*?" she clarifies.

"Leeds Gabriel." We're still swimming around each other in circles. She tilts her head and gives my name some thought.

"Leeds Gabriel is a front man kind of name. Why are you playing in someone else's band?" She keeps talking, apparently not really wanting an answer to that question. "Were you named after the town in England?"

"Yep. What's your name?"

"Layla." She whispers it like it's a secret.

It's the perfect name. The only name she could have said that would fit her—I'm convinced of that.

"Layla," someone says from behind me. "Open up." I look over my shoulder, and the bride is standing behind me, holding something out to Layla. Layla swims over to her, sticks out her tongue, and the bride places a small white pill in the center of it. Layla swallows and I have no idea what that was, but it was sexy as fuck.

She can see I'm transfixed by her mouth. "Leeds wants one," Layla says, reaching out her hand for another pill. The bride hands her another one and walks away. I don't ask what it is. I don't care. I want her so much I'll be the Romeo to her Juliet and take whatever the hell kind of poison she wants to put on my tongue right now.

I open my mouth. Her fingers are wet, and some of it has dissolved before it even hits my tongue. It's bitter and hard to get down without coating or water, but I manage it. I chew some of it.

"Who was the most important person in your life yesterday?" Layla asks. "Before I came along?"

"Myself."

"I've bumped you out of the number one spot?"

"Seems that way."

She moves fluidly and effortlessly onto her back, like she spends more time in a pool than on land. She stares up at the sky again, her arms stretched out wide, her chest rising with a huge intake of air.

I press my back against the side of the pool and stretch my arms out, gripping the concrete ledge. My heart is starting to pound. My blood feels thicker.

I don't know what kind of drug she gave me, probably Molly or some other kind of upper, because it's kicking in fast. I'm more aware of everything going on in my torso right now than any other part of my body. My heart feels swollen, like there isn't enough room for it.

Layla is still floating on her back, but her face is close to my chest. She's right in front of me. If I leaned forward a little, she wouldn't be looking at the sky. She'd be looking up at me.

Fuck, this is good shit.

I feel good. I feel confident.

The water is so calm around us it looks like she's floating on air. Her eyes are closed, but when the top of her head bumps against my chest, she looks up at me, her face upside down from mine, like she's expecting me to do something.

So I do.

I lean in just enough so that my mouth rests gently against hers. We kiss upside down, her bottom lip between both of mine. Her lips are like a soft explosion, igniting hidden minefields under every inch of my skin. It's weird and fascinating because she's still on her back, floating on top of the water. I dip my tongue into her mouth, and for whatever reason, I don't feel worthy enough to touch her, so I keep my arms where they are—gripping the pool on either side of me.

She keeps her arms outstretched, and the only thing she moves is her mouth. I'm thankful our first kiss is upside down because that leaves a hell of a lot of room to anticipate kissing her right side up for the first time. I'm never going to want to kiss a girl again without being high on whatever it is the bride gave us. It's like my heart constricts to the size of a penny and then balloons to the size of a drum with every beat.

It isn't beating like it's supposed to. There's no gentle *bom bom, bom bom, bom bom* anymore. It's a plink and a BOOM.

Plink BOOM, plink BOOM, plink BOOM.

I can't keep kissing her upside down like this. It's making me crazy, like we don't quite fit, and I want my mouth to fit perfectly against hers. I grab her waist and spin her on top of the water until she's facing me, and then I pull her to me. Her legs go around my waist, and both of her hands come up out of the water and grip the back of my head, which causes her to sink a little because now I'm the only thing keeping her above water. But my own arms are too busy sliding down her back, so we start to sink and neither of us does anything about it. Our mouths lock together right before we're submerged. Not a single drop of water passes between our lips.

We sink all the way to the bottom of the pool, still fused together. As soon as we hit bottom, we open our eyes at the same time and pull apart to look at each other. Her hair is floating above her now, and she looks like a sunken angel.

I wish I could take a picture.

Air bubbles cloud the space between us, so we both kick ourselves back to the top.

I break the surface two seconds before she does. We're facing each other, ready to start the kiss over again. We link together, back into the same position we were in. Our mouths seek each other out, but as soon as I taste the chlorine on her lips, we're interrupted by chants.

I can hear Garrett over several of the others, all cheering our kiss on from where they're seated. Layla glances behind her and flips them off.

She separates herself from me and pushes to the side of the pool. "Let's go," she says, pulling herself out of the water. She isn't graceful about it. She pushes up out of the deep end, five feet from the ladder, and has to roll onto the concrete to make it out of the pool. It's clumsy and perfect. I follow her, and a few seconds later, we're both running around to the side of the house where it's darker and more private. The grass is both cold and soft beneath my feet. Like ice . . . but melted.

I guess that would just make it water. But it doesn't feel like water. It feels like melted ice. *Drugs make things hard to explain.*

Layla grabs my hand and falls onto the melted ice-grass, pulling me down with her, on top of her. I hold myself up with my elbows so she can breathe, and I stare at her for a moment. She's got freckles. Not very many, and they're spread out over the bridge of her nose. A few on her cheeks. I lift my hand and trace them. "Why are you so pretty?"

She laughs. Rightfully so. That was cheesy.

She flips me onto my back, and then she pulls her dress up her thighs so she can straddle me. Her thighs suction to my sides because we're both sopping wet. I rest my hands on her hips and soak up the intensity of this high.

"Do you know why they call this place the Corazón del País?" she asks.

I don't know, so I just shake my head and hope it's a long story so I can hear her talk more than she has. I could listen to her voice all night. In fact, there's a room inside the bed and breakfast they call the Grand Room, and it's lined with hundreds of books on every wall. She could read to me all night.

"It translates to *Heart of the Country*," she says. There's excitement in her eyes and voice when she talks. "This location—this very piece of property you're lying on—is the literal geographical center of the contiguous United States."

Maybe it's because I'm very aware of my heartbeat right now, but that doesn't make sense. "Why would they call it that? The heart isn't really the center of the body. The stomach is."

She laughs her sharp, quick laugh again. "True. But *Estomago del País* doesn't sound as pretty."

Fuck. "You speak French?"

"Pretty sure that's Spanish."

"Either way, it was hot."

"I only took one year in high school," she says. "I have no hidden talents. What you see is what you get."

"I doubt that." I roll her off me and pin her wrists to the grass as I roll on top of her. "You're a talented dancer."

She laughs. I kiss her.

We kiss for the next several minutes.

We more than kiss. We touch. We move. We moan.

Everything is way too much—like I'm teetering on the edge of death. My heart just might literally explode in my chest. I'm starting to wonder if we should keep doing this. Drugs coupled with making out with Layla is one thing too much. I can't let her stay wrapped around me for another second, or I'll pass the fuck out from everything I'm feeling. It's like every nerve ending grew a nerve ending. I feel everything with double the magnitude.

"I have to stop," I whisper, unwrapping her legs from around me. "What the hell are we on? I can't breathe." I roll onto my back, gasping for air.

"You mean what did my sister give you?"

"The bride is your sister?"

"Yeah, her name is Aspen. She's three years older than me." Layla lifts herself up onto her elbow. "Why? Do you like it?"

I nod. "Yes. I love it."

"It's intense, right?"

"Fuck yes."

"Aspen gives it to me every time I drink too much." She leans in until her mouth is against my ear. "It's called aspirin." When she pulls back, the confusion on my face makes her grin. "Did you think you were high?"

Why else would I be feeling like this?

I sit up. "That wasn't an aspirin."

She falls onto her back in a fit of laughter, making a cross over her chest. "Swear to God. You took an *aspirin*." She's laughing so hard she has to fight to catch her breath. When she finally does, she sighs and it's delightful, and did I just fucking say *delightful?*

She shakes her head, looking up at me with a soft smile. "It's not drugs making you feel like this, Leeds." She stands up and makes her way around to the front of the house. Again, I follow her, because if that really was an aspirin, then I'm fucked.

I am fucked.

I didn't know another person could make me feel this good without some sort of substance running through my body.

Layla doesn't go to a bedroom once we're inside the house. She walks into the Grand Room, the one with all the books and the baby grand piano. When we're both inside, she closes the door and locks it. My jeans and her dress are leaving a trail of water behind us.

When I pause and turn to look at her, she's staring at the water pooling beneath my feet.

"The floors are old," she says. "We should respect them." She pulls her soaking wet dress over her head, and now she's standing in the dimly lit room five feet away from me in nothing but her bra and panties. They don't match. She's wearing a white bra and green-and-black-checkered panties, and I kind of love that she didn't put much thought into what she wore under her dress. I observe her for a moment—admiring her curves and the way she doesn't try to hide pieces of herself from me.

My last girlfriend had a body that could rival a supermodel's, but she was never comfortable with herself. It became one of the things that irritated me about her because no matter how beautiful she was, her insecurity was the loudest thing about her.

Layla carries herself with a confidence that would be attractive no matter what she looked like.

I do as she requested and remove my jeans, leaving on my boxers. Layla gathers our clothes and puts them on top of a rug that's probably worth more than the floors, but whatever makes her feel good.

I look around the room, and there's a brown distressed-leather couch against the wall next to the piano. I want to throw her on it and lose myself inside of her, but Layla has different plans.

She pulls the piano bench out and sits on it. "Can you sing?" she asks, poking at a few of the keys.

"Yes."

"Why don't you sing onstage?"

"It's Garrett's band. He's never asked me to."

"Garrett? Is that the lead singer's name?"

"That's the one."

"Is he as atrocious as his lyrics?"

That makes me laugh. I shake my head and join her on the bench. "He's pretty terrible, but he's not as bad as his lyrics."

She presses middle C on the piano. "Is he jealous of you?" she asks.

"Why would he be jealous of me? I'm just the bass player."

"He's not lead singer material. You are."

"That's a big statement. You've never even heard me sing."

"Doesn't matter. You could be terrible, but everyone else still fades into the background when you're onstage."

"Just like the rest of the crowd fades into the background when you're dancing?"

"I was the *only* one dancing."

"See? I didn't even notice."

She leans in after I say that, and I expect her to kiss me, but instead she whispers, "Play me something," against my mouth. Then she moves to the couch and lies down. "Play something worthy of that piano," she says.

She crosses her legs at her ankles and lets one of her arms dangle off the couch. She runs her finger against the hardwood floor while she waits for me to start playing, but I can't stop staring at her. I'm not sure there's another woman on this planet who could make me want to stare at her without blinking until my eyes dry up, but she's looking at me expectantly.

"What if you don't like my music?" I ask. "Will you still let me kiss you?"

She smiles gently. "Does the song mean something to you?"

"I wrote it using pieces of my soul."

"Then you have nothing to worry about," she says quietly.

I spin around on the bench and place my fingers on the keys. I hesitate for a moment before playing the song. I've never performed it for anyone before. The only person I've ever wanted to sing it for is my father, and he's no longer alive. His death is the reason I wrote this in the first place.

I've never been nervous while playing Garrett's songs onstage, but this feels different. This is personal, and despite the fact that there's only one person in the audience right now, it feels like the most intense audience I've ever performed for.

I fill my lungs with air and slowly release it as I begin to play.

That night I *stopped* believing in heaven

I can't believe in a god that cruel

Can you?

That night I stopped praying on my knees

But I don't pray standing either

Do you?

That night I closed the door and closed the window

I've been sitting in the dark

Are you?

That night I learned happiness is a fairy tale

A thousand pages read aloud

By you

That night I stopped believing in God

You were ours, he didn't care, he

Took you

So that night I stopped . . .

I stopped . . .

I just

Stopped.

That night I stopped.

I stopped.

I just stopped.

That night I stopped.

I . . .

When I'm finished playing the song, I fold my hands in my lap. I'm a little hesitant to turn around and look at her. The whole room got quiet after I played the last note. So quiet—it feels like all the sound was sucked out of the house. I can't even hear her breathing.

I close the cover to the piano and then slowly spin around on the bench. She's wiping her eyes, staring up at the ceiling. "Wow," she whispers. "I wasn't expecting that. I feel like you just stomped on my chest."

That's how I've felt since I first laid eyes on her tonight.

"I like how it ends," she says. She sits up on the couch and tucks her legs beneath her. "You just stop in the middle of the sentence. It's so perfect. So powerful."

I wasn't sure if she'd realize the intentional ending, but the fact that she does makes me all the more enamored of her.

"Where can I find the song? Is it on Spotify?"

I shake my head. "I've never released any of my own stuff."

She looks at me in mock horror, slapping the arm of the couch. "What? Why the hell not?"

I shrug. "I don't know." I honestly *don't* know. "Maybe because everyone in Nashville thinks they're a somebody. I don't want to be someone who thinks I'm a somebody."

She stands up and walks over to where I'm sitting on the piano bench. She pushes my shoulders until my back is leaning against the piano, and then she straddles me, both of her knees resting on the piano bench. I'm looking up at her now, and she's holding my face in her hands, her eyes narrowed as she speaks. "You're being selfish by keeping your songs to yourself. It's better to be a selfless somebody than to be a selfish nobody."

I think maybe I'm glad I met this girl.

Like *really* glad.

I grip the back of her head and bring her mouth to mine. I don't know what's happening here. It's been a hell of a long time since I've liked a girl enough to wonder where she's going to be the next day.

But . . . where will Layla be tomorrow?

Where was she yesterday?

Where does she call home?

Where did she grow up?

Who is *her* favorite person right now?

I want to know all the things. Everything.

Layla breaks our kiss. "Aspen warned me earlier tonight when she saw me staring at you. She said, *'Promise me you'll stay away from the musicians. They probably have chlamydia.'*"

I laugh. "Did you promise her you'd stay away from me?"

"No. I said, *'It's fine if he has chlamydia. He probably has condoms too.'*"

"I don't have chlamydia. But I also don't have a condom."

She separates herself from me and stands up. "It's okay. I have one in my room." She turns and walks toward the door.

I grab our wet clothes and follow her out of the room and up the stairs. She doesn't exactly invite me to her room, but I can tell she's expecting me to follow her because she's talking as she walks up the steps.

"It's been a while since I've done this," she says over her shoulder. "I only have condoms because they were party favors for the bachelorette party." She spins around, pausing on one of the steps. "I didn't realize how much harder it would be to get laid in the real world. You don't even have to make an effort in college, but after college . . . *ugh*." She turns and begins walking up the stairs again. She opens the door to her room, and I follow her inside. "The problem with sex after college is that I hate dating. It takes too much time. You dedicate an entire evening to a person you can tell in the first five minutes is a waste of your time."

I agree with her. I much prefer the idea of going all in. I've always wanted someone I could instantly click with and then just fucking *drown* in.

I don't know if Layla could be that person, but it sure felt like it when we reached the bottom of the pool. That was the most intense kiss I've ever experienced.

Layla takes our wet clothes out of my hands and walks them to her bathroom. She tosses them into the shower, and then on her way back into her bedroom, she says, "You should quit the band."

She has to be the most unpredictable person I've ever met. Even the simplest sentences catch me off guard. "Why?"

"Because you're miserable."

She's right, I am. We both make our way to the bed. "What do you do for a living?" I ask her.

"I don't have a job. I got fired last week."

She sits down and leans against the headboard. I lie on the pillow on my side, looking up at her. My face is near her hip, and it's both odd and sexy being this close to her thigh. I press my lips against it. "Why'd you get fired?"

"They wouldn't let me off for Aspen's wedding, so I didn't show up to work." She scoots down the bed and mirrors my position. "Your boxers are still wet. We should probably take off the rest of our clothes."

She's forward, but I like it.

I grab her by the waist and pull her on top of me. I place her so perfectly against me she gasps. I'm taller than her, so her face doesn't reach mine, but I want to kiss her. She must want to kiss me, too, because she crawls up my body until our mouths connect.

There aren't many items of clothing to remove between us as it is, so it only seems like seconds before we're naked under the covers and almost past the point of caring about a condom. But I don't know this girl and she doesn't know me, so I wait for her to fumble around the dark bedroom until she finds her purse. Once she retrieves a condom and hands it to me, I reach under the covers and begin putting it on.

"I think you're right," I say.

"About what?"

I roll on top of her and she spreads her legs apart, fitting me between them. "I should quit the band."

She nods in agreement. "You'd be happier playing your own music, even if you don't make money from it." She kisses me, but only briefly before pulling back. "Get a job you can tolerate. Release your music on the side. It's better to be poor and fulfilled than . . . poor and empty. I was gonna say *rich* and empty, but I don't think you're rich, or you wouldn't be playing for that band."

I would tell her I'm not poor, but admitting that I play for the band willingly and not out of necessity is kind of embarrassing, so I'd rather not say anything at all.

"If you're destined to be poor, it's better to be the happy kind of poor," she adds.

She's right. I kiss her neck, then her breast. Then my mouth is resting against hers again. "I think I'm glad I met you."

She pulls back a little, then smiles up at me. "You *think*? Or you *are*?"

"I am. I am *very* glad I met you."

She trails her fingers over my mouth. "I'm very glad I met *you*."

We kiss some more, and it's full of lazy anticipation, as if we know we have all night and there's no rush. But I already put on the condom, and she's already guiding me into her.

I still take my time with her. So much time.

Minutes feel like they matter more when they're spent with her.

~

She's on her stomach, and I'm trailing unworthy fingers up the smooth curve of her spine.

I reach the base of her neck and then sweep my fingers into her hair and begin caressing the back of her head.

"I'd kill for a taco right now," she says.

I've never wanted inside a girl's mind more than I want inside Layla's. Her mind doesn't work like other minds work. There's no filter between her brain and her mouth, and there's no conscience telling her she should feel bad for whatever it is she might have said. She just says things unapologetically and without any remorse. Even when her words sting.

I didn't know brutal honesty was sexy until tonight.

I told her a few minutes ago she was the best sex I ever had. I expected her to return the compliment, but she just smiled and said, "We always think that when we're in it. But then someone new comes along, and we forget how good we thought it was before, and the cycle starts all over again."

I laughed. I thought she was joking, but she wasn't. And then I thought about what she had said, and she was right. I lost my virginity at fifteen. I thought it was the best thing I would ever experience. But then Victoria Jared came along when I was seventeen, and she was the best sex I'd ever had. And then Sarah Kisner, and the girl who snuck into my dorm freshman year, and two or three after that, and then Sable. Each time, the aftermath made me think that was as good as it would get. But maybe they were all equally as good as the one before.

None of them compare to Layla. I'm certain of that. *As certain as I was all the times before Layla.*

"Are you religious?" Layla asks.

Her thoughts are as sporadic and intense as her actions. I think that's why I'm so intrigued by her. One minute she's on her back screaming my name as she digs her nails into my shoulders. The next minute she's on her stomach, telling me how badly she's craving a taco. The next minute she forgets about the tacos and wants to know if I'm religious. I love it. Most people are predictable. Every word and action from Layla is like being handed a gift-wrapped surprise.

"I'm not religious. Are you?"

She shrugs. "I believe in life after death, but I'm not sure I'm religious."

"I think existence is simply luck of the draw. We're here for a while, and then we're not."

"That's depressing," she says.

"Not really. Imagine what heaven is like. The incessant positivity, the smiles, the lack of sin. The thought of living eternally in a place full of people who spent their lives spouting off inspirational quotes sounds way more depressing to me than if it all just ends with death."

"I don't know if I believe in *that* kind of afterlife," Layla says. "I look at existence more as a series of realms. Maybe heaven is one of them. Maybe it isn't."

"What kind of realms?"

She rolls onto her side, and when my eyes fall to her breasts, she doesn't try to force me to make eye contact with her. Instead, she pulls my head against her chest as she rolls onto her back. I lay my head on her chest and cup one of her breasts as she casually fingers pieces of my hair and continues talking.

"Think of it like this," she says. "The womb is one existence. As a fetus, we didn't remember life before the womb, and we had no idea if there would be life after the womb. All we knew was the womb. But then we were born, and we left the womb and came into our *current* realm of existence. And now we can't remember being in the womb before this life, and we have no idea what comes after this life. And when our current life ends, we'll be in a different realm altogether, where we might not remember *this* realm of existence, just like we don't recall being in the womb. It's just different realms. One after the other after the other. Some we know for a fact exist. Some we only *believe* exist. There could be realms of existence we've never even entertained the idea of. They could be endless. I don't think we ever really die."

Her explanation makes sense, or maybe I'm just feeling agreeable because my mouth is on her breast. I grab another condom as I ponder her theory. It seems more probable to me than the idea of pearly gates or fire and brimstone ever has.

I'm still convinced that there is life and there is death and that is all there is.

"If you're right, then I like this realm the best," I say, covering her body with mine.

She parts her thighs for me and grins against my lips. "Only because you're in it."

I shake my head as I push into her. "No. I like it best because I'm in *you*."

CHAPTER TWO

I stare at her for a few minutes, hoping she doesn't wake up right away. Her hand is draped across my chest—a deadweight as she sleeps. I try to drag out the moment because I know how one-night stands work. I've had my fair share of them. I've snuck out of a lot of beds, but I don't want to sneak out of this one.

I'm hoping Layla doesn't want me to sneak out of this one.

She'll wake up soon, and I know how she'll feel as soon as she does. She'll probably shield her eyes from the sun and roll over while she tries to remember how we got here. Who I am. How she can get rid of me.

Her fingers are the first thing to move. She drags them from my shoulder, around to the back of my neck. She keeps her eyes closed as she pulls me against her so that she can tuck herself against me.

I'm relieved that I'm familiar to her—that she just woke up and knows exactly where she is and who she's with and isn't trying to pull away.

"What time is it?" she mutters. Her voice doesn't float out of her throat this early in the morning. It's a scratchy whisper and somehow even sexier than when she's wide awake.

"Eleven."

She looks up at me, her eyes puffy and smeared with mascara. "Did you know eleven in the morning is the deadliest time of day?"

That makes me laugh. "Is that a fact?"

She nods. "I learned that in college. More people die during brunch than any other time of day."

She's a hot mess. I love it. "You are so strange."

"Want to take a shower with me?"

I smile. "Fuck yeah."

⌒

I assumed we wouldn't actually shower in the shower, but it was a legitimate invite.

I'm massaging conditioner into her hair, asking her questions I normally wouldn't ask a girl after a one-night stand. There's just so much about her I want to know.

"Is Aspen your only sibling?"

"Yes."

"Do you like her?"

"I freaking *love* her," Layla says. "I don't really agree with her taste in husbands, but whatever works for her." She looks over her shoulder at me. "Do you know what his name is?"

"No. What's his name?"

"Chad Kyle."

"No way," I whisper.

"I'm serious. That's his actual name."

"Is it fitting or unfortunate?"

"Unfortunately, it's fitting," she says. "He's such a typical Chad. Frat boy, country club membership, a quarter-ton pickup, and a dog named Bo."

"That explains why he likes Garrett's Band." I grab the handheld showerhead and begin rinsing her hair. When it's wet, her hair goes down to the middle of her back. I've never washed a girl's hair before, but it's kind of sensual. So is the shape of her head. It fits perfectly against my palm. "Your head is sexy."

"How can a head be sexy?"

I cover her eyes with my free hand so soap doesn't run into them. "I don't know. But yours is. Or maybe it's just you." When I'm finished rinsing out her hair, I put the showerhead back on the holder. She spins around, and I pull her to me as the stream of hot water beats down on us. "I had fun last night."

She smiles. "Me too."

"The band is leaving in half an hour."

"I am too."

"Where do you live?"

"Chicago," she says. "I still live with my parents. Moved back in with them after college. I'm not sure where I want to end up yet. Definitely not Chicago."

"Why don't you like Chicago?"

"I do. I just don't want to live where I grew up. I want to experience the entire spectrum. City, country, condo, cabin in the woods . . ." She twists her hair to squeeze out the excess water. "Where do you live? Nashville?"

"Close to it. Nashville is pricey and I don't like roommates, so I lease a place in Franklin. If you're from Chicago, why did your sister get married in the middle of Kansas?"

"Chad Kyle is from Wichita," she says, slipping her arms around my waist. She looks up at my hair, then at my face, and sighs. "Do you know how lucky you are to be a man? You all look the same at the end of a shower. Maybe even a little sexier. Showers transform women. Leave us with flat hair, makeup smeared down our cheeks, concealer down the drain."

She talks like there's some drastic difference between the Layla I met at the wedding and the Layla standing in front of me right now.

If anything, this version of her is better. Naked, arms wrapped around me, covered in water. I like this version of her a lot. I lean forward and kiss her neck, gripping her ass with both hands.

She tilts her head to the side, giving me more access to her neck. "I think I could make a good country girl," she says. "I'd love to live here. It's beautiful. I could be happy running a bed and breakfast."

For a brief second, I forgot what we were even talking about because she has a two-track mind. Luckily one of them is on me. She lets herself fall against the wall of the shower as my hands roam over her body—my lips over her skin.

"I really love it here," she says quietly. "I like the seclusion. The quiet. No neighbors. Just transient guests I'd never really have to get to know."

I slide my tongue up her neck and then into her mouth. It's a deep, short kiss before I pull away. "It's the heart of the country," I say. "There's no better place on earth than right here."

In this moment, I absolutely mean that. No better place than right here, right now. She pulls my mouth back to hers, and neither of us flinches when someone knocks on the bedroom door. We're too preoccupied to care.

"Layla!" Aspen yells.

Layla groans at the sound of her voice, but she continues to kiss me while ignoring the knock. The pounding just becomes more incessant. "Layla, open up!"

Layla sighs, and I stop kissing her so she can get out of the shower. She wraps herself in a towel before walking out and closing the bathroom door. I'm left with a painfully hollow feeling in my stomach.

This can't be how we say goodbye. I just need one more day with her. One more conversation. One more shower. I can already feel the longing that'll fill me all the way back to Tennessee.

I turn off the water and grab my towel as Layla lets Aspen into the bedroom. I can hear every word when Aspen says, "Did you sleep with the bass player?" Their voices carry straight into the bathroom.

"Who's asking?" Layla says.

"Me. I'm asking."

"In that case, yes. Twice. Would have been three times if you hadn't interrupted us."

That makes me laugh.

"His band is looking for him. They're leaving."

"We'll be down in a few minutes," Layla says.

I hear the bedroom door open up again; then Aspen says, "Mom knows. She overheard one of them say, *'He shacked up with the bride's sister.'*"

I freeze at that comment. Why didn't I think about that? This is a wedding; of course their family is here. *Shit. Were we loud last night?*

"I'm twenty-two," Layla says. "I don't care if Mom knows."

"Just warning you," her sister responds. "I'm off to Hawaii. I'll text you when we land."

"Have fun, Mrs. Kyle."

When the bedroom door closes, I immediately open the bathroom door. Layla spins around, and the movement causes her towel to slip. She wraps it back around her as I drag my eyes up the length of her. She is so effortlessly sexy.

I tap my fist against the doorframe. "Let's stay." I'm casual about it, but that invite is anything but casual. Those two words are probably the most serious to ever leave my mouth.

"Stay where? Here?"

"Yeah. Let's see if we can keep the room for another night."

I like the look on her face—like she's contemplating the idea. "But your band is leaving. You said you have a show tomorrow."

"We decided last night that I should quit."

"Oh. I thought it was a suggestion. Not a decision."

I walk over to her and pull on the end of her towel tucked between her cleavage. It falls to the floor. She's grinning when my mouth meets hers. I can feel in the way she wraps herself around me that no part of her wants to leave. When she returns my kiss, that dreaded sense of longing that already formed in my chest instantly melts away.

"Okay," she whispers.

THE INTERVIEW

I've been talking for half an hour straight, and the man hasn't spoken a word. I would continue, but Layla hasn't let up this whole time. I need to make sure she's okay.

Or at least as okay as she *can* be while being held against her will by her own boyfriend.

"I'm sorry," I say to him, scooting my chair back. "I'll be back in a few minutes."

He hits the stop button with an understanding nod.

I walk up the stairs—*again*—to plead with Layla to trust me long enough to find answers. When I open the door, she's on her knees on the bed, doing her best to slip her hands out of the rope that's connecting her wrists to the bedpost.

"Layla," I say, defeated. "Can you please stop?"

She yanks her arms in the opposite direction of the bedpost in an attempt to break the rope. I wince. *That had to hurt.* I walk over to the bed and check her wrists. They're raw from all the times she's tried to break free. Her wrists are starting to bleed.

She mutters something unintelligible, so I remove the duct tape from her mouth.

She sucks in a huge gulp of air. "Please untie me," she pleads. Her eyes are bloodshot and sad. Mascara is smeared down her left cheek. It kills me seeing her like this. I don't want this for her, but I have no other choice. At least it feels like I have no other choice.

"I can't. You know that."

"*Please*," she says. "It hurts."

"It won't hurt if you stop trying to free yourself." I adjust the pillow beneath her and give the rope more slack so she can lie down. I know she feels like a prisoner. I guess, in a way, she is. But I've at least left her legs untied. If she'd just lie still and stop trying to fight me on this, she'd come out of it just fine. She might even get some much-needed rest. "Just give me a couple of hours. When I'm finished talking to him, I'll bring you downstairs with me."

She rolls her tear-rimmed eyes. "You're a liar. All you do now is lie to me."

I don't let those words penetrate the walls of my chest. I know she doesn't mean them. She's just scared. Upset.

But so am I.

I lean forward and press a kiss against the top of her head. She tries to pull away from me, but she can't go far. She's crying now, trying not to look at me. I hide my guilt behind a hardened jaw. "If you promise not to scream, I won't put the duct tape back on."

This is a compromise she's willing to make. She nods with a defeated look in her eyes, as if I won this round, but I'm not trying to win anything other than our normalcy back.

When I close the door and lock her inside, I can hear her begin to sob. I feel her pain in every part of me, crackling inside my bones. I press my forehead against the door for a few seconds and force myself to regain my composure before heading back downstairs.

When I'm back in the kitchen, there's a glass of dark liquor sitting in front of my chair. The man motions toward it.

"Bourbon," he says.

I sit down and sniff it, then take a sip, enjoying the burn as it slides down my throat. It immediately soothes my nerves. I should have poured myself a glass before we started this.

"What's your name?" I ask him. I only know the email address we've been using to communicate, but it was just the name of his business. Not his actual name.

He looks down at the shirt he's wearing. It's a Jiffy Lube shirt covered in oil stains with a name tag on it that says Randall. He points at the name tag. "Randall."

He resumes the recording, but we both know his name isn't Randall, and I know for a fact that isn't his shirt. But despite knowing he's not entirely forthcoming about his own identity, I still move forward with this interview, because he's the only person I know on this earth who can possibly help.

And I am desperate for help.

So desperate I'm making decisions I wouldn't have dared make if this were a few months ago.

It's interesting how much a person's belief system can be changed by things in this world that can't be explained. Hell, not just my belief system, but my morals. My values. My focus. My heart.

The Leeds from a few months ago would have slammed the door in this guy's face. Instead, I'm the one who reached out to *him*, begging for his help. And now that he's here, I can only hope I made the right decision.

"How long did the two of you stay here after you first met?" he asks.

"Three extra days."

"Did anything significant happen while you were here?"

"Not that I can recall. We stayed in our room most of the time. Only came down for meals. It was the middle of the week, so the place was relatively quiet."

"And then you went back to Tennessee? Layla to Chicago?"

"No. Even after four days together, we weren't ready to say goodbye. I invited her to come stay a week with me in Tennessee, but one week turned into two. Two turned into six, and then eight. We didn't want to be apart."

"How long have you been with her?"

"About eight months now."

"Have there been any significant changes in your life since you met her? Besides the obvious?"

I laugh half-heartedly at that. "I'm not even sure what you're referring to when you say *besides the obvious*. So much has changed."

"The obvious being everything that's happened in this house," he says. "What changed before that?"

I take another sip of the bourbon.

Then I finish it off.

I'm staring into the bottom of the empty glass, thinking about all of it. The picture I posted of us, the outcome of that, the fear, the recovery.

"Everything was perfect for those first two months."

"And then?"

That question elicits a huge sigh from me. "And then Sable happened."

"Who is Sable?"

"My ex."

CHAPTER THREE

I'm shoving a pair of jeans into my backpack. Layla is on my bed, reading a magazine.

"Did you pack a phone charger?" she asks.

"Got it."

"Toothbrush? Toothpaste?"

"Check, check."

"You should take a book," she suggests. "That's a long drive."

"I don't have any books."

Layla looks up from her position on my bed. She pulls her magazine to her chest and makes a face like I just offended her. "Leeds. It's been proven that people who read live longer. Are you trying to die young?"

Her brain is like a morbid version of Wikipedia. "I do read. I just read on my phone. I travel light."

She raises an eyebrow. "Lies. What's the last book you read?"

"*Confessions of a Dangerous Mind.*"

"Who is the author? What's it about?" She's smirking like I won't pass this interrogation.

"Can't remember his name. He hosted *The Gong Show* back in the seventies." I toss my backpack to the floor and grab my phone. I power it on for the first time since I shut it off last night. Layla leans onto her elbow, watching me as I wait for my apps to load. I sit down on the bed and pull the book up in my Kindle app. "Chuck Barris. He also created *The Newlywed Game.*"

"Is it an autobiography?"

"I think so. The guy claims to have been an assassin in the CIA, but I haven't finished it yet."

"The host of *The Gong Show* was an assassin?"

"Some people say he lied about it all. It's why I'm reading it."

"Wow. That's sexy."

"You think assassins are sexy?"

She shakes her head. "No. The fact that you *read* is sexy." She lifts her magazine from her chest and looks back down at it. "You're hot. You write songs. You read. Too bad you can't cook for shit."

I push her away from me and slap her playfully on the ass. She's laughing when she rolls back over. "Seriously. You can't even make a sandwich without screwing it up."

"Why do you think I've kept you?"

She rolls her eyes. I give my focus to my phone and begin checking all the messages I've missed in the last twelve hours since turning it off.

The first one is from Garrett, letting me know where and when to meet them tonight.

I never did quit the band. After Layla and I left the bed and breakfast, Garrett texted me like I didn't skip out on two shows in a row because of a girl I had just met. He said, Your vacation over yet? We need you to play tonight.

I didn't have a good enough excuse to *not* play that night, and knowing Layla would be going to the show with me made me dread it less. That was several weeks ago, and even though I still feel dead inside while I'm on that stage, Layla keeps all the other parts of me alive.

I'm not a cynic when it comes to love, but I've only been in a couple of relationships. I figured love would find me in my late thirties, when I was bored of travel and bored of life. I blame Jerry Seinfeld for my outlook on life.

I binge-watched every season of *Seinfeld* when I was fifteen and came out of it believing that Jerry was right—there's something annoying about every single human on this planet. Annoying enough to make relationships seem like torture. After witnessing all of Jerry's doomed relationships, I started seeking out the most annoying traits in people. Their laugh. The way they treat waitstaff. Their taste in movies, music, friends. Their parents. As soon as I would start dating a girl exclusively, I would find myself already planning ways to break things off.

Until Layla, that is.

We stayed three extra nights at Corazón del País when we met. And even after that last night, I didn't want to say goodbye to her. I didn't find a single thing about her annoying. In fact, the thought of being alone sounded more dreadful than being with her. That was a first.

I asked her to come stay a week in Franklin with me, but it's been over two months now and I've had more sex in these two months than I thought I'd be capable of in a lifetime. When we aren't fucking, I'm playing songs for her, or writing songs, or thinking about songs. I feel like my music has a purpose now that she's into it.

She believes I'm going to be a somebody, and her belief in me is actually making me start to believe it too.

It took some twisting of my arm, but three weeks ago she finally convinced me to release a few of the songs I've been sitting on. She posted me playing one of them to YouTube two weeks ago, and it has almost ten thousand views already.

I hate that I like that, but it feels surprisingly good to have someone in my life who makes me feel like my art is worth consuming. Even if she's the only one who ever consumes it, it'll be enough for me.

Garrett will be pissed if I officially stop playing with them and go solo, but bass players aren't all that hard to replace here in Nashville.

Layla comes with me to every show, no matter how painful they've been for us both. It helps that she spends the entire last song of each set re-creating her ridiculous wedding dance. At least I end the shows in a good mood now.

I love her.

I think.

No, I do. I love her.

Everything about her. Her confidence, her eccentricities, her drive, her body, her blow jobs, her spontaneity, her belief in me. I love watching her sleep. I love watching her wake up.

I'm pretty sure this is love.

It's only five o'clock in the afternoon and I leave in two hours, and I had to drag myself out of bed to finish packing. Garrett's Band is playing a beach festival in Miami, so Layla and I have spent all day in bed to make up for the three days we won't see each other. This will be the first show she hasn't gone to since I met her. There's not enough room for passengers in the van with all the equipment, and the idea of spending three days with Garrett and the guys isn't appealing to her. I'm not going to force her to endure that torture.

This whole day has been my favorite day with her. Neither of us turned our phones on when we woke up this morning. We kept the lights off and the curtains shut, and I had her for both breakfast and lunch.

The lamp beside my bed is on now as Layla flips through her magazine.

I open Instagram and immediately regret turning on my phone. I haven't looked at it since I posted a picture of us last night. It was the first time I've ever posted a picture with a girl. We were in bed, naturally. Layla was asleep on my chest and I really liked how I felt in that moment, so I held my phone up, snapped a picture of us, and left the caption blank.

I've gained almost a thousand followers since meeting Layla and releasing some of my own music, but that's still only five thousand people total. I would assume with only five thousand followers, there would be less of a reaction to the picture I posted of us. Call me naive, but I honestly didn't think I'd get much reaction at *all*.

Most of the comments I'm reading are from people congratulating us, but some of the comments are from other girls who are picking Layla apart. Luckily I didn't tag her in the photo. I'd hate for her to see what people are saying about her.

The more I read through the comments and private messages, I'm tempted to just delete my account altogether. I know if I ever get to the point of being able to pay a bill with my music, I'll be thankful for any followers I have. But right now, it's disturbing reading comments like, *Your girlfriend looks like a slut* and *You're hotter when you're single*.

The internet is fucking brutal. It makes me nervous to leave her here for three days by herself. I don't think she's seen the picture yet, so I don't even bother deleting the negative comments. I just delete the photo altogether and then set my phone facedown on the nightstand.

"You sure you're okay staying here alone?" I ask her.

She lays the magazine against her chest. "Why? Do you want me to leave?"

"No. Of course not."

"Are you sure?"

"I'm positive."

"We met two months ago and we haven't even come up for air yet. Surely you're sick of me crowding your space by now."

She has no idea how *not* sick of her I am.

Well, I guess she would have no way of knowing how I really feel about her since I've never said it out loud. I show her, but I don't say it.

I grab her magazine and toss it on the floor, then I roll on top of her. I love the look she always gets in her eye when she knows I'm about to kiss her. It's a gleam of anticipation. There's nothing better than knowing this girl anticipates my mouth on hers. "Layla," I whisper. "I am not sick of you. I'm in love with you."

I say it casually, but it only takes two seconds for my words to register. When they do, she covers her face with both hands. It's the first time I've ever seen her look shy. I kiss one of the hands covering her face right before she curls them into two fists against her chin. "I'm in love with you too."

I immediately press my mouth to hers, wanting to swallow those words. I imagine them typed out in Arial font, slowly bouncing around inside of me, ricocheting off my internal walls, endlessly twisting and rotating inside my stomach and my chest and my arms and my legs until every part of me has been touched by them.

I pull away from her, and I love that her smile is so wide. "I guess it's settled, then," I say. "We're in love, you're staying here while I'm gone, and I think this means we just officially moved in together."

"Wow. Maybe I should let my parents know I don't live with them anymore."

"You haven't been home since your sister got married. I think they're aware."

She wraps her arms around my neck. "This is a lot in one day. We said *I love you*, we moved in together . . . and we're *Instagram* official now." She says the last part like a joke, but my stomach drops knowing she saw the picture.

"You saw that?"

I can tell by the way her smile fades that she also saw the comments that accompanied the picture. "Yeah."

"Don't worry, I deleted it."

"You did? I didn't mind it."

"Either way, I don't think I was prepared for people I don't even know to have an opinion about us."

"You're not real to them. It's just how people are on social media." She kisses me. "It's your own fault for being so damn hot," she says with a grin.

I'm relieved she doesn't seem to be taking any of it personally. "I don't know if I want to post pictures of us together anymore. I don't want them to find your account and start bothering you."

Layla laughs. "Too late for that. You follow thirty people, and I'm one of them. They already found me."

I roll off her and sit up on the bed. "What do you mean they already found you?"

"It's just been one girl so far," she says. "Sonya? Sybil? I can't remember her name." Layla says it so nonchalantly, but I know exactly who she's talking about.

"Sable?"

She points at me with a wink. "That's it. *Sable.* I already blocked her, though."

I haven't heard from Sable since I blocked her number several months before meeting Layla. The fact that she's still looking at my posts confirms my concerns about her. "What'd she say?"

"I don't know. I had over twenty in-box messages from her when I turned on my phone this morning. I only read two of them before I told her to get a life. Then I blocked her." Layla walks her fingers up my leg, leaning in. She grins like she finds this amusing. "Did you sleep with her?"

Since I've known Layla, I've never once lied to her. I've never felt the need to. She's the least judgmental person I've ever met. "We dated for a couple of months. Figured out real quick that relationship was a mistake."

Layla grins, like she finds that amusing. "Well. She doesn't think it was a mistake. She thinks *I'm* the mistake."

Sable was the mistake, but I don't want to say anything about Sable that might worry Layla. But the girl is definitely someone worth worrying about. It took me several weeks to figure it out, though, probably because I was only paying attention to how much my dick liked her and wasn't aware that the way she felt about me was on a completely different level.

I initially thought our meeting was organic, but I found out from Garrett that Sable ran a fan club for me that she'd started a year before we even met. I confronted her about it, and things got weird after that. I tried to break it off, but she didn't take that very well. At first, it was just incessant phone calls. Messages. Voice mails. But then she started showing up to shows, demanding I give her another chance.

Garrett and the guys started calling her *Unstable Sable*.

We finally had to have security escort her out of a show one night—a couple of days before I blocked her on my cell and social media. I also blocked the account she used to run her Leeds Gabriel fan club.

The whole thing was bizarre. She was bizarre.

And it really unnerves me that she's still out there, watching my page, reaching out to people I post pictures with.

"It's people like Sable that make me question whether or not I want to be in the public eye at all. Why am I even trying when I hate everything it entails?"

Layla crawls on top of me. "Sadly, you can't really sell music without an online presence. Crazies and success are a package deal." She kisses the tip of my nose. "If you ever do become a household name, you'll have enough money to hire someone to delete the trolls *for* you. Then you won't have to deal with them."

"Good point," I say, even though I have enough money now to hire someone to deal with my social media. My finances haven't come up in conversation between me and Layla yet, though. She assumes I'm a starving artist yet somehow still loves me as if I could give her the world. There's no better feeling than being loved for who you are rather than for what you're worth.

Layla smiles. "I'm full of good points. That's why you're in love with me."

"*So* in love with you." I kiss her, but this kiss is coupled with concern.

In the beginning, I liked Layla. I was attracted to her. But concern for her didn't accompany those feelings. However, over the last few weeks, I've started to worry about her.

Concern might be the only difference between liking someone and loving someone.

I debate telling her to be extra careful while I'm gone because now I'm even more apprehensive. I'd like it if she'd never answer my door when I'm not here. I'd really like it if she'd delete all her social media accounts. But she's a grown-ass woman, so I don't say any of that.

I don't know why I have this pit in my stomach because essentially, I'm a nobody right now. One unofficial fan club and five thousand followers does not make me a somebody. A few comments from some fans online isn't really something that warrants an overprotective boyfriend. Even still, I'm having a security system installed while I'm gone. It'll put my mind at ease.

"I have to meet Garrett in two hours. And I still have to shower and finish packing."

Layla kisses me and then rolls off the bed. "I'll put a frozen lasagna in the oven so you can eat before you leave. Want some garlic bread with it?"

"Sounds perfect."

She closes the bedroom door, and I begrudgingly head to the bathroom.

Maybe we should get a dog. A protective one, like a German shepherd. It'd make me feel better when I have to leave Layla here by herself.

I turn on the water in the shower and take off my shirt, but before I unbutton my jeans, there's a knock at the door. I told Garrett I'd meet him at his house. *Maybe he got impatient.*

"I'll get it!" I yell out from the bathroom. I really don't want Layla answering the door after I read some of those comments. Not to mention, Sable knows where I live. She's slept in my bed.

"I've got it!" Layla yells back.

I'm picking up my shirt and pulling it back over my head when I hear a sound. It's like a single-shot firecracker. Pop!

My blood chills—as if my veins would shatter like glass if I moved. But I do move. I run.

When I reach the bedroom door, I hear the sound again. Another pop!

I swing open the door, and everything I know and everything I love and everything I live for is in a heap on my living room floor. There's blood pooling beneath her shoulder. In her hair. I immediately drop to my knees and lift her head.

"Layla," I whisper, right before feeling a sting in my shoulder.

Everything after that is a blur.

A nightmare.

Everything stops.

It just stops.

It just . . .

THE INTERVIEW

The man is quiet.

The whole *house* is quiet. Too quiet.

I need more bourbon. As if he knows this, he stands up and grabs the bottle. He brings it back to the table and slides it over to me. "What happened next?"

I shrug. Take a drink. "She survived."

"Who shot her? Sable?"

My jaw is tense when I nod. "Yes. Over a fucking *Instagram* post." My words are short and clipped. I'm sure the expression on my face shows just how done I wish I could be with this conversation.

"Was Sable arrested?"

I shake my head. "No."

The man is looking at me like he wants me to elaborate even more on that night, and I will, but not right now. I'm still trying to swallow everything that's led up to this point. I need to fully digest it before I spit it back out.

"I don't really want to talk about that right now," I say. "Not that it isn't important. I just . . ." I push back from the table and stand up. "I need to check on Layla again." My voice is dry from all the talking. He stops the recorder as I turn to walk up the stairs.

I pause halfway up the steps. I lean against the wall and close my eyes. It's still hard to wrap my mind around what's happening sometimes, even though I've been living it for weeks now.

I take a moment to separate everything I'm saying about Layla downstairs from what I need to say to her upstairs.

After a few long seconds, I push off the wall and head to our bedroom. I unlock the door and slowly open it, expecting Layla to be asleep. She isn't. She is lying down, though.

"I'm thirsty," she says flatly.

I pick up the glass of water by the bed and wait for her to sit up. I've given the rope plenty of slack so she can move around a bit, but she still winces when the rope rubs against her wrists. She leans forward until the glass meets her lips. She takes several sips before dropping against the headboard, exhausted.

"You should eat," I tell her. "What do you want me to bring you?"

She looks at me with disgust. "I don't know, Leeds. It's hard to see what's in the fridge when I'm tied to a bed."

Her anger slips into my skin with the ease of a sharpened scalpel. It mixes with the guilt I feel for keeping her here, but Layla's anger and my guilt combined still lack the capability to breach my conscience.

"I can make you a sandwich."

"How about you untie me and I can make it myself?"

I leave her while I go downstairs to make her a sandwich. Turkey and cheddar, no onions, double the tomato. I don't speak to the man while I make Layla her sandwich. I do have questions for him, but I'll get to those later. I just want to tell him everything I know first. I want to get it over with.

When I'm back upstairs, I set the sandwich and the bag of Cheetos I brought Layla on the bed. I also made her a glass of wine, so I place that on the nightstand.

"I'll untie you so you can eat, but don't try to run this time," I warn her. "You know it won't work."

She nods, and I can tell by the fear in her eyes that she doesn't want to experience that again. In fact, I can probably trust that she was so terrified by what happened the last time she tried to leave that she doesn't even need to be tied up. I doubt she'd even leave this bedroom willingly.

Unfortunately, I just can't risk it. I need her here.

When the rope is off her wrists, she pulls her arms down and massages her shoulder. I feel bad that she's sore, so I make room between her and the bed and I sit behind her. I rub her shoulders while she eats, wanting to ease some of her tension. She takes a small bite of her sandwich, then picks up a piece of tomato and lettuce that fell out onto the plate. She pops them both into her mouth and licks her fingers. Maybe she's just hungry, but she looks like she's actually enjoying this sandwich. It reminds me of how she used to tease me about my sandwich-making abilities.

"You used to hate my sandwiches."

She shrugs. "People change," she says between bites. "You also used to be a loving boyfriend who didn't hold me hostage, but look at you now."

Touché.

When her shoulders feel more relaxed, I leave her on the bed as I walk to the bathroom, trusting that Willow will stop Layla if she tries to escape again. I retrieve the first aid kit from beneath the counter, then walk back to the bed and apply antiseptic ointment to Layla's wrists between her bites of food and sips of wine. I bought this first aid kit at a gas station on our way here several weeks ago. I had no idea how much I'd end up using it.

We don't talk while she eats. The faster she eats, the better. I want to get these questions over with so we can start getting answers.

When she's finished, I wrap her wrists with a roll of ACE bandage to ease the pain from the rope. "Do you want me to tie you to the other side of the bed now so you can lie on your other side?"

She nods, holding her arms out for me.

I hate myself for this. Especially after spending the last hour talking about what it was like to fall in love with her. Remembering the agony that rolled through me when I saw her on my living room floor.

And now I have to spend the next hour talking about what everything has been like *after* that night. The hospital stay, the recovery, what it did to our private lives. The months of guilt. The betrayal, the lies. How I've manipulated her. *Not looking forward to this.*

"Try to get some sleep now."

She just nods this time. I think the exhaustion is getting to her.

I walk back downstairs, but the man isn't in the kitchen anymore. I find him in the Grand Room. He's moved the tape recorder to the piano, and he's sitting on the bench. "Thought I'd change up the scenery a bit," he says. I sit on the end of the couch closest to him, and he presses record again. "What happened after you were shot?"

"I called 911. Tried to keep Layla alive until they arrived. Then we were both taken into surgery."

"And after that?"

I tell him what I can remember, which isn't much. I woke up from surgery not knowing if Layla was even alive. I tell him about how I had to spend three hours in recovery with no word on her condition. I tell him about the agony of having to call her mother and sister to let them know what had happened, and the two hours I spent being interrogated while still not knowing if Layla had survived.

I tell him everything I can remember about the hospital stay, but none of it is all that important. Nothing about her survival or the recovery is nearly as significant as everything that started happening once we returned to the bed and breakfast.

"Why did you guys decide to come back here?"

"I wanted to get her out of Tennessee. Once her doctors gave her the all clear, I thought it would be good to get her away. And I know how much she loves this place." I pause when I say that, and then I backtrack. "Well . . . how much she *used* to love it."

"When did she stop loving it here?"

"I guess the day I brought her back."

CHAPTER FOUR

I ate a strand of Layla's hair this morning.

The thought crossed my mind that something as weird as eating your girlfriend's hair could be the starting point to even weirder behavior. It could be a precursor to cannibalism, much like harming animals as a child is sometimes a precursor to becoming a serial killer.

But eating her hair was nothing more than a slightly creepy last-ditch effort on my part to try and absolve myself from all the guilt. I dreamt that swallowing a piece of her hair tethered us together somehow, eliminating any fear that we might someday grow apart because of everything that happened. So, when I woke up, I plucked a strand from her head while she slept and put it in my mouth.

That was eight hours ago, and it feels like the strand somehow found its way around my heart and cut off the blood supply.

My heart is choking.

That would make a good lyric.

I open my phone while we wait in line to board the plane, and I type *my heart chokes on its own guilt* into my notes, beneath several other dismal lyrics I've pulled from random thoughts.

My lyrics have really taken a depressing turn lately.

"Leeds," Layla says, giving me a gentle nudge from behind. I'm holding up the line. I slide my phone into my pocket and head to our seats.

I packed very little for this trip. Two pairs of jeans, some shorts, a few T-shirts, and the engagement ring.

I tucked it into a sock and shoved the sock deep inside a pair of my running shoes. Layla has a separate suitcase, so there shouldn't be a reason for her to dig through mine, but I don't want her to find the ring. I bought it when she was still in the hospital. I knew it was premature, but I was overwhelmed with fears of the unknown. I thought buying the ring might put some kind of energy into the universe that would make her recover faster.

Her recovery has been better than expected, but I've yet to propose. She doesn't even know I bought her the ring. I'm still not sure when I'm proposing because I want it to be perfect. It might not even happen on this trip, but I'd rather have the ring and not need it than need it and not have it.

I booked this trip because the last six months have been horrendous. It has taken a toll on us, emotionally and physically. I'm hoping going back to the place where Layla and I met will feel like a reset on our lives. I have this notion that if I take us back to the starting line, we'll never cross the finish line.

Another potential lyric.

The man in front of me is attempting to shove his oversize suitcase into the overhead bin, so I take the pause in the movement of the line and type a tweaked version of that sentence into my notes. *I keep running back to the starting line because I don't want to be finished with you.*

Layla's recovery has been a lot more intense than my own. It was touch and go for an entire week. Once she was stable, it was still four weeks before she was discharged.

I blame myself daily for not being more careful. For not fearing Sable's instability all those months before, when she refused to stop contacting me.

I blame myself for ever thinking it was a good idea to put Layla's face out there while not expecting some sort of repercussions. I mean, it's the fucking *internet*. I should have known better. Every post has some sort of repercussion.

We desperately need this trip. We need the privacy. A break from the outside world. I just want to go back to how it all was in the beginning. Just the two of us, locked up in a bedroom, having the best and most random conversations between rounds of sweaty sex.

I shove Layla's carry-on into the overhead bin. We're in seats 4A and 4B, the last row in first class. Layla takes the window seat. She's been unusually quiet, which means she's probably feeling anxious.

I haven't told her where we're going yet. I wanted it to be a surprise, but the unknown might be feeding her anxiety. I hadn't really thought about that until this moment.

I sit down and fasten my seat belt while she closes the window shade. "Any guesses where we're headed?"

"I know we're flying to Nebraska," she says. "I don't even know what's in Nebraska."

"We're not actually staying in Nebraska. It's the closest airport to where we're going, though."

That should be a hint, but she doesn't seem to catch on to it. She grabs one of the small water bottles from between our seats and opens it. "I hope it's relaxing. I don't know that I'm in the mood for adventure."

I try not to laugh at the thought of that. What does she expect? That I would sign her up for rock climbing or river rafting after she's been in physical therapy for the past six months?

She's been through so much and I know I've been extremely overprotective, but we've slowly been easing back into our old routine. No one can bounce back from something like that and immediately fall back into being their chipper, happy selves, so there's still some ground to cover, but I'm confident our rhythm will come back with time.

Layla pulls her phone out of her purse before shoving the purse beneath the seat in front of her. "We need to post a picture of you on the plane," she says, lifting her phone.

I smile, but she shakes her head, indicating she doesn't want me to smile. I stop smiling. She snaps a picture of me and then opens it in an editing app.

It's hard not being a little bitter at the idea of fame after what happened to us. Layla never would have been injured if it weren't for social media.

She finishes editing the picture and holds it up for me to approve. I always approve them. I don't really care what she posts, to be honest. I nod when I see the picture, but then I groan when I see the hashtags. #Singer #Musician #LeedsGabriel #Model

"Model? Really, Layla? Am I trying to make it as a musician or an influencer?"

"You can't be the former nowadays without also being the latter." She posts the picture with the hashtags.

"They used to say MTV was the death of the ugly musician," I mutter. "Not even close. Instagram is the new grim reaper."

"It's a good thing you look like you do, then," Layla says. She kisses me and then puts her phone back into her purse.

I turn my cell on airplane mode and drop it into the back pocket of the seat in front of me, dreading the inevitable pictures Layla will force me to take before my head hits the pillow tonight. I know I should be more grateful to her for wanting me to succeed. It just all feels dirty now. Our story made a few headlines and circulated in the Nashville scene, so it gave me a small bump in sales and a huge bump in followers—I'm over ten thousand now. But I can't help but feel like I'm capitalizing off her injuries.

I feel like a sellout who never really had anything to sell out.

The plane begins to taxi, and Layla starts twisting the hem of her dress nervously. She's already downed both bottles of our water.

The attack changed a lot of things about her. It changed both of us.

A lot was taken from her because of me. Months of her life. Her confidence. Her security. She was left with anxiety, dependency issues, night terrors, panic attacks, memory loss. The carefree and confident girl I fell in love with no longer sits next to me. Instead, I sit next to a girl who seems like she's fighting not to crawl out of the skin she's in.

It's like all her resilience is buried beneath layers of scar tissue now.

Maybe that's why I've let her basically take over as my manager while she recovers. I do what she says because my career is the only thing that seems to give her a sense of purpose. Keeps her mind off everything that's happened.

And maybe that's how she deals with it—by turning the one thing that caused all of this into a positive thing. Every aspect of our lives other than my career has suffered. Layla says it's good we have that small sliver of positivity to hold on to. I don't want to deprive her of that, but I kind of miss the days when she didn't take my career as seriously. I miss it when she encouraged me to quit the band in order to preserve my own happiness. I miss how she used to pull my guitar out of my hands so she could crawl on top of me. I miss it when she didn't care about what was posted to my Instagram page.

But mostly, I miss just being myself around her. Lately, I feel like I've been inching away from the person I was so that I can become the person she now needs.

"Is the seat belt sign off yet?" she asks. Her face is buried in the sleeve of my shirt. She's gripping my hand. Honestly, I hadn't even realized we'd taken off. It's like I live inside my own head now more than I live in reality.

"Not yet."

She must be extremely nervous right now if she can't even lift her eyes to look for herself. I bring my hand to the side of her head and press my lips into her hair. She tries to hide it, but anxiety is not an invisible thing. I can see it in the way she holds herself. In the way her hands twist at her dress. In the way her jaw hardens. I can even see it in the way her eyes dart around when we're in public, as if she's waiting for someone to come around the corner and attack.

When a ding indicates the seat belt signs are off and it's safe to move around the cabin, she finally separates herself from me. Her eyes flitter nervously around the cabin as she takes a mental note of her surroundings. She lifts the shade and gazes out the window at the clouds, absentmindedly bringing her hand up to the scar on the side of her head. She's always touching it. Sometimes I wonder what she thinks about when she touches it. She has no memory of that night. Only what I've told her, but she rarely asks about it. She *never* asks about it, actually.

Her knee is bouncing up and down. She shifts in her seat and then glances back into coach. Her eyes are wide, like she's on the edge of a panic attack.

She's had two full-on panic attacks in the past month alone. This is how they both started. Her touching her scar. Her fingers trembling. Her eyes full of fear. Her breaths labored.

"You okay?"

She nods, but she doesn't make eye contact with me. She just blows out several slow and quiet breaths, as if she's trying to hide from me that she's attempting to calm herself down.

She closes her eyes and leans her head back. She looks like she wants to crawl beneath her seat. "I need my pills," she whispers.

I knew she didn't seem right. I reach to the floor for her purse. I look for her anxiety medicine, but it's not in her purse anywhere. Just a wallet, a pack of gum, and a lint roller. "Did you put them in the checked bag?"

"Shit," she mutters, her eyes still closed. She's gripping the arms of her seat, wincing as if she's in pain. I don't pretend to know what it's like, dealing with anxiety. She tried to explain it to me last week. I asked her what the anxiety felt like. She said, *"It's like a shiver running through my blood."*

Up until that point, I had always assumed anxiety was just a heightened sense of worry. But she explained it was an actual physical feeling. She feels it running through her body like tiny waves of electric shocks.

After she told me that, I just held her in my arms. I felt helpless. I always feel helpless now when it comes to her, which is why I go out of my way to make sure she's okay.

And she is not okay right now.

"Do you want to go wait it out in the bathroom?" I ask her.

She nods, so I grab Layla's hand and help her out of her seat. When we get to the front of the cabin, I lean in to the flight attendant. "She's having a panic attack. I'm going in with her until it passes."

The flight attendant takes one look at Layla, and her expression immediately turns sympathetic. She closes the curtain to block off the view of the bathroom door from the first-class cabin.

There's no room for us to move once I close the door. I wrap one arm around Layla's waist and pull her face to my chest. With my free hand, I wet a paper towel in the sink and then press it against the back of her neck while I hold her.

She told me last week that my arms work better for her than her weighted blanket. I don't know how I feel about that—being the one thing that seems to ease her panic. I'd like for her to figure out how to fight these without my help. I can't always be here with her, and I worry about what will happen if she has one when I'm not around.

I hold her for a moment, feeling her body trembling against mine. "Want me to tell you where we're going?" I ask her. "Maybe not knowing is making your anxiety worse."

She shakes her head. "I don't want to ruin your surprise."

"I planned to tell you after takeoff anyway." I pull her face from my chest so I can see her reaction. "We're going to the Corazón del País. I booked it for two whole weeks."

There isn't an immediate reaction. But then, after a few seconds, she makes a confused face. *"Where?"*

I try to hide my concern, but this has been happening a lot. Things she should easily remember take a moment to come back to her. The doctor said it's normal after brain damage, but it's still jarring every time I realize just how much she lost.

That took a long time to accept—that she has brain damage.

It's minor, but noticeable. Especially when it takes her a little longer to recall things that were huge for me. For us. I don't take it personal, but I still feel the sting.

"The bed and breakfast," I say.

Familiarity eases back into her expression. "Oh yeah. Aspen's wedding. Garrett's shitty band." There's a flicker of excitement in her eyes. "The *breakfast*."

"Actually, it's not a bed and breakfast anymore. The place is up for sale now; it shut down three months ago. I emailed the Realtor and asked if we could rent it for a couple of weeks."

"We have the whole place to ourselves?"

I nod. "Just me and you."

"What about the cooks? And housekeepers?"

"It's not a business anymore, so we'll cook ourselves. I already had groceries delivered." I can tell she's still trying to overcome the minor panic attack, so I continue talking to keep her mind off it. "Aspen and Chad want to come stay a night. It's only a couple hours from Wichita. They're thinking Friday."

Layla nods and then presses her cheek against my shirt. "That'll be nice."

I hold her for another couple of minutes—until she's no longer shaking. "You feeling better?"

"Yes."

"Good." I run my hand over her hair and kiss the top of her head. "We should go sit back down. Everyone on the plane will be talking about the couple who joined the mile-high club."

She doesn't release me. Instead, she brings her mouth close to mine and her hand begins to crawl down my chest, all the way to the button on my jeans. "Let's not make them liars." She stands on her tiptoes until her lips are pressed against mine.

I know she thinks this is probably some fantasy of mine—*I'd be lying if I said it wasn't*—but not right now. Not after she just came down from a panic attack. It feels wrong.

I take her face in my hands. "Not here, okay?"

She deflates a little. "We'll be fast."

I kiss her. "Not right now. Tonight." I back away from her and open the door, stepping aside to let her walk out.

She waves me out and shakes her head. "I want to use the bathroom first," she says with a weak voice. Her eyes look like they're frowning when I close the door. I walk back to my seat, feeling like a complete asshole for turning her down.

But it would have made me an even bigger asshole if I'd fucked her sixty seconds after she had a panic attack.

That's not something I want her to get used to.

I can't be the Band-Aid for her wounds. I need to be what helps them heal.

━

"How far away are we?" It's the first thing she's said since we got in the rental car. She fell asleep before we were even out of the airport terminal.

"About twenty minutes."

She stretches her legs and arms and lets out a moaning sound that makes me shift in my seat. I've been regretting not bending her over the airplane sink since I walked out of the bathroom earlier. The old Leeds would have taken her up on that offer. Twice, probably.

Sometimes I think I've changed more than she has. My love for her has been over-the-top protective since her surgery. I think I'm too careful with her now. I'm careful when I speak to her, careful when I hug her, careful when I kiss her, careful when I make love to her.

I flip my blinker on to take the next exit. "We need gas. This is the last store before we get there. You need a bathroom break?"

Layla shakes her head. "I'm good."

After we get to the gas station and I get the nozzle locked into place, I walk over to the passenger door and open it. Layla looks up at me, shielding her eyes from the afternoon sun. I grab her hand and pull her out of the car.

I wrap my arms around her, leaning her against the car, and then I kiss the side of her head. "I'm sorry."

It's all I say. I don't even know if she's disappointed that I turned her down or if she even knows what I'm sorry for, but she sinks into me a little more.

"It's okay," she says. "You don't have to want me every second of the day."

The wind is blowing her hair in her face, so I push it back with my hands. When I do this, I feel something in the strands of her hair. They're clumped together—sticky between my fingers. I lean in and inspect her head, even though she tries to pull away. Her hair is dark, so I can't see the blood, but when I pull my fingers back, the tips of them are red. "You're bleeding."

"Am I?" She presses her fingers against her head, right over her incision.

The gas nozzle clicks, so I release her and pull it out of the gas tank. "Let me park the car and I'll come inside and help you clean it up."

After I park the car, I search the store shelves until I find a small first aid kit. I meet Layla in the women's restroom with it. It's a one-person stall, so I lock the door to the bathroom behind me. She faces me, leaning against the sink. I take a cotton swab and some peroxide out of the kit and clean the dried blood out of her hair first, then from around the incision.

"Did you hit your head on something?"

"No."

"It's pretty bad." It should be healed by now. It's been six months since she got the scar, but every couple of weeks it breaks open again. "Maybe you should get it checked out this week."

"It doesn't hurt," she says. "It'll be fine. I'm fine."

I finish cleaning it up and then put some antiseptic ointment on it. I don't press her again about why it's bleeding. She'll never admit that she does it herself, but I've seen her picking at it.

I clean up the mess and close the first aid kit while Layla uses the restroom. She moves to the sink and washes her hands. I'm leaning against the bathroom door, watching her in the mirror.

What if I'm part of the problem? What if my hesitation to treat her exactly how I treated her before is holding her back somehow?

We make love a lot, but it's different than it was before. In those first couple of months together, we were a combination of everything that makes sex good. I was sweet and gentle with her, but also reckless and rough, sometimes all at once. I didn't treat her like she was fragile. I treated her like she was unbreakable.

Maybe that's where I've gone wrong. I need to treat her like the person she's trying to become again. The Layla who was full of strength and spontaneity before that was ripped from her.

She's watching me in the mirror as I set the first aid kit next to her on the sink. Our eyes stay locked together as my hand bunches up her dress and then slips slowly between her thighs. I can see the roll of her throat when I hook my finger around her panties and yank them down.

I place my right hand on the back of her neck and push her forward while I unbutton my jeans.

And then, for the first time in six months, I'm not gentle with her at all.

CHAPTER FIVE

I enter the pass code given to me by the real estate agent. The gate is wrought iron and shakes as it slides unsure across the gravel driveway, as if it's struggling to remember how to operate.

The bed and breakfast is a two-story old Victorian-style mansion overlooking acres of dense trees. It's stark white with a red front door, and from what I can remember, six bedrooms upstairs and a couple downstairs.

At first glance, the property looks the same as it did last year—just more vacant. The parking lot is empty. No guests walking the grounds. The first time I pulled into this place, I remember there being an energetic buzz as everyone was preparing for Aspen and Chad's wedding. It was in the height of the summer, so the grass was green and the lawn was manicured.

Right now, the grounds look to be in limbo, waiting for spring to bring back all the life that was murdered by winter.

"It looks the same," I say, putting the car in park, even though it doesn't really look the same at all. It looks . . . lonelier.

Layla says nothing.

I open my door and can't help noticing the emptiness in the air. No smells, no sounds, no birds chirping. It's quiet now, and I sort of like that. I welcome the idea of being in the heart of the country with Layla again, with the bonus of complete isolation.

We grab our suitcases from the trunk. I pull both of them up the porch steps while Layla uses the keypad and the code given to me by the Realtor to open the door.

I step inside first and immediately notice the smell is different. I don't remember it smelling like mothballs at the wedding last year. Hopefully there are candles we can light to overpower that scent.

Layla takes a step over the threshold, and as soon as she does, she shudders. She lifts a hand to the wall, like she's trying to steady herself.

"You okay?"

She nods. "Yeah. I just . . ." She closes her eyes for a few seconds. "It's cold in here. And my head hurts. I kind of want to take a nap."

It's not cold. It's actually kind of stuffy, but her arms are covered in goosebumps.

"I'll find the thermostat. Leave your suitcase, and I'll bring it to our old room for you in a second." I head into the kitchen to search for the thermostat. It's not in the kitchen, but I'm relieved to see the Realtor delivered the groceries. I wouldn't normally ask someone to grocery shop for me, but she offered, and I tipped her well.

I wasn't sure they'd allow us to stay here, so I alluded to the fact that I'm interested in buying the place and wanted a trial run. I haven't mentioned that to Layla, though. I wanted to check the place out first—see if we love it as much as we did when we were first there.

I'm not so sure the look that's been on Layla's face since we pulled into the driveway conveys a desire to live here, though. If anything, she looks ready to leave.

I walk toward the Grand Room to see if that's where the thermostat is located. I'm relieved to see the baby grand piano is still here. The lid is shut and there's a fine layer of dust over it, which makes me sad. A piano this beautiful deserves to be played, but by the looks of it, I might have been the last person to have touched it.

I run my finger across the top of the piano, clearing a line of dust away. I didn't know what to expect when I was told this place was vacant. I was worried that meant the owners moved the piano out, but all the same furniture is still here.

Layla knows this is as much of a work trip as it is a vacation. I have an album to write, so I plan on using the piano as much as I can without making Layla feel like music is my priority these next two weeks.

Hell, she'll probably make it my priority. She wants me to finish this album more than I want to finish it myself.

I leave the Grand Room after failing to find the thermostat. I glance down the hallway and see Layla peeking into a room. She closes the door and then continues walking and opens the door to a second room. She seems confused—as if she can't remember where our room was. She starts to close that door.

"It's upstairs, Layla."

She startles when I say that, spinning around. "I know." She points to the room she was about to walk past and heads inside. "I just . . . need to use the restroom first." She slips inside the bathroom and closes the door.

She just used the restroom twenty minutes ago at the gas station.

Sometimes I feel like her memory loss is worse than she admits. I've thought about testing her—maybe bringing up something that never happened just to see if she'd pretend to remember it.

That's conniving, though. I already feel enough guilt as it is.

I hear the water begin to run in the bathroom just as I locate the thermostat next to the stairwell. It reads seventy-one degrees. I'm not sure I want it warmer than that, but I bump it up a few degrees for her so that the heat can eat away whatever chill she's feeling.

I make my way to the living room, if only to inspect all the areas of the house I never entered last time I was here.

It has a very unwelcoming feel—as if the room isn't meant for living at all. A light cream-colored sofa and matching love seat are angled toward a fireplace. A stiff brown leather chair sits next to a table strategically piled with books.

There's only one window in the room, but the curtains are drawn, so the room is dark. I passed by this room a few times when I was here last, but I never utilized it. There were always people in here, but now those figures are replaced by shadows.

I don't necessarily like this room as much as I like the Grand Room. Maybe because Layla and I connected in the Grand Room. There's history for us in there.

This room feels unconnected to us. If this house is the heart of the country, this room is the gallbladder.

If we end up buying this place, this would be the first room I would strip bare. I'd knock out part of the wall and add more windows. I'd fill it with furniture that Layla could spill cereal on, or red wine.

I'd make it livable.

Nothing has felt like home to us since Layla was released from the hospital. Neither of us wanted to go back to my place in Franklin. Understandably. But I didn't feel right getting a new place without Layla having a say, so I leased a temporary apartment near the hospital, and that's where I took her when she was discharged. I've been dragging my feet on buying something permanent. I'm not sure I want a place in Franklin. Or Nashville, even.

I look at houses a lot, but until I saw this place for sale, I hadn't felt drawn to anything.

There's something about this place, though. Maybe it's because I met Layla here. Maybe it's because being in the literal heart of the country really is grounding in some way. Or maybe it's because it's an entire day's drive from Nashville, and I really like the idea of getting out of that town.

Whatever it is, I'm not here just because I wanted a vacation. I'm here because I want time to focus on my music and I want Layla to find peace. I feel like this is the only place that can give us that. The seclusion would be perfect for us. She'd feel safe.

I spin around at the sound of Layla screaming.

I immediately run across the room and toward the bathroom when I hear glass shattering.

"Layla?" I swing open the door, and she looks at me with two fearful eyes. I immediately reach for her hand because there's blood on her knuckles. Shards of mirror line the bottom of the sink. I glance up, and the bathroom mirror is shattered. It looks like someone put a fist right to the center of it. "What happened?"

Layla shakes her head. She looks from the broken mirror to all the glass in the sink. "I . . . I don't know. I was just washing my hands, and the mirror shattered."

There's an obvious indention in the mirror, as if someone punched it, but I can't imagine why Layla would do that. Maybe it was already broken before she started washing her hands and the movement jarred the glass out of place.

"I'll grab the first aid kit out of the car."

She's in the kitchen when I return from the van. And just like earlier, I care for her wounds. I don't ask her questions. She seems shaken up. Her hands are trembling. When I'm finished, I take the first aid kit with me and grab one of our suitcases. "I'll email the Realtor about the mirror," I tell her. "That could have done some serious damage."

She grabs the other suitcase and follows me upstairs. I can tell she's rattled from that incident.

I have to stop treating her like she's incapable of caring for herself, though. She's capable. She's strong. She's incredible. And I'm going to be the one to remind her of that, because she seems to have forgotten.

CHAPTER SIX

If I weren't striving to be a musician, I'd be a chef.

There's something calming about cooking. I never was much of a cook before Layla's surgery. She taught me a few things when she moved in with me, but after she got injured, I didn't feel comfortable with her exerting too much energy, so I started doing the cooking. I've mastered soup, mostly because it was all Layla was ever in the mood for while she was recovering.

She's upstairs unpacking. I made sure to unpack my shoes myself and put them in the closet so she won't see the ring. I came downstairs to start dinner. I wanted to try and start this trip out right, so I'm making pasta e fagioli. Her favorite.

I've learned a lot since she's been out of the hospital. Mostly from her mother, Gail. She stayed with us for the first few weeks after Layla's release. She wanted to take Layla back to Chicago with her, but thankfully Layla didn't want to go. I didn't want Layla to go. I felt like it was on me to help her recover since what happened to her never would have happened had I been more protective of her.

I have to admit it was an adjustment. I had only met Layla two months before she spent a month in the hospital. Right after that, her mother temporarily moved in to our already cramped, new apartment. In less than three months, I went from always having lived alone as an adult to living with my girlfriend, her mother, and a couple of times, her sister, Aspen. The apartment I leased was only one bedroom, so the couch was always occupied, and an air mattress took up most of the rest of the living room.

I was glad when her mother finally went back to Chicago, but not because I didn't like her. It was just a lot. Everything we had been through, not really feeling like we had our own space, and then watching Layla struggle to fall back into step with her life—I just craved normalcy. We both did.

But it wasn't all bad. I got to know Layla's family, and I quickly became aware of why I fell in love with her in the first place. They're all very charismatic, open people. Hell, I even kind of like Chad Kyle. I've only seen him once since the wedding, and like Layla suggested, he's a bit of a douchebag, but he's funny.

I'm kind of looking forward to their visit on Friday.

Once I get all the ingredients into the pot, I dry my hands on a dish towel and then run upstairs to check on Layla. She was unpacking when I decided to start cooking, but that was over half an hour ago, and it's been quiet upstairs since then. I haven't heard her walking around.

When I open the door, I find Layla asleep on the bed, the unpacked suitcases still open. She's snoring lightly.

It's been a long day. This is her first trip since being released from the hospital. I can imagine it's taken a toll on her, so I start quietly unpacking the suitcases while she sleeps.

Every now and then I'll glance at her, and I'm taken back to the days we first spent here. Every single second with her felt like an awakening. Like I'd never really opened my eyes until she came along.

I was blind but now I see.

That's how Layla made me feel. It was like someone let all the air back into my life when I had no idea I was even suffocating.

What I wouldn't give to go back to that feeling before we were unfairly robbed of it. We were comfortable in my house in Franklin.

Layla didn't have trouble sleeping at night. She wouldn't look over her shoulder every time we were in public.

I walk over to where Layla is asleep on the bed, and I touch her hair, pushing it gently behind her ear. They had to shave a section of her hair during the surgery, so she wears her hair parted now to cover up the regrowth. I brush her hair away and look at the scar.

I'm thankful for it.

I know she hates it and she does everything she can to cover it up, but sometimes I look at it while she's asleep because it's a reminder of what I almost lost.

Layla flinches a little, so I pull my hand away, just as the smell of something burning enters the room. I look toward the doorway, confused, because there's no way the soup could already be burning. It's been less than ten minutes since I turned the gas stove top on.

I walk to the top of the stairs and see a dark cloud of smoke drifting out of the entryway to the kitchen.

As soon as I start to descend the stairs, I hear a crash come from the kitchen.

It's so loud; I feel it in my chest.

I rush down the rest of the stairs, and when I get to the kitchen, soup is everywhere. I scan the stove, the floor, the walls. I wave the smoke out of my face and try to figure out what needs saving first.

There's no fire, though. Just a bunch of smoke and a huge-ass mess.

I'm staring at it all in shock when Layla runs down the stairs.

She pauses in the entryway to the kitchen and takes in the mess. "What happened?"

I walk to the stove to turn off the burner, but when I reach for the knob, the burner isn't even on. It's been switched to the off position.

My arm falls down to my side. I look at the burner, then look at the pan on the other side of the kitchen.

"Why is the sink on?" Layla asks.

There's a stream of water running from the faucet. I don't remember leaving the water on. I walk over to it to turn it off and notice something in the bottom of the sink.

A burnt rag.

The same rag I wiped my hands on right before running upstairs.

The rag obviously caught fire, because it's burnt to a crisp, but how did it end up in the sink? How is the water on? Who turned off the stove?

Who knocked over the pan of soup?

I immediately walk to the front door, but it's locked from the inside. Layla follows me. "What are you doing?"

I know there's a back door, but if someone knocked the pan off the stove as I was descending the stairs, I would have seen them heading toward the back door. There's no other exit to the kitchen.

I walk back to the kitchen and look at the window. It's also locked from the inside.

"Leeds, you're scaring me."

I shake my head. "It's fine, Layla," I say reassuringly. I don't want to worry her. If I act like I can't explain this, it'll cause unnecessary concern. "I caught the rag on fire. Accidentally knocked the soup off the stove trying to put it out." I rub my hands up her arms. "I'm sorry. I'll clean it up."

"I'll help you," she says.

I let her. I'd rather her be in the same room because I'm not sure what the fuck just happened.

THE INTERVIEW

The tape ends, so the man ejects it, flips it over, and presses record again.

I wonder if he knows how much easier using his cell phone would be. He's probably a conspiracy theorist who questions the government to the point that he refuses to even carry a phone.

"I want to see the stove," the man says. He picks up the tape recorder and walks with it back to the kitchen. I stay seated on the couch for a moment—wondering if asking him to come here was a mistake. Most sane people would call me crazy after hearing my story. And here I am trusting that this man won't leak my story straight into the hands of all those sane people.

Honestly? I don't even give a shit. My potential career, my meager following, the image Layla has been trying to build for me—none of it matters anymore. It all seems so insignificant now that I've seen what this world is capable of.

It's like I've lived my entire life in shallow waters, but in the last few weeks, I've sunk all the way to the Challenger Deep.

The man is staring at the stove when I walk into the kitchen—his head tilted. He presses the knob in, turns it, and waits for the gas flame to ignite. When it does, he watches it burn for a moment. Then he turns it off.

He waves his hand at the stove. "You have to press it in to get it into the off position. How'd you explain that to yourself?"

I shrug. "I couldn't."

He laughs a little. It's the first iota of expression I get from him. He takes a seat back at the table and places the recorder between us.

"Did Layla seem bothered by it?"

"Not really," I say. "I took the blame, and she didn't question me. We cleaned the kitchen together, and I ended up making plain pasta instead."

"Did anything else strike you as strange that first night?"

"Not like what happened with the stove."

"But something out of the ordinary did happen?"

"Several things happened over the course of the next couple of days that left me questioning whether or not I was going crazy."

"What kind of things?"

"Things that would have sent anyone else out the front door without a second thought."

CHAPTER SEVEN

Layla is picking at her pasta, moving it around with her fork more than she's eating it. She looks bored.

"You don't like it?"

She stiffens when she realizes I'm watching her. "It's good," she says, taking a small bite.

She hasn't had much of an appetite lately. She barely eats, and when she does, she picks out anything with carbs. Maybe that's why she's only taken three small bites—because everything in her bowl is a carb.

She weighed herself a week after she was released from the hospital. I remember I was brushing my teeth at the sink, and she stepped on the bathroom scale next to me. She whispered, *"Oh my God,"* to herself, and I haven't really seen her eat a full meal since then.

She chews her food carefully, staring down at the bowl in front of her. She takes a sip of her wine and then begins scooting pasta around again.

"When are Aspen and Chad coming?" she asks.

"Friday."

"How long are they staying?"

"Just one night. They have that road trip." Layla nods like she knows what I'm talking about, but when I called Aspen to tell her about this trip, she told me she hasn't spoken to Layla in two weeks. I checked Layla's phone later that night, and she had several missed calls from both her mother and her sister. I don't know why she's avoiding them, but she sends their calls to voice mail more than she doesn't.

"Have you talked to your mom today?" I ask her.

Layla shakes her head. "No." She looks up at me. "Why?"

I don't know why I asked that. I just hate that she's avoiding most of her mother's calls. When she does that, Gail starts texting me, wondering what's wrong with Layla. Then she texts Aspen and worries Aspen. Then Aspen texts me, asking why Layla isn't answering her phone.

It would just be easier for everyone if Layla updated them more often so they wouldn't worry about her so much. But they do worry. We all do. Another thing that's probably a setback for her.

"I wish my mother would get a hobby so she wouldn't expect me to talk to her every day," Layla says, dropping her fork to the table. She takes another sip of her wine. When she sets it down, she closes her eyes for several long seconds.

When she opens them, she stares down at her pasta in silence.

She inhales a breath, as if she just wants to forget the conversation.

Maybe she spent too much time with them when she was released from the hospital. She probably needs a nice break from them, much like I need a break from the rest of the world.

Layla picks up her fork and looks at it; then she looks down at her bowl of pasta again. "It smells so *good*." She says *good* in a way that makes it sound like a moan. She actually sniffs the pasta. Leans forward and closes her eyes, inhaling the scent of the sauce. Maybe this is her newest trick to dropping the fifteen pounds she keeps talking about— smelling food instead of eating it.

Layla grips her fork and twists it in the bowl. She takes the biggest bite I've ever seen her take. She groans when it's in her mouth. "Oh my God. It's so good." She takes another bite, but before she finishes swallowing, she's shoveling yet another bite into her mouth. "I want more," she says with a mouthful. She grabs her wineglass and brings it to her mouth while I take her bowl to the stove and refill it with more pasta.

She practically rips it from my hands when I sit back down at the table. She eats the entire bowl in just a few bites. When she's done, she leans back in her seat and presses a palm to her stomach, still gripping her fork tightly in her right hand.

I start laughing because I'm relieved she's finally eating, but also because I've never seen anyone so animated while they eat.

She closes her eyes and groans, leaning forward. She props her elbows up on the table and moves her hand from her stomach to her forehead.

I take a bite of my own pasta right when she opens her eyes. She looks straight down at her empty bowl and makes this horrific face like she regrets every carb she just ate. She covers her mouth with her hand. "Leeds? My food is gone."

"Do you want more?"

She looks up at me—the whites of her eyes more prominent than I've ever seen them. "It's *gone*," she whispers.

"Not all of it. You can have the rest if you want it."

She looks horrified when I say that—as if I'm insulting her.

She looks at the fork still in her hand and studies it as if she doesn't recognize it's a fork. Then she drops it. Tosses it, really. It slides across the table, hitting my bowl just as she scoots back and stands up.

"Layla, what's wrong?"

She shakes her head. "Nothing. I'm fine," she says. "Just . . . ate too fast. A little nauseous." She turns and leaves the kitchen, then rushes up the stairs.

I follow her. She's behaving like another panic attack might be on the horizon.

When I get to the bedroom, she's rifling through the dresser drawers, muttering, *"Where is it?"* When she doesn't find whatever it is she's looking for, she opens the door to the closet. I panic a little—thinking maybe she might find the ring by accident. I walk over and grab her hands, pulling her attention to me and away from the closet.

"What are you looking for?"

"My medicine."

Of course.

I reach into the top drawer of the dresser and pull out her bottle of pills. I open them and hand her one, but she looks like she wants to take the bottle from me and down every single one of them. I have no idea what has her so spooked, but as soon as she has the pill, she goes to the bathroom and turns on the faucet. She places the pill on her tongue and then takes a sip straight from the sink. She tilts her head back to swallow it, and it reminds me of the night in the pool when Aspen gave her medicine.

The thought makes me smile as I lean against the doorway. Layla seems a little bit calmer now that she's taken the Xanax, so I try to distract her from her own anxiety by making conversation. "Remember when I thought your sister gave me drugs?"

Layla swings her head in my direction. "Why would I remember Aspen giving you *drugs*?" As soon as she says that, I can see the regret in her eyes. She drops her head between her shoulders and grips the sink. "I'm sorry. It's been a long day." She blows out a breath and then pushes away from the sink. She walks over to me and snakes her arms around my waist, pressing her forehead against my chest.

I hug her, because I have no idea what it must be like inside that head of hers. She's doing her best, so I don't let her mood bother me. I hold her for several minutes—feeling her heartbeat as it gradually slows down.

"You want to go to bed?" I whisper.

She nods, so I slip my hands up her back and ease her out of her shirt. Somewhere between the bathroom door and the bed, we start to kiss.

It's become our nightly routine. She stresses out. I soothe her. We make love.

I took a shower after Layla fell asleep. I still couldn't sleep after that, so I went downstairs and crammed in an entire day's worth of stuff in the span of two hours. I've shaved, washed the dishes, written some lyrics for a new song.

It's now one o'clock in the morning, and I'm finally back in the bed with Layla, but my mind still won't settle down.

I close my eyes and try to force myself to sleep, but my mind is racing. I thought today would be different for Layla. Stress-free. I thought maybe it would be like the first time we were here—but it hasn't been. Today has been like all the other days since the hospital. As much as I don't want to suggest it again, I really think she needs to start seeing a therapist. The doctor recommended it. Her mother and sister recommended it. But she insisted she would be fine. Until now, I've been on her side. I thought if I supported her through her recovery, the anxiety would pass. But it's getting worse.

I'm staring at the alarm clock when I feel Layla's side of the bed shift. I hear her stand up and walk across the hardwood floor.

At first, I think maybe she's heading to the bathroom. But the sound of her walking ceases, and she doesn't move for a while. I can feel that she's not in the bed, though, so I turn over to see what she's doing.

There's a standup mirror on the wall a few feet away from the bed. Layla is staring at herself. It's dark in here, other than a little light from the moon shining through the window, so I'm not sure what she's trying to see. She turns from left to right, inspecting herself in the mirror. It's strange how long she stares at herself. I wait another couple of minutes, thinking she'll come back to bed, but she doesn't.

She steps closer to the mirror, lifting a hand to the glass. She traces her index finger over the mirror as if she's outlining her body.

"Layla?"

Her head snaps back in my direction. Her eyes are wide with embarrassment—like she got caught doing something she shouldn't have been doing. She rushes back to the bed and slips under the covers with her back to me. "Go back to sleep," she says in a whisper. "I'm fine."

I stare at the back of her head for a while, but then I turn away from her. I certainly can't sleep, though. Especially now.

I'm staring at the alarm clock when it turns over to 1:30 a.m. Layla has already fallen back asleep. She's snoring lightly.

I can't sleep, no matter how long I lie here.

I sneak out of bed, grab my cell phone, and go downstairs. I take a seat on the couch in the Grand Room. It's 1:35 here, but it's only 11:35 back in Seattle. My mother never goes to sleep before midnight, so I text her to see if she's up. She responds with a phone call.

I lie against the arm of the couch and swipe my finger across my phone screen. "Hey."

"You guys made it to Kansas?" she says.

"Yeah. Got here around five o'clock."

"How's Layla?"

"Fine. Same."

"How are you?"

I sigh. "Fine. Same."

My mother laughs because she can tell when I'm full of shit. But she also knows I'll tell her what I feel like telling her when I feel like telling her.

"How's Tim?" He's the first guy my mother has dated since my father died. I've met him a couple of times. He seems all right. Meek. Gentle. Just the kind of guy I'd want for my mother.

"He's fine. His morning class didn't have enough students, so it got dropped. Now he has an extra free hour in the mornings. He's really liking that."

"Good for him," I say. And then, before I can even think about the words coming out of my mouth, I ask her, "Do you believe in ghosts?"

"That's random."

"I know. I just don't remember you ever talking about ghosts."

"I'm kind of indifferent to the idea of them," she says. "I don't *not* believe in them, but I don't know that I've ever had an experience that would make me believe in them." She pauses for a moment, then says, "Why? Do you?"

"No," I say. Because I don't. "But earlier . . . I don't know. Something weird happened. I almost caught the house on fire while I was cooking. I was upstairs before I noticed the smoke. When I got back to the kitchen, the rag I had left on the stove was in the sink. Water was running on top of it. The pan had been knocked to the floor, and someone turned off the burner. Layla was upstairs the whole time, so it couldn't have been her."

"That is weird," she says. "Does that place have a security system?"

"No. But the house was locked up from the inside. Even the windows, so no one could have put a fire out and then left without being seen."

"Hmm," she says. "It's definitely weird. But if someone saved the place from burning down, it sounds like you have a guardian angel. Not a ghost."

I laugh.

"Or a haunted house . . . *keeper*," my mother says, laughing at her own pun. "What else is going on?"

I sigh again, but don't elaborate on the sigh.

"It's okay to feel what you're feeling, Leeds."

"I didn't say I was feeling any certain way."

"You don't have to. I'm your mother. I can hear the stress in your voice. And guilt has always been your worst trait."

She's right about that. I press my palm to my forehead. "I don't know what's wrong with me."

"Let's see . . . ," she says. "You were attacked in your own home. The girl you love almost died. You spent an entire month by her side in

76

a hospital, and even longer after that caring for her. I can imagine that's pretty stressful," she says. "And to top all that off, you have a ghost."

I laugh, feeling the tension ease from my shoulders. She's always had a way of justifying everything I don't even have to tell her I'm feeling.

"You know what I miss?" my mother asks.

"What?"

"You. It's been six months since I've seen you, and those weren't good circumstances. When are you coming to Seattle?"

"Soon. Now that Layla has been cleared to travel, I'll see what she wants to do. Next month sound good?"

"I don't care when you get here as long as you eventually get here."

"Okay. I'll call you tomorrow after I talk to her."

"Sounds good. Miss you and love you. Hug Layla for me."

"I will. I love you too."

I end the call and stay motionless in my defeated position on the couch. *Maybe I'm depressed. Maybe I need therapy.*

As shitty as it is to think, I kind of hope everything I've been feeling lately is a result of depression. A chemical imbalance of some kind. I could take a pill every day and then hopefully start to fall back in love with my life.

This all sounds like it could be a song. I reach over to the end table where I left my laptop earlier, and I open a Word document. I start typing out lyrics.

I'd feel nothing if you punched me in the heart
I'd feel even less if you stabbed me with a knife
But I didn't fall out of love with you
I fell out of love with life

I study the lyrics, convinced I've never written truer words. Nothing excites me anymore, it seems. Not even writing music. It feels like I'm opening wounds I've been trying to heal.

I should just buy this place. We could stay here forever, plant a garden, get a dog and some cats. Maybe some chickens. We could reopen it as a bed and breakfast and watch people get married in the backyard every Saturday.

I minus out the Microsoft Word app and open Google. I type in the Realtor's website and search for the house. I have the listing saved in my favorites because I've looked at it almost daily since I found out it was for sale. It's not hard to imagine me and Layla building a life here.

Maybe I could accept growing the public side of my career if I also had an extremely isolated private life. I'm sure there's a way to find a good balance between both.

Her recovery would probably be less stressful here, especially if I installed a privacy fence and an electronic gate. Get her out of the city where all our bad memories began.

I click on the email icon to email the Realtor. I have some questions about the property, and I'd like her to meet us here at the house so Layla can be a part of the decision.

As soon as I'm finished typing the email, I move the cursor to send, but before I click it, my laptop slams shut—right on top of my hands.

What the fuck?

I toss the laptop away from me. It's a gut instinct to throw it, even though it pains me as I watch it crash against the hardwood floor.

But what the fuck was that?

I look down at my hands. I look at the laptop that's three feet away from my feet. There's no way to explain that. It closed with enough force that two of my knuckles are red.

I immediately run up the stairs. When I get to the bedroom, I lock the door behind me.

I think of all the things that could have caused that to happen, but I come up empty. That can't be blamed on a broken hinge, or a faulty appliance, or wind.

I don't believe in ghosts. This is stupid. Fucking stupid.

Maybe I'm delirious. I woke up at 4:00 a.m. in Tennessee yesterday so I could get us packed for our trip here. I've been up almost twenty-four hours now.

That has to be it. I just need sleep. Lots of it.

I crawl into bed, my heart still pounding. I pull the covers over my head like a scared toddler trying to shut out the monsters.

I'll go find a Best Buy tomorrow. Figure out what's wrong with my laptop. While I'm there, I'll buy cameras. Some kind of security system that can be connected to an app on my phone.

From this point forward, anything weird that happens in this house will be recorded.

CHAPTER EIGHT

It's almost nine in the morning when I wake up. It took me forever to fall asleep last night. I feel like I still have hours of potential sleep left in me, but I want to get up before Layla. The idea of coffee and isolation on the front porch is all I really want right now after last night.

After I get the pot of coffee started, I open the refrigerator to look for the creamer, but I immediately pause when I catch something out of the corner of my eye.

My laptop is sitting on the kitchen table.

I stare at it—afraid to move. *Did I dream that last night?*

I hate that I immediately begin to question myself. I never get my reality confused with my dreams, but this feels like maybe I have, because I know this laptop was on the floor in the Grand Room last night. I threw it there after it slammed shut on my hands.

Maybe Layla got out of bed after I fell asleep. I don't know why she'd use my laptop, though. She has her own.

I walk over to the table and take a seat in front of it. I slowly open the laptop and then move my finger over the track pad to wake up the computer. I want to look at the browsing history and see what Layla thought I was up to.

When the computer powers on, the Word document I wrote the lyrics in last night is pulled up. I specifically remember minimizing this document before I opened Google, which means Layla definitely used my computer after I fell asleep.

A sinking feeling settles in my stomach, as I realize Layla read the few lyrics I've put into this document. Does she assume they're about her?

I go to minimize the document, but before I do, I notice in the left-hand corner at the bottom it says there are two pages.

I only wrote four sentences.

I didn't write anything else that would have created another page in this document.

I scroll down until I get to something on the second page I'm certain I didn't write. It's just five words, but it's enough to make my blood run cold.

I'm sorry I scared you.

I read and reread the words typed into my document no less than twenty times before Layla comes downstairs. As soon as she walks into the kitchen, I say, "Did you use my laptop last night?"

She shoots me a funny look, like that's a stupid question. "No." She walks straight to the coffeepot. Her back is to me now, but I'm not sure I believe her.

Does she not like it here? Is she trying to scare me into leaving?

She probably saw my browsing history and is worried I'm buying the house. Maybe it's not something she wants anymore. But why go to such elaborate lengths to move my laptop and then make me think she didn't type these five words? Why wouldn't she just tell me she doesn't want to live here?

Someone is fucking with me, and since Layla is the only one in this house, it has to be her. But the kicker is, she's too fragile for me to confront her about it. I'm afraid if I accuse her of lying to me, she'll feel attacked and she'll go upstairs and pop another pill and zone out.

I read the words again before closing out the document, but I don't bring it up to Layla. She either already knows about it and is the one who wrote it, or she's going to freak out if I tell her someone moved my laptop while we were sleeping.

Neither of those outcomes is okay.

"You need to post something today," she says. She's at the coffeepot, stirring Splenda into her cup of coffee. "Maybe a shirtless selfie by the pool," she says with a wink.

I can't think about my fucking platform right now. Either I'm sitting across from someone who is trying to manipulate me, or I'm sitting in a house where someone—or some*thing*—is fucking with me.

Either way, I need a security system.

I google where I might be able to find one, but the nearest Best Buy is hours from here. The nearest Walmart is sixty-three miles away. *Damn, we really are in the middle of fucking nowhere.* I could order it online, but that would take a few days before anything is delivered.

"Want to run into town with me?" I ask Layla. "I need a few things."

She makes a face. "Town? Leeds. There is no town we can *run into.*"

I close my laptop. "It's just an hour away. I'll take you to lunch."

Layla looks like she's contemplating it as she sips her coffee. But now that I'm thinking about it, she might question me when I start buying a security system for a house she assumes we're only staying in for two weeks.

"Or I can go alone," I say. "It's fine if you want some alone time."

She thinks about it for a moment, and then gives me a sheepish look. "Is it okay if I don't go? I couldn't sleep last night. I'll probably just go back to bed for a couple of hours."

"Yeah, babe. Totally fine." I kiss her on the forehead before I leave the kitchen. "I'll be back after lunch. Text me if you need anything."

THE INTERVIEW

I'm leaning forward with my elbows resting on the table. The talking is becoming less of a nuisance. Maybe because we got past the hardest part.

"Why did you buy a security system?" the man asks. "Why didn't you just leave?"

I pick at a chipped fingernail. "I have no idea. Maybe because it was the first thing to happen to me in a while that I actually felt."

"What do you mean by that?"

"I was numb inside. Had been for a while. But the things that were happening in the house were as fascinating as they were inexplicable. I didn't leave, because in some twisted sense . . . I think I was *enjoying* it."

"So you stayed out of boredom?"

I think about that for a moment. "Not boredom, really. I had Layla. But I certainly wasn't scared of whatever was happening. It's hard to find something threatening that you don't believe in. I thought the security system was going to explain away everything that had happened."

"How about now? Do you feel threatened now?"

I think back on all that's happened since we've been here. There have been times I've wanted to leave . . . to run from it all. Things have happened that were downright terrifying. But even through it all, I'm resolute in my answer when I say, "No. I don't feel threatened. I feel sympathetic."

"That's usually not the reaction people have in these situations."

"I know. It's why I reached out to you, though. It isn't because I feel threatened. It's because I want answers."

"Did the security system help you find any?"

"Not at first. But . . . eventually. Yes."

CHAPTER NINE

I put one security camera in the kitchen and one on a bookshelf in the Grand Room. The cameras are connected to an app on my phone, so anytime there's movement, I get a notification.

That was two days ago, and so far the only times it has gone off are when Layla or I walk into view of the cameras.

I came here to focus on Layla, but to say I've been distracted would be an understatement. I'm always looking over my shoulder, waiting for something to happen. So much so I disguise my late nights as work, but all I've been doing is sitting in the Grand Room, browsing websites about supernatural shit. I stayed up so late last night I ended up falling asleep on the couch.

I just woke up. It's still dark out now. I'd guess it's probably around five in the morning. I'm still on the couch, but I haven't moved since I opened my eyes.

I'm trying to think about what position I was in when I fell asleep, what I was holding, the fact that I wasn't covered up. Because I don't remember the blanket I'm clutching. I remember it being on the back of the couch, but I don't remember using it to cover up with.

When I fell asleep on this couch last night—this blanket was folded and draped over the back of it.

I know Layla more than likely came downstairs and covered me with it, but I still mentally retrace my steps before opening the app.

Layla doesn't know about the security cameras. I'm not trying to hide anything from her, but I did set them up while she was asleep. I just figured if she saw one and mentioned it, I'd tell her they were here when we showed up so she wouldn't grow concerned.

But watching the videos recorded by the app is an invasion of her privacy. I just don't want to tell her I have access to the footage because I don't want her to worry unnecessarily. I also don't want her to feel like I'm spying on her.

But in a way, I am. I set the cameras up as a way to catch her in the act. Because who *else* am I going to catch? A ghost that I don't believe in? An intruder that can somehow bypass dead bolts?

I move for the first time since opening my eyes a few minutes ago. I sit up slowly on the couch and reach for my phone. I open the app and notice my fingers are trembling as I skip the video back to the moment I fell asleep. *Why would my hands be shaking if I think it's just Layla?*

I fell asleep around two in the morning, so I set the video to play around that time. I remain seated on the couch, half-covered with the blanket, and I watch the footage closely, fast-forwarding every few minutes.

At three twenty in the morning, a shadow appears in the doorway to the Grand Room.

Layla isn't anywhere in the frame, but I can tell it's her shadow.

A few seconds later, she walks slowly into the Grand Room. She stares down at me as I'm sleeping. Then she covers me with the blanket.

It was Layla.

I'm an idiot. I'm getting inside my own head. Now I'm forcing myself to assume things are happening without some explanation behind them.

I move my finger to stop the video, but my finger hovers over the screen because something Layla does on the video catches my attention.

After she covered me up, her eyes moved straight to the security camera in the Grand Room.

I watch the video with a lump in my throat. Layla peers at the camera for a good fifteen seconds before moving toward it. She walks across the room with a curious expression on her face and then stops right in front of the camera. She doesn't pick it up. She doesn't even touch it. She just stares into it as if she wants me to see her.

A moment later, she turns and walks out of the room, leaving me asleep on the couch.

The whole interaction between Layla and the camera is so bizarre; I rewind it and watch it again. But this time, I keep watching the video long after Layla has left the room. There are a couple of times I roll over on the couch, but other than those two movements, nothing else happens in the room.

Until it does.

At approximately 4:29 in the morning, the camera view changes abruptly, and then the video goes black.

I pause the video and look at the security camera perched on one of the bookshelves. It's pointed toward the wall now.

I immediately stand up and walk over to the camera. I adjust it so that it's pointing at the Grand Room again.

There's no way this camera could have turned on its own.

I watch the video no less than fifteen times in an attempt to figure out how the camera could just turn itself, but it can't. And there was no one in the Grand Room at that point other than me.

I begin pacing the room.

I can't explain that.

No one can explain that.

And if I were to show it to someone, I'd be accused of faking the video.

Maybe because the video *is* a fake? Is that possible? Maybe the camera was made to move on its own?

I walk over to the camera again. I pick it up and inspect it for a second time, as if I'm going to find something in the camera that could explain how it could move itself.

What if the app company has a hacker? I could see that happening. Some guy sitting at his computer, manipulating camera angles and positions to scare people.

It's the more plausible explanation, but I still find myself at the kitchen table on my laptop ten minutes later, researching ghosts and haunted houses.

I create an account using a fake name in a paranormal chat room. I read through the posts in the forum until the sun has fully risen outside.

I roll my eyes at every single one of the stories I read. People who claim to have seen a shadow, or heard a noise, or had a light flicker. All things that can easily be explained.

This shit can't be explained.

How does a camera move by itself? How does a stove-top burner turn off by itself? How does a rag move from the stove to the sink? How does a laptop type messages to itself and move from one room to another?

I can feel the certainty in my beliefs being chipped away at as I make my own post in the forum. I title it "Skeptic."

Then I write:

> *I don't believe in ghosts. Not even a little. But things have happened that even my skeptic self can't explain. Appliances turn off by themselves. Objects move themselves. My laptop slammed shut on my hands. My initial thought is that my girlfriend is pranking me, but the timelines and her placement in the house don't add up with the things that have happened. I'm not sure what I'm expecting you guys to say. I guess I just want another skeptic to explain these things away for me. But how many*

*things have to happen before they can no longer
be explained?*

When I hit post, I feel like a damn idiot.

I shut my laptop and stare at it.

I'm losing my mind.

Not because weird things are happening—but because I've allowed myself to believe they can't be explained. There's an explanation for everything. I just have to figure it out.

"You're up early."

My whole body jerks at the sound of Layla's voice. I didn't even hear her coming down the stairs. She leans in and kisses me before walking to the coffeepot. I made a fresh pot, but that was two hours ago—back when I used to be an idiot and chose to spend an entire morning online reading ghost stories.

I'm no longer that same idiot. I've matured in the last two minutes. I've come to my senses.

"What are your plans today?" Layla asks. She's looking down at her cell phone, sipping from a coffee cup.

"I don't know. Figured I'd work on some music. You?"

She shrugs. "I'm thinking about having a pool day." She sets her phone and the coffee on the counter and walks over to me. She slips between me and the table, so I push my chair back a little so she can straddle me. She's wearing a fitted T-shirt that doesn't even cover her stomach, and a pair of pink panties.

Anytime Layla is wearing something this revealing, it's the first thing I notice. And then once I do notice, she usually ends up no longer wearing whatever it is she was wearing because we end up naked in the bed, or in the shower, or on the couch.

Yet . . . I didn't notice her this time until she sat on my lap.

I slide my hands to her ass and bury my face in her neck. This is further proof that my focus has been skewed since the day we arrived here.

"Didn't you say the pool was heated?"

"Yep."

"You should take a break and have a pool day with me," she says.

A pool day actually sounds good. Being outside sounds good. Spending time in the water with Layla might feel reminiscent of the first time we were in that pool together, and that sounds *really* good.

I slide my hands up her back and smile at her. "Bathing suit pool day or naked pool day?"

"That's a stupid question." She smiles, and it's the first genuine smile I've seen on her face in a long time. I love it so much I kiss that smile.

I also find that smile misleading. Why hasn't she asked me about the camera?

Maybe she assumes it belongs to the owner of the house.

I'll just let her keep assuming that.

＝～

Layla found an oversize float with cup holders and a Bluetooth speaker, so we're on it together in the middle of the pool. She's on her stomach attempting a tan, even though it's in the low sixties right now. She might even be asleep. I'm lying on my back, shamefully and secretly interacting in the paranormal forum.

It's late afternoon now and even though I decided I'm no longer the same person I was this morning when I stupidly posted to that forum, I'm still reading the comments like I can't devour them fast enough.

How long have you lived in the house?

Dude, get the heck out of there.

Has anyone ever been murdered in the home?

I answer a few of them with one reply:

We don't live in this house. It's for sale, but we're only here for a short-term rental. I was thinking about buying it but now I'm not so sure. And I don't know the history of the home. How could I find that out?

I hit post, just as Layla groans. "You've been on your phone for two hours," she says. She grabs my phone out of my hands, and I try to snatch it back from her, because the paranormal forum is still pulled up, but she doesn't look at the screen. She just stretches out her arm and sets it on the concrete next to the pool to keep me away from it.

I feel bad. She's right. I haven't put my phone away once today.

Layla rolls over onto her back. The float bobs up and down from the movement. Her eyes are closed, and she's relaxed as she lazily drapes her arms over her head. I stare at her for a moment—my eyes following the length of her. She looks insanely sexy right now.

"Have you ever had sex on a pool float?" I ask her.

She doesn't open her eyes. She just grins and shakes her head. "No. But I'm definitely up for the challenge."

⌒

The lack of food coupled with the alcohol led to us failing at trying to fuck on the pool float. We fell off it three times. We didn't give up, though. We just moved to one of the nearby lounge chairs to finish.

The wind picked up as the sun was beginning to set, and no matter how warm the water was, the air was getting too cold to remain outside.

We've been inside for several hours now, relaxing on the bed. She's been watching movies, and I've been on my laptop attempting to browse the forums, but it's difficult trying to keep the screen out of her line of sight with as much as she moves around.

I finally decide to take my browsing downstairs. I reach over and turn off my lamp.

"You going to sleep too?" Layla asks, her voice muffled by the pillow she's snuggling.

"I'm gonna work on a song for a little while." I lean over and kiss her. "Text me if the piano is too loud."

She nods, her eyes closed. "Can you turn off the TV?"

I turn it off and head downstairs.

Today was nice. Layla seemed relaxed. Content. There was a moment right after we finished having sex when I almost told her about how I'm considering buying the property. I was kissing her neck, thinking about how nice the day was. How nice all the future days could be. I wanted to ask her opinion on buying the house, but I couldn't get the words out.

Buying a house is a huge commitment.

Buying a house with a girl I've known less than a year is an even *bigger* commitment.

Today was damn near perfect. But there's still an uncertainty that lingers, not only with the strange things that have happened in the house, but with whether Layla would even want to make a decision that huge.

I chose not to say anything. Not yet, anyway.

When I get to the Grand Room, I sit at the piano, but I'm really not in the mood to work on my music tonight. I set my laptop on top of the piano with the intention of checking my email, but I don't. I go straight back into the forum I posted in this morning and start reading the replies in my thread.

> Why is the place for sale? You should ask the previous owners why they left.

That comment piques my curiosity. This place wasn't for sale when we were here the first time. And I remember Layla saying something about how Aspen had to book a year in advance in order to secure the venue. If they were booking out that far in advance, they couldn't have been hurting for business. Why would they shut it down and put it up for sale so suddenly?

I continue scrolling through the comments until I come across someone with the username UncoverInc. I click on his profile, and the description makes me laugh. *Ghosts are people too.*

Wow. They really take this shit seriously.

I scroll back to his comment and read it.

Have you tried talking to your ghost yet?

That one comment started a thread of other comments.

I can't even read them. I can't take any of them seriously when they're claiming to have had conversations with ghosts.

I close my laptop, feeling sympathy for all the people who spend so much time in that chat room.

Even if ghosts existed, how the hell would I *communicate* with one?

As much as I'm trying to put my own intellect above all the people in that forum, I still catch myself looking around the Grand Room. I look behind me, in front of me.

I make sure Layla isn't anywhere near me when I whisper, "Is someone here?"

Nothing happens.

No one responds.

That's because *ghosts don't fucking exist, Leeds.*

"Jesus Christ," I mutter. I'm now on the same playing field as the crazies in the forum.

I stand up and stretch my arms over my head. I look around the room, waiting another few seconds, as if someone is actually going to respond to that question.

I finally shake my head at how absurd my thoughts have been the last few days. I walk toward the door and grip the handle, and then an unexpected sound forces me to pause in my tracks.

One of the piano keys just played.

It was so loud I recognized exactly which key it was that made the noise. Middle C.

I close my eyes.

That did not just happen.

I slowly turn around, eyes still shut, not sure what I'm expecting to find when I open them. Maybe my laptop fell onto the piano keys? My pulse is pounding so violently—I can feel it in my neck.

I open one eye . . . then the other.

There's no one at the piano. No one in the room but me.

I immediately pull my phone out of my pocket, open the app for the security cameras, and watch the playback of the last thirty seconds.

The app shows me standing up from the piano. Stretching. I keep my eyes on the footage of the piano. As soon as I reach out for the door handle, middle C on the piano is pressed by nothing.

The key just . . . *played* itself.

There was nothing there. Absolutely nothing.

There is no way that can be explained.

My first instinct is to run, but my second instinct—the part of me that finds this fascinating—wins out.

"Do that again," I say, walking closer to the piano.

A few seconds pass, and then the same key plays itself again.

I take a quick step back.

My knees feel like they're about to give out. *"Fuck."* I bend over, staring at the piano. I take in a slow breath.

I want to ask another question. I want to ask a million questions. But the reality of this moment is too heavy for me to accept. This is where I draw the line, apparently, because I'm walking toward the door.

Rushing. Running. Halfway up the stairs, I pause and press my back against the wall.

I think back to every ghost story I've ever laughed at. Every fairy tale I've never believed in.

Could I really be wrong?

Incredulity begins to simmer inside of me, or maybe it's fear. How can I have been wrong my whole life? I've always been able to explain everything. These last few days have been the only time in my life I haven't been able to explain something away.

I can either continue to run from that, or I can confront it. Figure it out. Put my mind at ease.

I think about the idiots in scary movies that never run when they should, but I empathize with them now. The need to disprove the thing that's scary is greater than the need to run from the potential harm it might bring.

I'm not convinced this is something I should be scared of. I'm convinced it's something I should investigate.

When I'm back in the room, I close myself inside. I realize most sane people would be in the rental car right now, getting the hell away from this place. I'm still not sure that won't be me in a few minutes.

"Who are you?" I ask, staring at the piano, my back pressed to the door in case I need a quick escape.

I wait for an answer but realize a question like that can't be answered with the stroke of a piano key.

I hesitate before finally walking to the piano. I look behind it. Beneath it. Inside of it. There are no wires . . . no setups that would allow someone to be doing this.

"Press a different key."

The D key is played this time, almost immediately.

I cover my mouth with my hand and mutter "Holy shit" against my palm. I have to be dreaming. That's the only explanation.

"Press the A key."

The A key makes a sound.

I don't know what's happening, but I completely suppress the skeptic in me and just go with my instinct this time. "I have questions," I say. "Press middle C for yes. D for no. A if you don't know the answer."

Middle C presses lightly, which means yes. My voice comes out a little shaky when I ask, "Are you dangerous?"

I don't know why I ask that. Any dangerous entity would surely deny they're dangerous.

The D key is pressed for *no*.

"Are you a ghost?"

I don't know.

"Are you dead?"

I don't know.

"Do you know me?"

No.

I start pacing the room. My legs feel like they're floating because I no longer have feeling in them. My skin is tingling with excitement. Or fear. They feel the same to me sometimes.

"I'm having a conversation with a piano," I mutter. "What the fuck is happening?"

I have to be dreaming. I'm asleep right now. Either that, or someone is punking me. I'm probably on some prank show. Hell, Layla probably signed us up for a prank show to get me more notoriety.

Maybe someone outside the room is getting a kick out of this. I should ask questions no one would know the answer to unless they were here with me. I look up at the security camera. *Maybe that's it?* Someone from the security company thinks this is a funny prank? I take the cover off one of the throw pillows on the couch. I toss it at the camera and cover it up.

I hold up five fingers.

"Am I holding up three fingers?"

No.

"One?"

No.

"Five?"

Yes.

I drop my arm. "Am I going crazy?" I whisper to myself.

I don't know.

"That question wasn't for you." I sit on the couch and rub my hands down my face. "Are you alone?"

Yes.

I wait for a while before asking another question. I'm trying to soak up everything that's happened in the last half hour, but I'm still trying to throw explanations at myself.

No keys are pressed while I sit in silence. My adrenaline has never been this high. I want to wake up Layla and show her what's happening, but I'm reacting to this like I found a stray dog and not some entirely different . . . *realm.* Layla said that once. That she thinks there are different realms. *Fuck. Maybe she was right.*

It makes me want to tell her about this even more, but I'm worried it'll freak her out. She might want to leave. We'll have to pack our things and get in the car, and then I'll never get answers to all the thousands of questions that have formed in the last few minutes. Like what is this thing? *Who* is this thing?

"Can you show yourself to me?"

No.

"Because you don't want to?"

No.

"Because you don't know how to?"

Yes.

I run my hands through my hair and then grip the back of my neck as I walk over to one of the bookshelves that line the walls. I need more proof that this isn't a prank. It's not that easy to suspend an entire lifetime of beliefs in one day.

"Pull a book off one of these shelves," I say. A hacked security camera won't be able to pull that off.

I stare patiently at the bookshelf in front of me.

Ten very quiet and still seconds go by; then the book I'm focused on slides out of the bookshelf and falls to the floor with a thud. I look at the book in complete disbelief.

I open my mouth, but nothing comes out of it.

I pace the room for a few minutes. I think about everything that's happened up to this point, and I think maybe I'm numb. In disbelief.

"Do you have a name?"

Yes.

"What is it?"

Nothing happens. No keys are pressed. I realize the question can't be answered using one of the piano keys. I've started working out a way words can be spelled out using piano keys when I hear a noise. I look over at my laptop, which is sitting on top of the piano. It's opening.

My Word document pulls up.

Letters are being typed into the Word document.

W . . . i . . . l . . . l . . . o . . . w . . .

I take a quick step away from the laptop.

I'm extremely uneasy now.

Before, with the piano, I felt like I still had a small sliver of a chance at explaining it away. A faulty piano key. A mouse in the strings. *Something.*

But after the book, and now this—this is a full-on conversation with . . . *nothing.* No one is here but me, so that only leaves one explanation.

Ghosts are real.

And this one's name is Willow.

I stare at the computer for so long the screen goes dark. Then my laptop shuts, all by itself, no wires attached, no explanation—this is insane, *good fucking night.*

I leave the room.

When I get up to the bedroom, I open the drawer where Layla keeps all her medicine. She has three prescriptions. One is for her anxiety, one is to help her sleep, one is a pain medication.

I take one of each.

THE INTERVIEW

"Why did you walk away when she told you her name?"

I laugh. "Why didn't I walk away when the stove turned off by itself? Or when the laptop shut on my hands? I don't know. I was a hard sell, I guess. It's not easy for a person to just change their entire belief system in the span of half an hour."

The recorder is still going when he says, "Did anything else happen that night?"

I open my mouth to say no, but both of us look up at the ceiling as soon as we hear a crash. I leave the kitchen and run up the stairs.

Layla is still tied to the bed, but the lamp on the nightstand has been knocked over. She's looking at me calmly. "Let me go or I'll break something else."

I shake my head. "I can't."

She lifts her leg and kicks at the nightstand. It scoots a foot across the floor, and then she kicks it again, knocking it over.

"Help!" she screams. "HELP ME!"

She knows someone is downstairs, and even though she knows someone is in the house, she has no idea he isn't here to help her escape. "He's not here to help you, Layla," I say. "He's here to help us get answers."

"I don't want answers! I want to *leave*!"

I've seen her upset since all of this started, but I'm not sure she's been *this* upset. Part of me just wants to cut her loose and let her go, but if I do that, it will only mean trouble for me. She'd go straight to the police. And what would my excuse be? A ghost made me do it?

If they don't arrest me, they'll send me to a psychiatric hospital.

I take Layla's face in my hands. My grip is firm, but she won't be still, and I need her to look me in the eyes. "Layla. Layla, *listen* to me."

Tears are streaming down her cheeks. She's breathing heavily, inhaling shaky gasps. The whites of her eyes have turned red from all the crying.

"Layla, you know this is out of my control. You *know* that. You saw the video." I wipe the tears from her cheeks, but more follow. "Even if I were to untie you, you'd be unable to leave."

"If I can't leave, then why do I have to stay tied up?" Her voice is tearful—a guttural ache. "Untie me and let me go downstairs with you. You can tie me to the chair, I don't care. I just don't want to be alone up here anymore."

I want to. But I can't. I don't want her to hear everything I'm about to admit to the man downstairs. I know she's scared, but she's safe in here. Even if she doesn't feel like it.

"Okay. I'll bring you downstairs with me." Her eyes grow hopeful, but that hope fades when I say, "Soon. I need twenty more minutes, and then I'll come back up here." I press a kiss against her forehead. "Twenty minutes. I promise." I put the nightstand back near the bed. I place the broken lamp on top of it, and then I go back to the kitchen. My feet feel heavier as I descend the stairs. The longer I keep Layla tied up against her will, the guiltier I feel, and the harder it's going to be for her to forgive me.

Is this even worth it? Are answers for me and for Willow worth what I'm putting Layla through?

"Is she okay?" the man asks when I walk back into the kitchen.

"No, she's not okay. She's tied to a bed." I sit down with a thud and press my face into the palms of my hands. "Let's just get this over with so I can figure out what to do with her."

"Does she know why I'm here?"

"No."

"Does she know anything at all?"

"A little. But she thinks it's all related to her head injury. The memory loss. She doesn't know it has nothing to do with her."

"What does she think about you keeping her locked inside this house?"

"She thinks I'm a monster."

"Why don't you just let her leave?"

It's such a simple question to have so many complicated answers. "Because maybe she's right. Maybe I'm a monster."

He nods, almost sympathetically. I don't know how he can look at me without judgment, but that's exactly how he's looking at me right now. Almost like he's seen this before. "After the incident with the piano, did you speak to Willow again that night?"

I shake my head. "No, I fell asleep. Slept for twelve hours because of the pills I took. When I woke up, Layla decided she wanted another pool day, despite her sunburn. She stayed under the canopy and read a book in the shade. I joined her because I just wanted to stay out of the house. I was uneasy after what had happened the night before. But the whole time we were outside, I was on my phone. Distracted by the cameras, waiting for something else to happen. Speaking to people in the forum."

"Did you speak to Willow again that day?"

"Chad and Aspen ended up showing up around five o'clock in the afternoon. I didn't even try to communicate with Willow. I tried to forget it had happened, but Willow made that impossible."

"How so?"

"She joined us for dinner."

CHAPTER TEN

"You guys have any plans for your anniversary?" I ask. I'm trying to keep up with the conversation—pretend I'm mentally involved in this dinner. But my mind hasn't been on dinner at all.

"Just practicing our baby making on our road trip," Chad says, grinning in Aspen's direction.

"We are not. I'm still on birth control," Aspen says.

"That's why I said *practicing*," Chad says. He looks at me. "We took a detour to Hutchinson on our way here today. Ever been to the Salt Mine Museum?"

I take a long swig of my beer and then say, "No."

"We had sex in the mine," Chad says, shooting Aspen a grin.

I look at Layla. She's cringing.

Aspen groans and says, "Please stop talking about our sex life."

"Yes," Layla says. "Please."

I want to beg him to stop, too, but I'm honestly barely even in this conversation. Chad was tolerable when they got here a few hours ago, but that was before eight beers.

"I can't wait until the honeymoon phase is over," Aspen mutters. "You're wearing me out."

Chad laughs and picks up her hand, kissing the back of it. Aspen seems to melt a little with that action.

Layla is still holding her fork, cringing at Chad.

"How's the stay been so far?" Aspen asks. "It's kind of weird seeing this place so empty."

"It's been good," Layla says, seeming relieved by the change of subject. "Having the pool to ourselves is my favorite part, even though I'll probably start blistering if I don't stay inside."

"It's crazy the place is for sale now," Aspen says. "How cool would that be to own a bed and breakfast?"

"Sounds like a lot of work," Layla says.

I sink a little at that reply, wondering if Layla really feels that way now. She cuts a tiny bite of her pizza. It's a homemade pizza—Aspen cooked it. Layla used to make it, but she hasn't cooked since her surgery. The crust is thick, and the toppings are an inch high, so it's hard to eat with your hands. Chad is the only one at the table not eating it with a fork.

"I'd hate to live here," Chad says. "Do you know how far away the liquor store is? Far. *And* we're out of beer."

Aspen grips the bottle of wine sitting in the center of the table and slides it over to him. "There's a few of these left," she suggests.

"I'd rather you not drink all my wine," Layla says. "There's a liquor cabinet above the sink."

Chad perks up at that comment. I wish she wouldn't have said that. Chad reached his limit about three beers ago, but he stands up and heads straight for the liquor anyway.

Aspen pours herself more wine.

I'm staring at Layla, because she just stiffened in her seat. Sometimes when that happens, it's because of the anxiety.

I stay focused on her, watching her every movement, hoping she's not experiencing the onset of a panic attack—but something about how she's holding herself now is concerning me.

She sets down her fork and picks up her slice of pizza with her hands. She takes a huge bite of it. Then another. She holds the pizza with her right hand while she picks up her wineglass and sips from it.

"This is so *good*," she says, her voice on the edge of a moan, like she hasn't eaten in days. It catches everyone's attention. She shoves the rest of the pizza in her mouth.

Aspen looks at her like Layla was looking at Chad earlier—with a little bit of disgust. Layla lifts out of her chair and reaches toward the pan of pizza, picking up another slice with her hands.

She plops back down in her seat and stuffs as much of the pizza in her mouth as she can. She's doing that thing again—eating like her life depends on it. Aspen just continues to stare at her in horror as she shovels half the slice of pizza in her mouth.

"Gross," Aspen says. "Use your fork."

Layla pauses and looks at Aspen; then she gives her attention to me. Her eyes are suddenly apologetic. Embarrassed. She takes another quick, huge bite and then downs her entire glass of wine in one go.

As soon as Layla sets down the glass, she hesitates. Then her hand goes to her forehead and she groans, squeezing her eyes shut. "Oh, God. My head hurts." She massages her forehead and then lowers her hand, opens her eyes, and . . . *screams*.

The unexpected noise makes all of us jump in our chairs.

Her scream makes *Aspen* scream. "What is it?" Aspen says, pushing back from the table. "Is it a spider?" She crawls up into her chair. "Where is it?"

Layla is shaking her head but doesn't say anything. She's staring at her empty plate of food. She stands up and backs away from the table—a look of sheer terror on her face.

"Get her some water," I say to Aspen as I stand up. I walk over to Layla, and her back is flat against the wall now, her body trembling. She breathes in and then out very slowly, but still hasn't taken her eyes off the table.

I place a gentle hand on her cheek and pull her gaze to mine. "Layla, are you okay?"

She nods, but her hands are shaking as she grasps for the glass of water Aspen brings her. She downs it all and then almost drops the glass as she hands it back.

"I don't feel well," she says, turning to exit the kitchen.

I follow her up the stairs, and as soon as she gets to our room, she goes straight to the dresser and fumbles with her bottle of pills. Her hands are unsteady, and she spills some of the pills when she gets the lid open.

I bend down and pick them up, then take the bottle from her and put the stray pills back inside. She's crawling into the bed when I close the dresser drawer.

I sit down next to her, and she's curled into a fetal position in the center of the mattress. I pull the covers over her, running my hand soothingly through her hair. "What happened down there?"

She shakes her head, dismissing my question. "Nothing. I just don't feel good."

"You think you ate too fast?" I suggest.

She rolls over and pulls the covers up to her chin. "I didn't *eat*," she says. Her words come out clipped—full of anger and confusion. I want to ask her what she means by that, but part of me already knows.

She's having blackouts. Silent seizures, maybe? She's had one before—in the hospital. But it was just the one, so they decided not to put her on medication for it. I should call her neurologist tomorrow.

I turn off the lamp beside the bed and then kiss her. "I'll come check on you soon."

She nods and then pulls the covers over her head.

She's been sleeping a lot. More than usual. Coupled with the blackouts and the strange behavior—I really do think she needs to see a neurologist.

But I'm also afraid it has nothing to do with her head injury.

I sit by her side for a few minutes, hesitant to go back downstairs. Part of me doesn't want to leave her alone, but I need to go clean up the kitchen.

The wheels are turning in my mind as I make my way downstairs.

Aspen is in the process of loading the dishwasher when I rejoin them. Chad has face-planted on the table, a glass of some kind of liquor in his hand. He isn't fully passed out because he's muttering something unintelligible.

"She okay?" Aspen asks.

I don't even try to cover for Layla because I'm confused and full of questions. "I don't know. She says her head hurts."

"I'm sure she'll have migraines the rest of her life," Aspen says. "Side effect of getting shot in the head, unfortunately."

Aspen would know. She is a nurse, after all. I'm sure she's seen a lot worse recoveries than what Layla is going through.

Aspen puts the last plate in the dishwasher. "I need to get Chad upstairs. Can you help me?"

I shake Chad until he opens his eyes, and then I pull on his arm and say, "Let's go to bed, buddy."

He groans. "I don't want to go to bed with you, Leeds." He tries to push me away from him, but I wrap his arm over my shoulders.

"I'm taking you to your wife's bed."

He stops pushing me away at that comment. He lifts his head and looks around the room until he finds Aspen on the other side of him. "Am I too drunk to fuck?"

Aspen nods. "Yeah, babe. Way too drunk. Maybe tomorrow."

He drops his head like he's disappointed in himself, but we get him out of the chair and to a standing position. He mopes the entire time we help him up to his room. Once we've got him tucked into the bed, Aspen walks me to the bedroom door. "We'll probably be on the road before you wake up. If I don't see Layla, tell her we had fun."

"It wasn't that fun," I say with a laugh.

Aspen shrugs. "Yeah, I'm trying to be nice. Maybe we can stop back by before you guys leave. It's not too far from Wichita."

I tell her good night and leave the room, then check on Layla. I don't know if she's asleep yet, but she still has the covers pulled over her head. I leave the door to our bedroom open because I want to be able to hear her if she calls for me. I go downstairs to the Grand Room and take my phone out, then take a seat on the couch.

I watch the video from dinner three times on my security app. Every time, I notice small things that make the entire event seem weirder and weirder. There was a change in her posture. A difference in the way she went from being invested in the conversation to completely ignoring everyone around her. The way she held her head before she screamed. The whole thing was strange.

But what is normal anymore?

It could be a blackout. It could be silent seizures. But those two minutes were so uncharacteristic of her as of late. Just like when she freaked out after eating the pasta.

I can't stop thinking about the three words she said as I was tucking her in.

"I didn't eat."

I grab my laptop and go to the kitchen. I open the same Word document that has the words *I'm sorry I scared you* in it and the name *Willow*.

I completely suspend my disbelief for a few seconds and type out a question.

Was that you?

I push the laptop a few inches away from me and watch it intently. Almost immediately, letters appear on the screen.

Yes.

I feel those three letters like punches in my gut, my back, my jaw.

I think I've finally accepted that this house came with a spirit of some kind, but believing that spirit can take over Layla's body is an entirely new thing to process.

This is real. It's fucking real, and I can't deny it anymore.

I start thinking back on the days we've been here. That first night—when Layla was staring at herself in the dark. The dinner where Layla ate more carbs in two minutes than she's eaten in six months. Her behavior at dinner *tonight*.

None of those moments were Layla.

How many other moments weren't Layla?

My heart begins to pound harder. Not necessarily faster—just harder and louder, making me aware of its beat in more than just my chest. I feel like I should be scared, like my heart rate should be out of control, but I'm not scared. If anything, I'm angry. Whatever this is—whoever this is—I don't like that they've used Layla like they have.

But I'm also angry at myself, because I need to see it again. I need to know that this isn't Layla going crazy. I need to know that this isn't *me* going crazy.

I need answers to every single question I never knew I had.

I want you to do it again, I type. *I want to be able to have a real conversation with you.*

I close the laptop, not giving whoever I'm speaking to a chance to refuse my request. But I also don't move. If this is really happening—I want them to prove their existence in some other way. I want to see the change in Layla with my own two eyes while I know exactly what's happening.

I don't go upstairs. I want whoever this is to come to me, so I remain seated in the kitchen for several minutes. My heart just beats harder and harder as I wait.

I don't hear a door open, but I do hear footsteps as they begin to descend the stairs. It's a slow descent, with each step cracking beneath the weight of whoever is approaching the kitchen.

I don't look behind me as whoever it is enters the room. My gaze remains transfixed on the table in front of me.

I smell Layla's perfume before I see her, so I know it isn't Aspen or Chad. Chills crawl up my spine and spread out over my shoulders and arms as she walks around me. I still don't look at her. It's the first time I've felt truly afraid since this began because I don't know what to expect.

Is it Layla? Did she come downstairs with strangely impeccable timing?

Or is Layla asleep somewhere in there?

I finally make eye contact with her when she pulls out the chair to sit down. It's Layla.

But it isn't.

There's something different about her—as if she's staring back at me like she's just as unfamiliar with me as I am with her. She looks scared. Or maybe it's curiosity rather than fear.

She pulls a leg up and places a bare foot on the chair, wrapping her arms around her knee. She lays her head on her knee and just stares at me.

"Layla?" My voice is a whisper, but not because I'm trying to be quiet. I just don't have much of a voice right now because there's more trepidation caught in my throat than air.

She shakes her head.

"Willow?"

She nods.

I lean forward over the table and blow out a deep breath, massaging my forehead with my hand. *What the fuck?*

"You aren't going to run?" she asks. Her voice is Layla's voice, but it comes out different. Her voice sounds full of amusement, unlike Layla's voice.

"Should I?"

"No."

This is so strange. How can I be looking at Layla while seeing someone else entirely stare back at me?

I've officially lost my mind. Isn't the average age of onset for schizophrenia in males the early twenties? Maybe that's it. Maybe I'm just schizophrenic. I'd believe that before I'd believe I'm witnessing a spirit possess a body. "Am I going crazy?"

She shrugs. "You've asked that before. I still don't know the answer." She looks over her shoulder at the refrigerator. "Can I have some juice?"

Juice?

She wants juice?

I nod and start to scoot back in my chair, but she holds up a hand. "I can get it." She walks over to the cabinet and grabs a glass. She opens the refrigerator and pulls out the bottle of orange juice. I just watch her, kind of captivated by the whole thing. She carries herself differently than Layla. There's almost a whimsical way to how she moves, as if there isn't an ounce of anxiety holding her back.

She leans against the kitchen counter and downs the juice. She sighs, pressing the glass against her cheek for a moment when she's finished with it. Her eyes are closed as if she's savoring the way the juice tastes on her tongue. "This is so good." She washes the glass and then puts it back in the cabinet.

"Do you do that a lot?"

"Do what?" She sits back down at the table, pulling her leg up again. "Steal your groceries?"

I nod.

"No. I need a body to do that. I don't like using Layla's body unless I have to. It's a little weird."

"A little?"

"My normal and your normal aren't the same."

"What's your normal?"

She looks up at the ceiling in thought. "Nothing."

"What do you mean?"

"My normal is nothing. I just . . . exist. But I *don't* exist. I don't know—it's hard to explain."

"Are you a ghost?"

"I don't know."

"How long have you been here?"

"I don't know. Time is weird. It's like it doesn't count for me." She traces an old scratch on the table with her finger. "I once stared at a clock on the wall in the living room for eight calendar days, just to see how long I could stare at the wall."

"You don't sleep?"

"Nope. Don't sleep, but I'm always tired. Don't eat, but I'm always hungry. I can't drink, but I'm always thirsty. I'm starting to think maybe this is hell because there is nothing worse than being eternally hungry."

This is surreal. She's in Layla's body right now, but she is so different from the Layla I've been with all day. "Are there others here like you?"

She shakes her head. "Not in this house. I'm alone."

"Can you leave?"

She shrugs. "I don't know. I'm too scared to try."

"What are you scared of?"

She lifts a shoulder. "Other things like myself, maybe?"

I raise an eyebrow. "A ghost afraid of other ghosts?"

"It's not that far fetched," she says. "Humans are afraid of other humans."

"Are you afraid of me?"

Again, she lifts a shoulder. "I don't know. I don't think so. But it could just be that I'm inside Layla's body right now, so I feel some of her feelings. You make her feel comfortable."

That's good to know. "How did you feel when we showed up here?"

She lowers her leg and leans back in her seat. "Nervous. I didn't want you here. It's why I closed your laptop when you were emailing the Realtor about buying this house."

"So that was you?"

"I don't normally do things like that. I try to keep our worlds separate."

"You aren't right now."

"That's because you asked me to do this—to talk to you through Layla. I don't *want* to do this."

112

"But you have. Twice, already. Maybe three times. Right?"

She blows out a frustrated breath. "Yes, but that's only because it's torture sometimes. I can't help it." She stands up and begins rummaging through the cabinets. She finds a bag of potato chips and then comes back to the table, but she sits *on* the table this time, placing her feet in her chair. She pops a chip into her mouth. "I didn't know I could do it at first," she says. "Not until the night you guys showed up. There have been other people here before, but I've never tried to get inside of them. I didn't even know I *could*. But I was so hungry." She eats another chip. "You have no idea what it's like to know what hunger feels like . . . and thirst . . . but not be able to eat or drink. And it's been so long since this place has been open. I missed the smell of food, and pasta must be my favorite thing because when I was watching Layla pick at it, all I wanted to do was taste it. It just sort of happened. I didn't mean for it to."

"How many times have you done that?"

"Just a few times," she says, wiping crumbs from her fingers onto Layla's shirt. "Twice at dinner. Once while you were sleeping on the couch. And once when I was looking at her in the bedroom mirror upstairs. I try to be inconspicuous, but you notice every time."

"You aren't inconspicuous. It's an obvious change when you're inside of her."

"I'm a bad actor, what can I say?"

"What do you look like when you aren't inside Layla?"

She laughs. It's *Layla's* laugh, though, which causes my heart to constrict a little. It's weird—someone else laughing Layla's laugh. It's been so long since I've heard it.

"I don't look like anything. I don't exist in a physical form. I can't see anything when I look in the mirror. It's not like the ghosts in the movies with the flowy white gowns. I'm just . . . *nothing*. I'm thoughts. Feelings. But they're not really attached to anything tangible. It's weird, I guess, but it's all I know."

I'm trying to think of more questions to ask, but it's hard when I'm full of this much adrenaline. I feel like we've cracked some code by communicating this way. Or maybe we've broken some unspoken rule.

I want to get excited about the idea of it all, but twenty-five years of disbelief is hard to just let go of.

"Layla . . . if this is some kind of prank . . ."

She shakes her head. "It *isn't*. I'm not Layla. I'm Willow."

The idea that Layla would go to these lengths to lie to me for no reason is somehow more unbelievable than Layla being possessed by a ghost. All I can do is believe this girl—or at least *pretend* to believe her—while I try to get more answers. "How old are you?"

"I don't know. I don't even know that I have an age, if that makes sense. Like I said earlier, time isn't really a thing for me."

"So you don't feel like there's an end to your life?"

"I just don't think about it. Not like humans do. When there's literally nothing I can do or look forward to . . . not even meals or naps. Or the bigger things, like aging and death . . . what importance is time?"

She eats several more potato chips in silence. Then she grabs a soda from the fridge and sits back down in the chair while she drinks it. Every time she takes a sip or a bite of food, it's like she appreciates it with the feelings of a million taste buds. It makes me feel like I've taken everything I've ever tasted for granted.

"Does it feel different being in her body?"

She nods immediately. "Yes. It's really confusing. There are memories that don't belong to me. Feelings that aren't mine. But that's the thing—when I'm *not* inside of her—I feel very little, and I have no memories at all. So I kind of like being inside of her, even though it feels wrong, like I'm not supposed to do this."

"You have her memories?"

She nods. "Yes, but I'm trying not to be intrusive."

"Can you remember things that happened between me and Layla?"

She looks down at her can of soda. I see her cheeks flush a little with embarrassment, and it makes me wonder what memories caused that feeling in her.

"You met her here."

I nod to let her know that memory is right.

She smiles. "She loves you."

"You can feel that?"

"Yes. She loves you a lot. But she's also worried."

"About what?"

"That you don't love her as much as she loves you."

I can feel my face fall a little at that confession. I don't want Layla to feel that way. I don't want her to feel loved less than she is, or full of anxiety, or scared.

"Will she remember this conversation? You taking over her?"

She shakes her head. "No. She didn't remember the times I ate her food. She just thinks she's having memory issues." Her eyes narrow. "Something bad happened to her. It affected her. A lot."

"Yeah. It did."

A door opens upstairs and steals my attention. We both look at the entryway to the kitchen. *Shit.* I forgot Aspen and Chad were still here. "Can you leave her body? That's probably her sister."

Willow shakes her head. There's a new look of unease about her. "I don't know if that's a good idea. Layla will freak out if I leave her body right now. She'll be in the kitchen when she wakes up and will have no memory of getting down here."

Aspen appears in the doorway. "Thought I heard you two." She walks over to Layla—*to Willow*—and grabs the bag of chips from her. Aspen takes a seat next to Willow. "Chad pissed the bed. I changed the sheets, but I'm pretty sure the mattress will need to be cleaned now." She looks at Willow. "Your fault for showing him where the liquor was."

Willow looks at me wide eyed, like she's scared to say anything to Aspen.

I push my chair back. "I'll take care of it tomorrow. No big deal." I look at Willow. "You ready for bed, Layla?"

She nods and starts to stand up, but Aspen grabs her hand and pouts. "No, stay. I never get to see you anymore, and I can't sleep."

Willow looks at me and then Aspen and then back to me. She reluctantly sits back down. I don't want to leave her down here alone, so I sit back down with her. Aspen looks relieved to have the company, but Willow looks afraid to speak—as if Aspen will immediately know that she isn't Layla right now.

"Did y'all finish off the pizza?" Aspen asks.

"No, it's still in the fridge."

She walks to the refrigerator to grab the pizza, and Willow leans her elbows onto the table, gripping her forehead. She mouths, *What do I do?*

I honestly don't know. And it's weird that she's asking *me* how to handle this, like I have any experience at all with these things. I try to sidetrack Willow with the only thing I know about her. She likes food. "Want some pizza?"

She pauses for a beat, and then nods with the slightest grin. "I do, actually. Two more pieces. And another soda."

The entire next few minutes are surreal. I make Willow a plate, and then Aspen sits down next to her. Aspen has been talking nonstop while Willow mostly just eats. I keep Aspen talking, making up almost half of the conversation so Willow doesn't have to speak much. She's a little more relaxed than when Aspen first came down here. She's focusing mostly on the food in front of her.

That lasts until Aspen says, "Did you tell Leeds what happened while I was cooking the pizza?"

I look at Willow, and her eyes grow wide.

"Oh my God," Aspen says. She starts to laugh while waving her hand from Layla to me. "Tell him, Layla. It was so funny."

I can see the fear in Willow's eyes—like we're about to be caught. I know Willow said she has access to Layla's memories, but I'm not sure how accurate they are. And if Willow wasn't in the kitchen while they were cooking pizza, she wouldn't have that memory.

"She already told me," I say. I have no idea what Aspen is talking about, but I don't want to put Willow on the spot. I stand up. "We really need to get some sleep."

Willow nods and pushes back from the table. "Yeah, I'm exhausted. And still have that damn headache." She leans down and hugs Aspen. "Good night. Thanks for coming."

Aspen throws a hand up in the air. "Seriously? I've seen you twice since I got married."

I'm pulling Willow by the arm as we back out of the kitchen. "Why don't you guys stay longer tomorrow?"

Aspen rolls her eyes. "We can't. We're supposed to be in Colorado by tomorrow night, and Chad will make me drive most of it until his hangover wears off." She waves toward the stairs. "You two go to bed. I'll clean up my mess."

Willow doesn't waste any time. She says good night again and rushes up the stairs. I follow her, but when we're in the bedroom and I close the door, I have to lean against the door and exhale several times to settle my nerves.

The entire last fifteen minutes with Aspen had me on edge more than the fact that there's a ghost using my girlfriend's body.

"That was intense," she says, pacing the room. "I have to be more careful."

"They leave in the morning, and then it's just me and Layla again. You don't have to worry about anyone else."

She pauses. "You're . . . staying?"

I nod. "Yes. We don't leave until next Wednesday."

"You aren't mad at me?"

"For what?"

She waves a hand down the length of her body. "For this. For using Layla."

Should I be? I don't know.

I kind of feel sorry for Willow—not mad at her. This goes beyond anything I can even begin to wrap my head around, so my reactions probably aren't at all adequate for what's actually happening here.

"I'm not mad. I'd actually like to talk to you again if it doesn't affect Layla. I don't want her to find out about you yet. I'm not sure she'll understand it."

"Do *you* understand it?"

I shake my head. "Hell no. I feel like I'm going to wake up tomorrow and laugh at how insane this dream was."

Willow looks at the bed, and then back at me. "I can't slip out of her without her being asleep first. I don't want her to get scared."

I nod. "It's fine. I'll sit in the chair until you're asleep."

"You sure?"

"Yeah. But I do want to talk to you again. Maybe tomorrow night?"

She nods but doesn't say anything else. She just crawls into the bed, pulls the covers over herself, and closes her eyes.

I watch her for half an hour. And then, slowly, Layla's body relaxes.

I saw nothing that would prove Willow is no longer inside her, but I can tell she isn't. She just changed, ever so slightly, and now Layla looks peacefully asleep. She looks like the same Layla I tucked into this same bed earlier tonight.

I look around the room, knowing Willow can probably still see me. Still hear me. I whisper, "Good night," and then I crawl into bed with Layla.

I spend the next hour running question after question over in my mind, wondering if Layla will remember any of what happened.

And what does this mean for Willow? What happens when Layla and I leave next week? She'll just be completely alone again?

I fall asleep feeling more sympathy course through me than fear or guilt.

THE INTERVIEW

It's been a lot longer than twenty minutes since I last left Layla upstairs. Layla lets me know this by yelling my name over and over and over.

The man pauses the tape recorder. "She sounds angry."

I nod. "I told her I'd bring her downstairs. She wants to meet you."

"Layla does?"

"Yes. Is that okay?"

"What was the reason you gave her for my being here?"

"I haven't really told her much at all yet. She knows something strange is going on with her behavior. I told her you might have answers."

The man nods. "Bring her down, then."

I pour myself another sip of bourbon before going back upstairs to untie her.

When I walk into the bedroom, she's trying to reach the knot on the rope but can't. I made sure of that when I tied it, but I admire her tenacity.

She hears the door shut, so she swings her head in my direction. "Twenty minutes? It's been an *hour*."

"I'm sorry." I start to untie her hands and notice she's been attempting to pull out of the ropes to the point that her bandages have come undone. Her wrists look even worse now. I don't know what else I could use to restrain her that wouldn't hurt. I don't have any handcuffs, and I don't trust her enough to leave this house to go buy any. "I need you to promise me you won't try anything stupid. I hid all the knives."

"Did you hide the forks? Those hurt too."

I don't even respond to that comment. Once she's untied, she says, "I have to pee first." She goes to the bathroom, so I follow her and keep an eye on her.

She's not as scared as she was earlier. She seems more angry now. Her movements are full of temper as she flips on the water to wash her hands.

"So who is this guy?" she asks, following me out of the bathroom.

"I found him on the internet."

She pauses as I open the bedroom door. "You're kidding, right?"

"What am I supposed to do, Layla? Call up the police and ask them to help?"

"You brought in an internet quack to solve this?"

I put my hand on her lower back and guide her out of the bedroom. "I'm doing my best. Grasping for straws now. It's all I can do."

She stomps down the stairs, and I keep my hand on her back, not because I'm fearful she'll fall, but because I'm worried she might try to run. I added a couple of dead bolts to the doors leading to outside, so she won't have time to open a door and escape. It's the only reason I'm allowing her to come downstairs in the first place.

She walks into the kitchen and pauses at the sight of him. She looks from the man, to me, back to the man. "You're a detective?"

"Sort of," he says. He reaches his hand out to shake hers. "I'm Richard."

"Randall," I correct him.

He looks down at his shirt. "Oh. Yeah, Randall. Name's Randall."

This was a bad idea.

"You don't even know your own name?" Layla asks.

"It's Randall Richard," he says, covering up his lie.

Layla slowly turns her head to find me. She raises an eyebrow and then looks back at him. "You a doctor?"

"Somewhat."

Layla laughs half-heartedly. "*Sort of* a detective. *Somewhat* of a doctor. You either *are* or you *aren't*."

"I used to be a doctor. Now I'm a detective."

"Of course," Layla says flatly.

The man sits back down at the table, motioning toward the chair opposite him.

Layla says, "I'd rather stand." She turns her attention back to me. "Did you do a background check on this guy before you brought him here?"

I don't lie to her. I just shake my head.

Layla laughs. "This is brilliant." She walks toward the exit to the kitchen. "Just great." She pauses and looks at me, and it's the first time she's ever looked at me with hatred in her eyes. "I'm *leaving*. And if you try to stop me this time, I will scream until someone hears me or until I die. I don't really care which comes first."

"I'm not the one who stopped you from leaving last time, Layla."

I stay where I am as she brushes past me, but I watch as she crosses the foyer and heads toward the front door. She gets the top lock unbolted before she stops, pauses, and then backs away from the door.

She turns around to face me, and I can tell Layla isn't the one looking back at me right now. It's Willow.

"She's really upset," Willow says. Her eyes are full of concern. "I think you need to tie her up again."

I nod and walk back up the stairs with Willow and into the bedroom. She sits down on the bed, and I notice a tear fall down her cheek as she lifts her hands up to me.

"Don't feel bad," I say, even though I know she does. We both do.

"I can't help it. I hate that we're doing this to her. She thinks you're evil and that she's going crazy."

I rewrap her hands before I tie them with the rope, hoping Willow will stay inside her long enough for Layla to fall asleep. "Have you been downstairs with us this whole time?" I ask her.

Willow nods. "Yes, but he hasn't offered up any advice. No explanations."

"I know, but he's getting there. I don't have much more to tell him, and then he could know exactly how to help you. It's why we have to keep Layla here until we're finished. We might need her."

Willow is crying a little bit harder now. Her tears are different than Layla's. Layla cries out of anger and fear. Willow cries because she's sympathetic toward Layla.

God, what a tangled web we've woven.

I grab a tissue from beside the bed and wipe the tears from her cheeks. I tilt her face up. "We're going to figure this out. I promise. Can you try to make Layla fall asleep?"

She nods. I lean forward and kiss her on top of the head; then I go back downstairs. When I walk into the kitchen, I feel guilt, but it's also accompanied by a little bit more hope than it has been lately. This man has seen Layla. He's seen what Willow can do. None of it seemed to faze him, though, so that gives me a sense of optimism. If it didn't faze him, maybe he's seen things like this before. And if he's seen things like this before, maybe he really can help.

"Is Willow making you do this?" the man asks as I take a seat.

I'm not sure how to answer that. She doesn't want us to leave. She's made that clear. But I also haven't fought back very hard. "I don't know. I think this is a mutual effort, unfortunately."

"Why won't either of you let Layla leave?"

I don't answer that, because the answer makes me feel like a monster.

The man leans forward, tilting his head. "Are you in love with her?"

"Of course. She's only tied up because I want to keep an eye on her, but I can't do that if she leaves."

"I wasn't talking about Layla."

My eyes fall to the table when I realize what he's insinuating. I can feel the heat in my chest spread to my neck . . . my cheeks. "No. It's not like that."

"Not like what?"

"It's not . . . I don't know. I care about Willow. But I'm in love with Layla."

"But you've developed a relationship with Willow. Enough of one that you would put Layla at risk in order to help Willow."

"I don't feel like Layla is at risk," I say.

"You certainly aren't keeping her out of harm's way by forcing her to stay here."

"But I'm also not doing it out of a lack of concern for her." I'm getting agitated at his line of questioning. "Look, it doesn't matter why I'm choosing to keep Layla here. She's seen too much. That's a good enough reason alone." I wave my hand toward him. "Ask me something else."

He rolls his eyes a little. "All right. How often do you and Willow use Layla's body without her knowledge?"

"Not as much as we did at first."

"How often did it happen in the beginning?"

"A lot."

CHAPTER ELEVEN

The way a person wakes up in the morning reveals a lot about the stage they're at in life. Before I met Layla, I was a hard wake. I'd hit snooze on my alarm five times if there was somewhere I was meant to be. And if there wasn't, I'd sleep until my body ached; then I'd roll myself out of bed like a deadweight and drag my feet all the way to the shower. I lived a life with very little that excited me.

After I first met Layla, I was eager to wake up. My eyes would open and immediately search her out. If the alarm was set, I'd silence it at the first sound, fearful it would wake her because I wanted to be the thing that woke her. I'd kiss her cheek or drag my fingers up her arm until she smiled. I wanted to see her before she saw me, but I also wanted to be what she woke up to.

Today, I wake up in a similar, yet entirely new way—my skin already buzzing with anticipation before I'm fully alert. My eyes pop open, and I immediately search out Layla, but not because I want to be the thing that wakes her. I want the opposite. I want to slip out of our bed undetected so I can hide in the bathroom and rewatch footage from last night.

I lock the bathroom door, turn on the shower to drown out the noise from my phone, and then I lean against the counter. I skip the footage back to the moment Willow walked into the kitchen and sat at the table. I rewatch my entire conversation with Willow, just to make sure it actually happened and I didn't dream the whole thing.

I didn't dream it at all.

I close my phone app and stare into the bathroom mirror. It's insane how two mornings ago, I woke up confident in my view of the world. But now that confidence has vanished and has been replaced by curiosity, fascination, and a new, intense need to uncover everything else in this universe that I'm unaware of.

Knowing there's more to this life than meets the eye makes everything around me feel insignificant. My career feels insignificant. My love for Layla feels like it matters less to the timeline of my life than it did two days ago.

Most of the things that have ever caused me stress all seem so unimportant now that I know there's so much more out there than what I've led myself to believe.

My *own* existence feels less important to me now.

My priorities have shifted in the last twenty-four hours, yet I have no idea what my new priority is. It's been Layla for so long now, but even everything Layla and I have been through feels less traumatic when you consider the possibility that not only do other humans have it worse than we do—but other realms of existence have it worse than we do.

I always tell Layla everything, but I'm still not sure I want to bring this up to her. But there's a part of me that believes Layla knowing the truth about this could somehow help her. If she knew for a fact that there were other planes of existence than the one we're currently in, maybe what happened to us would feel less significant. Maybe, in some warped way, this would be just as intriguing to her as it is to me, and it could possibly help with everything she's been struggling through.

It has certainly freed me from the emptiness I've been feeling lately. I'm not sure what it is I'm filled with now, maybe just curiosity and a shit ton of questions. But it's been a while since I've woken up with this much enthusiasm for the day.

I'm ready to speak to Willow again.

I look around the bathroom, wondering if Willow is in here right now. Does she watch us all the time? What does she do all night if she doesn't sleep? What is she doing right now?

I have so many questions for her; I don't even want to waste time on a shower. I turn off the water and slip out of the bathroom. Layla is still asleep on her stomach.

I leave her in bed and go down to the kitchen. I start a pot of coffee and look around the kitchen, wondering if she's here. We need a way to communicate when she's not using Layla.

"Are you in here?" I ask.

I say it quietly because I'm not sure it'll ever feel normal—talking to nothing.

I don't get any type of response, so I repeat myself. "Willow? Are you here?"

I spin around when the water in the sink faucet begins to drip. I turn and observe the drips of water until they change into a steady flow, then a heavy stream.

Then the water turns itself off completely.

I realize fear should be coursing through me, but the only thing I feel right now is eagerness. I want to continue where we left off in our conversation last night. I look around the kitchen—wondering how we can do that. I have a phone in my hands. I can use my phone. Willow can use my laptop.

I retrieve my laptop and sit at the kitchen table. "I don't know if you know much about technology," I say out loud. "But since I know you can type, we can use the messenger app." I open it and point to the screen, assuming she's following along if she's in the room. "I'll use my cell. You can use the laptop." I slide it to the left of me and then rest my elbows on the table, holding my phone in my hands. I'm staring at the keys on my laptop as they begin to depress, quickly, several letters in rapid succession. She types fast. That could be a clue as to what she did in her past life.

A message appears on my phone. *I'm very good with technology.*

I can't help but smile at the message.

This is surreal. It is so much bigger than anything I've ever imagined would happen in the span of my lifetime. The idea of marriage, having kids, building a music career—it all seems like filler now. What if I have some sort of sixth sense? What if I'm supposed to do something with that? What if I'm meant to be something else besides a musician?

The keys on my laptop are being pressed again. She's typing something else.

I know things—like how to cook. How to use a computer. How to use a cell phone. But I have no idea how I know those things.

I don't use my phone to respond to her. I just speak out loud since Layla is still asleep upstairs. "I wonder if that could be a clue to how recently you died. I would assume if your death happened decades ago, you'd speak differently, or act differently."

You seem so sure that I used to be alive. What if I've just always been here?

"Maybe you have, and you've just picked knowledge up along the way. You say you watch television sometimes, right?"

Yes.

"There are things we could do to try and pinpoint a timeline."

Is that important to you? Knowing if I was once alive?

"Is it not important to you?"

I don't know. Not really, I guess. What would it matter?

"If you knew what your life was like, maybe you could figure out why you're stuck here."

I don't necessarily feel stuck.

"But are you happy?"

No. I already told you what it's like here. You and Layla showing up is the most exciting thing to happen to me.

"What if I'm here to help you? Do you even want help figuring this out?"

That's pretty egocentric of you to assume I'm the one who needs the help. What if I'm here to help you?

I stare at that comment for a moment, allowing it to get tangled up in all my other thoughts. "I've never thought of it like that." I lean forward on the table, bringing my fingers to a point against my chin. "Maybe you're right—maybe we're both where we belong. But if that were the case, why would you be crossing into *this* world? You're the one who misses things I still have. Food. Water. Sleep. You're never satiated where you're at. Everything tangible is in this realm, and it seems like you miss those things, which means maybe you had them at some point in the past."

My laptop slides several inches across the table until it's sitting directly in front of me. The sudden movement causes me to flinch.

"Why'd you let me sleep so late?" Layla asks. My eyes dart up, and she's standing in the doorway to the kitchen, stretching her arms above her head. She yawns as she heads for the coffeepot.

"It's not that late," I say, slowly closing the lid to my laptop.

Layla pours coffee into a mug. "It's eleven o'clock."

"The deadliest time of day," I say teasingly.

She eyes me curiously. "It's *what*?" She has both hands wrapped around her coffee mug now as she sips from it. I walk over to her and kiss her on the forehead.

"Eleven in the morning—the deadliest time of day," I say, repeating one of the many facts she's told me.

Her eyes squint in confusion. "Weird. You'd think it would be nighttime."

A blanket of guilt feels like it drapes over my shoulders. There are so many things I take for granted that Layla is still slowly recovering—the conversations we've had, the memories we've made, all the perfect moments we've spent together. It's like someone took a pair of craft scissors and cut slivers of her life out of her mind, leaving them in scraps on the table.

I feel like I sometimes don't appreciate the severity of her injuries. I've spent the last six months since it happened walking on eggshells, trying not to point out the obvious, not wanting her to feel like she's lost as much as she has. But what if indulging her desire to avoid talk of that night has inadvertently made it all worse?

A brain injury has to be similar to a physical injury. You exercise a physical injury. You work harder to gain back all the strength you lost. I went through three months of physical therapy for the wound to my shoulder, but we did the exact opposite with Layla's injury.

We didn't exercise her brain . . . we put it on bed rest.

We've avoided the damage—put her wounds on respite in the hopes everything would heal on its own. But it hasn't. Physically, yes. But mentally—I'm not so sure.

"Were you on the phone just now?" she asks.

"No. Why?"

"I thought I heard you talking when I was coming downstairs."

"I was," I say quickly. "To myself. Not on the phone."

She buys my explanation and walks to the refrigerator and opens it. She stares at the shelves, but grabs nothing before closing the door.

"Want me to make you some breakfast?" I ask her.

She groans. "I've gained two pounds this week. I'm not eating breakfast anymore."

"We're on vacation. You still have at least eight more pounds left to gain before we can even consider this a successful trip."

She smiles. "You're sweet. But eight more pounds on me would mean no more naked pool days. I wouldn't be able to look at myself."

I walk over to her and pull her against me. I don't like hearing her talk like this. I don't like that something as simple as a little weight gain on vacation would even stress her out. I try to think back on our relationship—recall anything I might have said that would make her think I care about her body more than I do her. I do tell her she's sexy a lot, but I mean that in a positive way. But maybe reinforcing my attraction to her looks is causing her to put more importance on her appearance than she should.

I take her face in my hands. "I love you, Layla. That love doesn't fluctuate with numbers on a scale."

She smiles, but her smile doesn't reach her eyes. "I know that. But I still want to be healthy."

"Skipping meals isn't being healthy."

"Neither are Pop-Tarts or Twinkies, but this kitchen is full of nothing but junk food."

"It's *vacation*," I say. "That's what you do on vacation. You eat crap that's bad for you while being lazy and sleeping too late." I kiss her. "You need to get in vacation mode before our vacation is over."

She wraps her arms around my waist and presses her forehead against my shoulder. "You're right. I need to relax and enjoy this next week." She pulls back. "You know what I can't say no to? Mexican food. Specifically tacos."

"Tacos sound good."

"And margaritas. Where can we go around here to get tacos and margaritas?"

I fill with hesitation when she suggests leaving the house. I do want to get her out of here, and I like that she seems excited about the idea of tacos, but I also have fifty thousand questions left for Willow. I won't be able to ask her those questions if we leave and I'm driving and preoccupied with Layla.

"You sure you want to leave? It's at least sixty miles to the nearest restaurant."

Layla nods emphatically. "Yes. I need out of this house." She stands on her tiptoes and kisses me. "I'm gonna go shower."

She walks out of the kitchen, and I head straight for my laptop and open it.

"Are you still here?" I ask, hoping to get some kind of response.

I stare at my laptop, but nothing happens. I wait patiently until I hear the shower running upstairs. I repeat my question. "Willow? Are you still here?"

The seconds are slow as they pass without action. But then the keys begin to press down, and I breathe a sigh of relief as she types something out.

Sorry. I'm here now. I left the room when Layla got down here. It feels weird watching the two of you without your permission, so I don't.

"Where do you go when you leave the room?"

I was in the Grand Room.

"Do you ever go upstairs?"

Sometimes. Not when you're both up there, though.

That's not entirely accurate. "You were upstairs the night you slipped into her and got out of bed to look in the mirror."

I thought you were both asleep. I try not to spy on you when you're together. It feels wrong. But I have weaknesses . . . like when I smell the food you're eating.

"But you spy on us when we're alone?"

Spy is a strong term. I'm curious. Lonely. So yes, sometimes I watch you live your lives. There's nothing else to do around here.

"What will you do when we leave next week?"

Sulk. Maybe try to beat my eight-day record of staring at the clock.

I don't laugh at her self-deprecating joke. The thought of her being completely alone makes me feel bad for her. It's weird—feeling sorry for a ghost. A spirit. Whatever she is.

I wonder what happened in my childhood that makes me take on so much guilt, even when I'm not responsible for whatever is wrong. I take on the weight of Layla's sorrows. Now I'm taking on the weight of Willow's.

Maybe I *should* buy this house. I know Layla wouldn't want to live here full-time, but we could come here for vacations. That way Willow wouldn't always be alone.

"We're leaving soon, but we'll be back this evening."

Where are you going?

I guess she really wasn't in here for Layla's and my conversation. I find it humorous that a ghost has morals in the same way humans do. She doesn't want to be intrusive, even though we wouldn't be aware of her presence.

"Layla wants tacos. And I'm sure she'll want to shop while we're in town. We'll be gone all afternoon."

Tacos sound so good.

"Want me to bring you some?"

It's a nice gesture, but I think you forget that I can't eat.

"You could tonight. After Layla goes to sleep." There's a moment of stillness before she begins typing again.

You're okay with me using Layla again?

I shouldn't be okay with it, but it doesn't seem to be harming Layla in any way. If anything, she's getting some much-needed calories from it. "Sure. Tacos are important. You want beef or chicken?"

Surprise me.

I close the laptop and head upstairs, skipping every other step. I'm looking forward to spending the day with Layla. But I think I'm looking more forward to talking to Willow again tonight.

There's definitely some deceit going on here—I'm fully aware of that. But it's hard to know where to draw the line when the lines aren't even in the same world.

CHAPTER TWELVE

There were more options in Nebraska than anywhere within an hour of Lebanon, Kansas, so we crossed the state line and went to a city called Hastings.

I was starving by the time we got there, but Layla wanted to shop first, so we went to a few boutiques before going to the restaurant. It was a smart choice on her part, because she had four margaritas with just one taco, so she was barely able to stand without assistance by the end of dinner.

She wasn't too drunk not to question why I wanted to order tacos to go. I told her it was because she didn't eat enough at dinner, so I wanted to take food home in case she got hungry later.

When I said that, she smiled and leaned across the table to kiss me but knocked over one of her margarita glasses. It went crashing to the floor, and she was so embarrassed she was apologizing to everyone in the restaurant while they cleaned up her mess. She even apologized to the glass she broke. That's when I knew she'd exceeded her limit.

It was only an hour's drive back, but Layla had to stop twice to pee because of all the margaritas. I kept talking to her in an attempt to keep her awake. It was still fairly early in the evening on our drive back to Lebanon, so I didn't want her sleeping in the car and then staying up late.

I felt a twinge of guilt for that—being excited for her to go to sleep at the house so Willow could take over.

But not guilty enough to stop myself from doing everything I could to keep her talking.

We arrived back at the house right as the sun was setting. Layla wanted to sit outside and watch it, so that's what we're doing right now. Sitting on the grass near the pecan tree, watching as the sun is swallowed up by the earth.

It's a painfully slow process.

I keep checking the time on my phone as if I have somewhere to be. I have nowhere to be, but I've never wanted Layla to want to go to sleep as much as I wish she would right now. But she's still drunk. Still laughing at nothing and at everything.

I have so many questions for Willow, and I just want to go inside, but Layla has other plans.

She places her hand on my chest and pushes me onto my back as soon as the last sliver of sun disappears. She leans over me, dropping her hand to the button on my jeans, just as she lowers her mouth to mine. The sour taste of lime still lingers on her tongue.

I kiss her back because that's what I'm supposed to want to do. I'm supposed to crave her, to want her tongue in my mouth, my hands on her body, to push myself inside her. But it's not what I want right now. All I feel right now is overwhelming impatience.

I don't know how to separate my desires now. I came here so Layla and I could regain our footing, but I have a feeling our worlds are going to grow further apart the longer we stay here. I'm becoming too fascinated with the world we aren't in, and that's going to affect us. Somehow. I don't know how yet, but I know what I'm doing is wrong. Allowing Willow to use Layla's body is a terrible form of deception. Yet, it's a deception I find myself justifying every time I start to question it.

Layla's hand slips between my jeans and my stomach. I can feel her deflate when she grips me and finds that I'm not nearly as into this as she is right now.

"You okay?" she asks. This normally doesn't happen. When she wants me, all she has to do is kiss me, and that's enough to make me hard. But right now it's not enough. My mind is everywhere but here, and I can tell in her eyes that she feels it's somehow a reflection of how I feel about her. It's not. I'm just preoccupied.

I bring my hand up to her cheek. "I'm good," I say, brushing my thumb over her mouth. "There's just a rock or something digging into my back." I roll her over so that I'm looking down at her now. "Maybe we can finish this later tonight. In our bed."

She smiles. "Or right *now* in our bed." She pushes me off her and then stands up. She's wobbly when she's on her feet, so I stand up and steady her. She brings a hand to her forehead. "Wow. I am so drunk."

I help her back to the house, hoping she's too drunk to want to continue this upstairs.

She doesn't forget, though.

She starts kissing me as soon as we're inside the house. She tucks her hands into my jeans and tugs me toward the Grand Room. "Let's just do it on the couch," she says.

I pause, wondering where Willow is right now. It feels weird, knowing she can see this.

I don't want to fuck Layla in the Grand Room. I don't want to fuck Layla at all right now. It feels awkward, knowing someone else is in this house with us. Layla is loud during sex when she thinks we're alone. And yes, technically we're alone, but we're not.

Our vacation here isn't over, though, and I can't avoid having sex with her for the remainder of our trip. She'll know something is up. She'll take it personal. And the last thing I want is for her to start feeling like I made her feel in the airplane bathroom.

"Let's go upstairs," I say, pulling her away from the door to the Grand Room and toward the staircase. She pouts, but lets me take her hand. She holds on to the railing all the way up the stairs. I hold on to her because I don't want her to fall.

When we get to the bedroom, I close the door, confident that Willow remained downstairs.

Layla takes off her jeans and kicks them toward the bed. She pulls her shirt off, but gets caught up in it and almost falls. I help her out of her shirt. She's laughing when I toss it to the floor.

That's when Layla gets my full attention. She's in a good mood. She's *laughing*. She's drunk and carefree in this moment. It's very rare that Layla lets loose like this anymore. I can count on one hand the times I've heard her giggle since her surgery.

I like it. I *miss* it.

Maybe this house and this vacation really are helping us.

I kiss her this time, and I'm relieved when I do, because all the *want* is back inside me. I force Willow out of my mind and focus on Layla as much as I possibly can. She wrestles my shirt off me, and we're still standing next to the bed when I unfasten her bra. She presses her body against mine, and we kiss until I can feel her becoming unbalanced, her body leaning to the right.

She gasps as I spin her around and bend her over the mattress. Her gasp is followed by a giggle, and *my God, I love that sound so much*. I don't even remove her panties. I just pull them aside and then shove myself into her like I'm afraid this feeling will pass if I don't rush it.

She moans, and it's loud, and I don't want her to be loud tonight. I reach around and cover her mouth with my hand as I fuck her. All the noises she makes remain stifled against the palm of my hand.

I don't make a single noise when I come.

And then when I roll her onto her back and reach between her legs, I kiss her the whole time I'm touching her.

Willow may be in the back of my mind, but that means she's still in my mind, and for whatever reason, I don't want her hearing this right now.

When we're finished, I fall on top of her, breathing heavily. Layla is running her fingernails down my back, but my eyes are closed, my face pressed into the mattress.

I should be satiated, but I'm full of impatience, even still.

I want to go downstairs and talk to Willow.

I think about that—how I brought Layla back to this place so I could focus on her, but that focus is beginning to blur.

Layla has a right to know what's going on in this house around her. She's ignorant of Willow's presence. Ignorant of Willow's use of her body at night. Ignorant of my culpability in the situation.

Yet I do nothing to change any of that.

Layla shoves against my chest until I roll onto my back. She walks to the bathroom to clean herself up. I lie on my back and stare up at the ceiling, wondering how long it'll be before Layla goes to sleep. It's not very late. Four margaritas would normally be enough to ensure she calls it an early night, but she slept until eleven this morning.

I can hear the shower kick on in the bathroom, and I groan. Showers wake her up even more when she's drunk. It's like they breathe new life into her. She's probably going to emerge from the shower and ask to binge-watch an entire Netflix series in one go. It could be hours before she falls asleep now.

I button my jeans and walk to the dresser. I study her prescription bottles, reading the names to see which one she normally takes to help her sleep.

I open the lid to the Ambien, shake one into my hand, and then put the bottle back in the dresser.

I go downstairs to make Layla a glass of wine. Wine mixed with margaritas will make her sleepier. The sleeping pill will exacerbate that.

It's not like she doesn't take them on her own every night anyway. I'm just accelerating the process.

I use the back of a spoon to crush the pill up on the counter. I scoop up the powder and mix it into the wineglass until it's completely dissolved.

I turn to walk out of the kitchen, but I don't make it far.

The glass is knocked from my grip and shatters against the kitchen floor, several feet away from me.

I look at my empty hand, and then I look at the droplets of red wine as they stain the white cabinets on their descent to the floor.

The wine is everywhere. I just stand still, completely shocked. Instantly regretful. The glass was knocked out of my hand with enough force to send it across the kitchen, and there's only one explanation as to why that happened.

Willow saw what I was doing, and it obviously upset her.

The severity of what I was about to do finally catches up to me. I look up at the ceiling and drag my hands down my face.

What was I thinking?

I leave the kitchen and head back upstairs, embarrassed that Willow saw that. Embarrassed I would even consider slipping Layla her own medication so that she'd fall asleep faster.

My desire to speak to Willow fades immediately and is now replaced by a heaping pile of shame. I open the bedroom door just as Layla walks out of the bathroom wrapped in a towel. She points at the floor near my feet. "Toss me your T-shirt."

She catches the shirt and pulls it over her head, dropping the towel in the process. The hem of it falls to the middle of her thighs, and I take in the fact that my clothes swallow her. She's petite and quite possibly underweight now that she barely eats; yet I was about to slip her a dosage of her sleeping medication, along with even more alcohol, not knowing how that might affect her. Especially if she would have taken her usual nightly pill along with that.

This is not who I am.

I wrap my arms around Layla, pulling her against me, silently apologizing for something I'll never admit to almost doing. I close my eyes and press my face into her damp curls. "I love you."

"I love you too," she says, her words muffled against my skin.

I hold her like that for a long time. Several minutes, as if it'll somehow absolve me of my guilt.

It doesn't. It just makes it worse.

Layla yawns against my chest and then pulls back. "I'm so tired," she says. "I think I drank too much. I'm gonna go to bed."

"Me too," I say. She leaves my T-shirt on and crawls under the covers. I change out of my jeans, pulling on a pair of sweatpants. I normally sleep in boxers, but I don't know if Willow is going to show up tonight. I want to be prepared if she does.

⁓

I wasn't tired when I lay down with her, and even though an hour has passed since we crawled into bed, I'm still not tired. I don't even close my eyes. I watch Layla sleep, waiting for Willow to take over, but she still hasn't.

She could be upset with me. Or maybe she has to wait until Layla is in a deeper sleep. I don't know. I don't know the rules. I don't know if there *are* rules.

I want to explain my actions to Willow, but I can't do that if she doesn't slip into Layla, and I can't do that from up here because I need my laptop to communicate with her.

I ease myself out of bed without waking Layla, and I head downstairs to the kitchen.

I pause in the doorway, shocked by what I see. Or by what I *don't* see, actually.

There isn't a single trace left of what happened earlier. The spilled wine has been cleaned up. The shards of glass are gone. It's as if it never happened.

I walk over to the trash can and lift the lid. Right on top of the trash are the bits of glass that were all over the floor an hour ago.

Willow cleaned up everything while I was upstairs with Layla.

I take a seat at the kitchen table, but I don't open my laptop. I open the security app on my phone first. I skip it back and watch as the wineglass is knocked out of my hands by nothing. I fast-forward it, and approximately ten minutes after I went upstairs earlier, the video shows the lid as it slides off the trash can.

I watch in fascination as the kitchen is slowly cleaned by nothing. The wine stains disappear. The shards of glass move from the floor to the trash can. The lid eventually slides back over the top of the trash can, and all traces of the broken glass are gone.

I close out the app and lay my phone facedown on the table.

I tried to stop understanding the world around me the day after we arrived here. Watching a tape of a ghost cleaning a kitchen doesn't even faze me at this point. At least in this element.

I don't know what that says about me.

I also don't know what it says about me that I almost slipped Layla medication without her knowledge.

Maybe this house is messing with my head. Unraveling the threads of my morals.

I'm not even sure where to start the conversation with Willow. *How* to start the conversation. Do I apologize? I don't want Willow to think I'm the type of guy who would drug his girlfriend, but . . . that's exactly what I was about to do before she prevented it from happening.

Did she prevent it because she didn't like what I was doing or because she didn't want Layla's body to be too hard to wake up?

I don't know if Willow's actions were selfless or selfish, but I'm not really in a position to judge, considering my actions were completely selfish.

I hear our bedroom door open.

My spine stiffens, and I immediately get out of my chair. I don't know if Layla or Willow is walking down the stairs right now, but I'll feel equally ashamed, no matter whose eyes I'm about to look into.

I suddenly don't know how to act natural or what to do with my hands. I grip the counter behind me and lean against it, staring at the entryway.

She walks around the corner. I can tell it's Willow immediately. She's pulled a pair of Layla's shorts on and is still wearing my T-shirt. I can tell it's Willow because of the way she's looking at me—as if I have a lot of explaining to do.

"I'm sorry," I say immediately.

She holds up a hand and then pulls out a chair and sits down. "Not yet. She's really drunk; I need to sit down for a second." She drops her head into her hands. "Can you pour me a glass of water?"

I turn around and grab a glass from the cabinet. I fill it with ice and water and hand it to her, then take a seat at the table. She downs the glass and then sets it back on the table in front of her.

She stares at the glass for a quiet moment, gripping it with both hands. "What was it?"

"What was what?" I ask, needing clarification.

She drags her eyes to my face. "What kind of pill did you put in her wine?"

My jaw twitches. I lean back in my chair, folding my arms over my chest. "Ambien. A sleeping pill. I don't . . . I've never done that before. I just really wanted her to go to sleep."

"Why? So you could talk to me?"

I nod.

"That's dangerous, Leeds. She was drunk. And what if she would have taken another pill on top of what you were already giving her?"

I lean forward, running a hand through my hair. I grip the back of my neck and blow out a breath. "I know. I wasn't even thinking. It was like I was acting on impulse."

"If your need to speak to me makes you act on impulse like that, I'm not sure it's such a good idea we do this anymore."

The thought of her putting an end to this makes my chest tighten. I have so many more questions. "I would never do anything to intentionally hurt Layla. It won't happen again."

Willow's eyes are searching mine for truth. She must accept whatever it is she sees because she nods and says, "Good." Then she leans forward, pressing a palm to her stomach as it rumbles. "Does she ever eat? *Christ.* She's always starving."

I stand up, remembering the tacos. "I brought you tacos." I retrieve the to-go box from the refrigerator. I had them separate the condiments and the meat from the taco shells so they'd be easy to assemble and heat. "She only ate one taco at the restaurant, but that's probably because she drank four margaritas." I heat up the food while Willow remains seated at the table. "What do you want to drink?"

"Water is fine. I don't think her body can handle anything stronger than that right now."

I refill her water and then assemble the tacos. When I place them in front of her, her eyes are practically shimmering. She picks up one of the tacos and takes a bite.

"Holy shit," she says with a mouthful. "These are so good." It's funny how small differences, like the way they eat food, are so noticeable between the two of them, even though it's the same body. "Did Layla ask why you were getting tacos to go?"

"I just told her she didn't eat enough." I tilt my head as I think more about Willow's question. "You have her memories when you're inside of her, right? Can't you remember us being at dinner even though you weren't there?"

Willow grabs her napkin and wipes her mouth. She takes a sip of water. "I'm sure I could, but it takes too much effort for me to do that. Her thoughts are really . . . cluttered. I try to stay out of her head when I'm inside of her."

"How do you do that?"

Willow leans forward a little, lowering her voice as if someone might hear us. "It's like reading a book. How you can read an entire page before you realize you didn't process any of what you read because your thoughts were somewhere else entirely. That's how it is being in her head. If I want to, I can focus harder and intentionally take in all the information. But I'd rather just be distracted." She picks up her glass and downs the rest of her water. "Her head isn't a fun place to be sometimes."

"What do you mean by that?"

Willow shrugs. "I don't mean anything negative by it. We all have thoughts we'd never speak aloud. It's weird being able to see those thoughts, so I'd rather not look at them. I think about other things when I'm inside of her."

I want to ask her what some of Layla's unspeakable thoughts are, but I don't. I already feel like I've crossed one too many lines tonight with the Ambien. Not to mention the line I'm crossing right now—allowing Willow to use Layla's body so she can eat tacos. Tacos can excuse a lot of bad decisions, but I'm not sure they're worthy enough to excuse a possession.

"Can we go swimming?" Willow asks.

I'm caught off guard by her question. "You want to go outside? I thought you didn't leave the house."

"I never said that," she says. "I said I've never left the property. The idea of it makes me nervous, but I've been wishing I could go swimming for as long as I can remember."

I'm not sure what I expected tonight, but I certainly didn't expect Willow to want to go swimming. But the water is heated, so why not? "Sure," I say, amused by the turn of events. "Let's go swimming." She's eaten two tacos and left one on the plate, but she pushes it away from her like she's full. I take the plate and dump the food in the trash. "Layla has a couple of bathing suits upstairs." I set the plate on the counter, and then Willow follows me up to the bedroom.

I open the third dresser drawer and take out a pair of swim trunks for myself. Layla brought two bathing suits, and as much as we've swum, she hasn't worn either of them. "Which one do you want? Red or black?"

"I don't care," Willow says.

I hand her the black one. It's not as revealing as the red one. Not that it would matter—she doesn't have anything I haven't seen before, or touched.

But it does matter. She's not Layla, so it doesn't feel like her body is something I should look at in the same way I do when Willow isn't occupying it.

Willow changes in the bathroom while I change in the bedroom. When she walks out, she's holding two towels. I can't help it when my eyes wander down her body—but it's hard not to be enthralled by the fact that it's not her body, yet she makes it her own somehow. Her strides are longer, her shoulders set farther back when she walks. She even holds her head differently.

When my eyes meet hers, I immediately clear my throat and look away. "Ready?"

I walk out the door, down the stairs, and all the way to the pool without making eye contact with her again.

I jump into the deep end as soon as I reach the pool, needing the refreshing water to reset my focus. I stay under the water for a moment, long enough to see Willow's feet as she dips them into the water.

Her legs dangle over the ledge in the deep end. I push myself up out of the water, and she's sitting near the spot where I sat when I spoke to Layla for the very first time.

That was back when I thought the hardest part of life was playing bass in a slightly successful band I couldn't stand.

So much has happened since then. I've changed as a person in more ways than one. *That happens when you're forced to take another person's life.*

I don't allow myself to think about it a lot. I did what I had to do, but it still doesn't take away that guilt, no matter how justified it was.

I sink back under the water, hating that my thoughts have gone back to that night. I don't want to think about it. I don't want to think about anything right now. I just want Willow to enjoy being able to feel water for the first time.

I push myself off the bottom of the pool and break the surface. She's still sitting in the same spot, staring at the water surrounding her calves. "You getting in?" I ask her.

She looks at me and nods. "Yes, but I'm kind of scared. What if I can't swim?"

"Only one way to find out." I swim closer to her and reach out my hand. "Here. I'll help you."

She hesitates before taking my hand. She slips slowly into the water and sinks down to her chin before she squeals and grabs hold of my shoulder with her other hand. She starts moving her feet to try and stay afloat, but she's too scared to let go of me.

She's smiling, though, so I know she isn't scared. This is just new to her. She releases my shoulder and starts to move her arm, but she's still holding on to my hand.

"You got it?" I ask.

She nods, taking in accidental gulps of water as she barely keeps her head above the surface. She spits it back out and says, "I think so." She's breathless in a giddy way. It's like watching a child try to swim for the first time. I release her hand but stay near her. When she doesn't immediately sink, her eyes grow wide with excitement. "I'm doing it!" she says. "I'm swimming!"

Her pride makes me laugh. She stretches her arms out in front of her and parts the water. Maybe swimming is a natural instinct, even for ghosts, but she pushes off the wall and dog-paddles to the middle of the pool by herself. She spins and then swims back. She's already got the hang of it, which proves she's done this before.

"It's like riding a bike," I say.

She laughs. "I wouldn't know. I've never done that either."

"You probably have—you just don't remember being alive."

My words make her smile disappear.

She stays in the same spot, moving her arms and legs to keep herself afloat. "You really think I died?"

She asks me in a curious way, not an offended way. "If theories about ghosts are accurate, I feel like maybe you had a life before this. You just don't remember it."

She watches me for a moment before swimming back to the ledge of the pool. She holds on to it. "Do you think I'm a stereotypical ghost, stuck between death and an afterlife?"

"I'm not sure why else you would be here. What do *you* think?" I ask her.

"I don't know. I never really thought about it until you showed up here and started trying to figure me out."

"Do you wish I'd never showed up?"

She doesn't answer that.

Instead, she looks away from me and presses her back against the concrete ledge. She tilts her head back until she's staring up at the stars. "I'm kind of scared to find out why I'm here. It's why I've never left this property to search for answers, or to search for others like me. Because what if you're right? What if I'm stuck between life and death?" Her eyes seek mine out again, but she looks scared when we make eye contact this time. "What if I find answers and then it's over?"

"And then *what's* over?"

"This. *Me.* What if I find a way to leave this existence, only to discover there's nothing after it? What if I just . . . disappear? Forever?"

"Would that make you sad?" I ask. "You talk like it's a miserable existence."

She stares at me for several long seconds. Then she says, "It used to be." She lets herself sink below the surface as soon as she says that.

Her response was heavier than I expected it to be.

When she comes back up, she's closer to me. She regards my shoulder with curiosity, reaching out to touch it. She runs her finger over the scar from the wound I was left with six months ago. "Is this where you got shot?"

"Yes." It feels odd—her touching my scar. Layla has never touched it. Not once. Every time we make love, she deliberately runs her hands around it, near it, but she never touches it. I've always wondered if it brings back bad memories for her, or if she's just scared it might hurt me if she touched it.

"Who shot you?"

"Sable. The same girl who shot Layla." I lift her hand and bring it to the scar on Layla's head. "Feel that?" Willow touches Layla's scar with her fingertips, running her fingers back and forth over it. Then she brings her hand back to my shoulder and runs her finger over my scar.

"Yours feels healed. Hers doesn't."

"She messes with hers a lot," I say.

"Why?"

"I don't know. You're the one inside her head. You tell me."

She stares at me for several seconds, and I think maybe it's because she's sifting through Layla's memories. I want to ask her what Layla remembers, but I don't want to use Willow to pry into Layla's mind without her permission. What we're doing with Layla's body is wrong enough.

Willow swims back to the ledge and rests against it. She drops her chin to her arms and looks out over the backyard. I swim up next to her and do the same. I watch her, but she doesn't look at me. I'm not sure what she saw in Layla's head—or if she even saw anything at all—but her quietness stirs up an uneasiness inside me.

She lays her cheek on her arm and looks at me. "She fell in love with you in this pool."

"Did she?"

Willow nods, but the nod isn't accompanied by a smile or a look of fondness while she thinks back on it. She just whispers, "Yes," and then turns away from me. She lays her opposite cheek on her arm and looks in the other direction. I swim around her, wanting to see the look on her face. When we make eye contact, her eyes are rimmed with tears.

"What's wrong?"

She laughs, embarrassed, and wipes at her eyes. "It's just confusing. I have her feelings when I'm inside of her. I guess she's sad right now."

"How do you know the tears aren't yours?"

Willow regards me with a stoic expression. "I guess I don't." She slips beneath the water, and when she comes back up, she wipes her burgeoning tears away along with the water.

I feel conflicted.

She's inside Layla's body, and if Layla is the one who is sad right now, I want to comfort her. Pull her against me and kiss away her pain.

But she isn't Layla, so the need to comfort her and the knowledge that I can't leave me feeling empty. It feels a little like longing, and I don't like that feeling. This is all starting to become muddled.

"We should go back inside," I say. "I'll need to wash and dry her bathing suit before I go to sleep so she doesn't notice it was used."

Willow concedes, even though she seems like she isn't ready to stop swimming yet. She swims to the edge of the pool and lifts herself out of the water. She grabs a towel and wraps herself in it, her back to me. Then she walks back toward the house, never checking to see if I'm following her. I'm still in the middle of the pool, watching as the door closes and she disappears inside.

I sigh heavily and then sink to the bottom of the pool, holding my breath until I can't hold it anymore.

Willow is wearing my T-shirt when I get back to the bedroom, but she's not wearing the shorts this time. When I close the bedroom door, my eyes linger on her thighs for a moment.

"I put her shorts back in the drawer where I found them," Willow says. "I don't want her to question herself by waking up in something she didn't fall asleep in."

"It's fine," I say. "Where's the bathing suit?"

She motions toward the bathroom door. "I hung it up on the shower door."

I walk toward the bathroom, but pause before I go inside. I'm not sure Willow is ready to leave Layla's body. "You want to watch TV while I shower?"

She nods, so I grab the remote and turn on the bedroom television. I toss the remote to the bed and then go inside the bathroom.

I take a long shower—not because I'm trying to avoid Willow, but because I need time to clear my head. This whole thing feels wrong, but how does one properly interact with a ghost? It's not like there's a handbook, or people who could tell me if what I'm doing is morally corrupt.

Who would I ask? A psychiatrist would tell me I'm schizophrenic. A doctor would send me to a psychiatrist. My mother would tell me the stress from all that's happened is getting to my head, and she'd beg me to move back home.

Layla would probably leave me if she knew what was happening while she slept. Who wouldn't? If she told me she was allowing some spirit from a different realm to inhabit my body to fulfill some gaping hole in her life, I'd have her committed and then I'd run in the opposite direction.

There isn't a single person I can talk to about this.

But that also means there isn't anyone to tell me that what I'm doing is wrong.

It's after midnight now, and I don't really feel like staying up for an entire washing machine cycle just for a bathing suit, so I hand-wash it in the sink and then take it down to the laundry room and throw it in the dryer. While I'm downstairs, I pop a bag of popcorn in the microwave.

Willow is sitting up in bed, half-covered with the blanket when I bring it to her, along with another glass of water. She looks elated when she sees the popcorn. She sits up straighter and grabs for the bowl before I'm even seated on the bed.

"What are you watching?" I ask.

She shoves three pieces into her mouth. "*Ghost*." I raise an eyebrow, and it makes her laugh. "I know. I'm a ghost, watching the movie *Ghost*. Ironic."

"I've never seen it."

Her eyes grow wide. "How have you never seen this movie?"

I shrug and take a handful of the popcorn. "It released before I was born." My comment makes me wonder if that could be a clue. If she's seen this movie before, how long has she been in this house, watching movies when no one's around? "How old do you think you are?"

"I already told you I don't know. Why?"

"You seem young. The way you talk. The fact that you know how to use a computer. But then you act like it's crazy that I've never seen a movie that came out thirty years ago."

Willow laughs. "I don't think that's a clue. This movie is like a rite of passage; pretty much everyone alive has seen it. Everyone but you. Hell, I've seen it, and I don't even really exist."

"Stop saying that."

"What?"

"That you don't exist. You've said it at least three times since we met."

"It's no worse than you calling me *dead*." She shoves more popcorn in her mouth and leans back, focusing on the movie again. I watch a little bit of it with her, but the irony of our situation is too much.

"This is so weird," I say.

"The movie? Or watching a movie called *Ghost with* a ghost?"

"All of it."

She raises an eyebrow. "You know what would be even weirder?"

"What?"

"If another ghost showed up," she says, grinning. "Then there would be a ghost watching a ghost watch *Ghost* while in someone else's body."

I study her for a moment, then take a few pieces of popcorn and toss them at her face. "You are so strange."

Kernels of popcorn are all over her shirt, in her hair. She pulls a piece from her shirt and then eats it. I sit back and look at the TV, because looking at her is starting to stir something up inside me. Normally when Layla says something I find funny, I'd laugh and then kiss her.

There are moments when I forget that Willow isn't Layla while she's using her body.

I can't react with her how I would react with Layla. But it's instinctual for me to just want to grab her hand, or kiss her. But then I remember she's not the girl I'm in love with, and it's confusing.

Maybe I shouldn't put myself in situations like this. Familiar situations where I'm sitting on a bed in our bedroom. It makes everything dangerously blurred.

I let Willow finish her movie, but I go downstairs and check the dryer. The bathing suit is almost dry, so I set it for five more minutes and go to the kitchen. I sit at the table and open my laptop, then go straight to the paranormal forum. I'm curious if anyone has said anything else that might give me any answers as to why Willow is here.

I never updated the group to let them know I did, in fact, speak to the ghost. I certainly haven't updated them to tell them I communicate with her through Layla. Those two things seem too far fetched, even for a paranormal forum.

I have a notification in the top-right corner of my screen. I open the private messages in the forum and have one unread message from the forum member UncoverInc. I click on it.

Did you ever communicate with your ghost?

I don't respond to his message. I'm not sure anyone would even believe me at this point. I hit delete, and my in-box is empty again, but then I get a ping and a box pops up in the left-hand corner of my screen. It's from the same username.

I've been waiting for an update. Your post has me intrigued.

The message is live, sent just now in a chat box. I move my mouse over the X to minimize it, but I don't minimize it. I'm anonymous in this forum, so what would it hurt to talk to this guy? I type,

Let's just say I'm no longer a skeptic.

I hit send and immediately see that he's typing something out. I watch the chat box until his next message comes up.

So you've communicated?

Yes.

Are you still there at the house? Or did you leave?

I'm still here.

Is there a reason you chose to stay? Most people would have left if they were in your situation.

She doesn't seem dangerous.

Hopefully. They usually aren't.

I stare at that sentence for a beat. This person hasn't hesitated at all while chatting with me. What if whoever this is has had an experience like mine? I type out another question:

She has no memory of her life. I don't know how to help her. I'm not even sure she wants help.

Ghosts have no capacity to hold specific memories. Only feelings, so that's not unusual. But her lack of desire for answers could be an indicator that she might be a fairly new spirit. It takes its toll after a while. They're usually more than ready to move on the longer they've been around. It's not a fun place to be.

I reread the response, wanting to believe this person knows what they're talking about, but this is the internet. Chances are the person on the other end of this conversation is laughing at my gullibility.

I would like to help your ghost find answers. It's what I do.

I start to type a response to that, but my fingers grow still on the keyboard. How could this person possibly help without me having to give him personal information, like where the ghost resides or how to contact me? I can't tell a complete stranger who I am. I learned my lesson the hard way that privacy is a precious and fragile thing.

My entire body jerks when the buzzer from the dryer sounds off. I quickly close my laptop, go get Layla's bathing suit, and head back upstairs.

Willow is staring at the TV as the credits roll, her eyes full of tears. She doesn't even look away from the TV when I close the door behind me. I put Layla's bathing suit back in the dresser and then grab the empty popcorn bowl from Willow. She finally breaks her stare and follows me with her eyes as I set the bowl on my nightstand. "It's such a terrible ending," she mutters. "I always forget how bad the ending is."

"How does it end?"

"He finds closure and goes to heaven," she says with a pout.

I laugh, not understanding why that's a bad ending. "If heaven exists, isn't that what a ghost should want?"

She waves her arm angrily at the television. "What about Molly? She's all alone now. She has to live the rest of her life knowing her husband is gallivanting around in eternity while she still has to work and pay the bills and . . . *live*."

She says *live* like it's such a bad thing. I take a seat on the bed. "Let me make sure I have this right. You're sad for the human? Not the ghost?"

"Of *course* I'm sad for the human. Wow, *great ending*, the ghost became an even ghostlier ghost," she says sarcastically. "Big freaking deal, we knew he was dead since it happened in the beginning of the movie. But where does that leave *her*? She got proof he was dead, and then she got even *more* proof that he was dead. How is that romantic? She had to grieve *twice*! It's the worst movie I've ever seen."

"I thought you've seen it before."

"I have, but not while I was in a body with a heart that could break and tears that could form. I didn't feel all this when I watched it before. This *sucks*." She drops down onto the bed and hugs Layla's pillow. "I don't like all these feelings."

I point the remote at the TV and then hit the power button. The room grows dark. I set the remote on the nightstand and then lie down in the bed and pull the covers over me. Willow turns to face me, curling her hands beneath her cheek. "Patrick Swayze died, right? In real life?"

"Yeah."

"You think he's a real ghost now? You think he could be like me?"

"Maybe. But you've never left this property, so how can you know what else is out there? *Who* else is out there?"

She grins. "I'd leave this property for Patrick Swayze."

"Maybe that's what you need to do. Leave. Travel. Go see if there are others like you."

"But it feels like I'm supposed to stay here."

"Why?"

She shrugs. "I've just always felt that way. Surely there's a reason I'm here, in this random house in the middle of nowhere."

"Maybe you used to live here. Maybe you died here."

She thinks on that for a moment. "It doesn't feel like home, though. Not that anywhere could, I guess."

"What if there was a way you could find out where you're from? Who you are? Would you do it?"

Her eyebrows furrow. "What do you mean? Like hire a detective?"

"Something like that. I might know a guy."

She laughs. "You *know* a guy?" She rolls her eyes as if that's far fetched. But honestly, not much seems improbable to me anymore. She covers her mouth and yawns. "Layla's really tired. She'll have a hangover when she wakes up tomorrow."

"Will I see you tomorrow night? I want to talk more about how I can help you find answers."

Willow adjusts the pillow beneath her head. "I don't really want help, Leeds. Every time you bring it up, it gives me a Dr. Kevorkian vibe."

I laugh, confused. "What?"

"How would you feel if I told you that you should move on from *your* existence? It's like encouraging me to commit suicide."

Wow.

I roll onto my back, clasping my hands together over my chest. "I didn't think about it from your point of view. I'm sorry I keep bringing it up."

"It's okay," she says. "And I'm not saying I'm opposed to searching for answers someday. I'm just not sure I'm brave enough to take that step yet. For now, I just want to enjoy this last week of being able to hang out with you."

I don't look at her, but I can feel her staring at me. *She enjoys hanging out with me.* It's not an inappropriate thing to say, but the reaction I have in my chest to those words might be bordering on inappropriate.

I don't respond to her. It's during the moments of silence between us when I feel the guiltiest.

Silence is where all the mistakes happen.

I roll over and close my eyes. "Good night, Willow."

THE INTERVIEW

The man stops the recorder.

I tilt my head back, feeling uneasy about where this conversation is headed. I want to be honest with him, but the truth that's about to come up doesn't paint me in a good light.

Nothing else I say tonight will paint me in a good light.

"Do you have a restroom I can use?" he asks.

I point down the hallway. "Third door on your right."

He gets up and leaves the room. I would go check on Layla, but it's finally quiet upstairs. Hopefully it stays that way for a while. I open my laptop to see if Willow is in the room with us.

"Are you here?" I ask her.

I scoot the laptop over to an empty seat next to me, and she immediately types a response.

Yes.

"What do you think?"

I haven't been down here for all of the conversation because I wanted Layla to fall asleep, so I don't know what all you've told him, or what he's suggested.

"I've told him almost everything, but all he's done is listen so far."

Almost everything? What have you left out?

I roll my head and then lower it to my arms. "I haven't told him everything that happened the night Layla and I were shot."

Leeds . . .

"I know. I'll get to that. I just . . ."

The man walks back in the room, so I clamp my mouth shut and don't finish my sentence. He eyes me carefully as he takes his seat at the table. "Were you just speaking to Willow?"

I nod.

"How?"

"Through my laptop. I talk to her out loud, and she responds using the computer."

The man stares at me in thought. "Fascinating," he says.

I turn the laptop toward him. "Do you want to watch her do it?"

He shakes his head. "I don't need to see it. I believe you." He leans forward and hits record. "So what happened the next morning?"

CHAPTER THIRTEEN

I wake up to the smell of eggs. I roll over, and Layla isn't in bed. There's a popcorn kernel next to her pillow, so I quickly snatch it up and take it with me to the bathroom, tossing it into the trash can.

After I brush my teeth, I head downstairs, not exactly sure what to expect. Layla doesn't usually cook anymore, but *someone* is cooking.

I walk into the kitchen, and she's still in the T-shirt Willow was wearing when we crawled into bed last night, but I'm not certain this isn't still Willow.

It's the first time I'm not able to tell who is who. Did Willow wake up as Layla?

I quietly observe her from the doorway. *Would Willow ever pretend to be Layla to trick me?*

I immediately feel bad for even thinking that. Willow is protective of Layla. She knocked the wineglass out of my hand last night. I doubt she'd do anything deceptive now that I know about her.

As soon as she looks up from the stove and I make eye contact with her, I know instantly that it's Layla. Her voice is heavy with sleep when she mutters, "Morning." Her eyelids are drooping a little. She looks tired. Hungover.

I walk over to her and kiss her on the cheek. "Morning." I look down at the pan, and she's scooting around scrambled eggs with a fork.

"You want some?" she asks. "I read eggs help with hangovers."

"Nah, I'm good." I make myself a cup of coffee and lean against the counter, watching Layla. I'm curious if she has any memories at all of last night.

"What time did you wake up?" I ask her.

"Five. Couldn't go back to sleep. I have a horrible hangover." She spins around and says, "Want to know something weird?"

"What?"

"I had a piece of popcorn stuck in my tooth when I woke up."

My spine stiffens at that comment. I turn away from her and pour creamer into my coffee cup. "Yeah, we watched a movie in bed last night. You were pretty drunk."

Layla laughs, but it's a painful laugh. She's touching her forehead when I turn back around. She winces and then says, "Wow. I don't remember that at all."

She scoops a pile of eggs onto a piece of toast and sits at the table to eat. I can't stop looking at her eyes. Her pupils are dark and wide—like two black marbles have covered the greens of her eyes.

She takes a bite of her eggs and toast with a fork, then taps her fork repeatedly on the table as she chews. Her knee is bouncing up and down, like her hangover is oddly coupled with a lot of pent-up nervous energy.

"How much coffee have you had today?"

She swallows her bite and then wipes her mouth with a napkin. "Four cups already. I thought it might help with the hangover."

That explains her behavior. I was beginning to think she might be Willow again, but she isn't. She's eating like Layla eats. Small bites, always with a fork. Willow would have devoured that whole plate of food by now.

"Maybe you should relax today," I suggest. "Have another pool day."

She motions toward the kitchen window. "I can't—it's supposed to storm."

I walk to the window and push the curtain aside. The entire sky looks like deep-blue rolling hills. I open the weather app on my phone, and it says it's supposed to rain for the next two days. I look back at Layla. She's only eaten half of her toast and eggs, but she's already pushed her plate away and is scrolling through her phone. "Then what do you want to do today?" I ask.

"You really need some new social media content," she says. "We haven't posted anything since the picture on the plane. I can take some sexy pictures of you in the rain. That might make a really great album cover."

That actually sounds like a nightmare. Layla can see on my face that I'm not in the mood to pose for pictures.

"I know you don't want to think about work, but this house is huge. There are so many potential backdrops for photos. Just give me two hours with the camera, and then I'll leave you alone about it until Wednesday."

"Why Wednesday?"

"That's when we leave."

Her voice is delicate, but those words feel dense and unintentionally harsh. We'll be leaving Willow here alone in just a matter of days. I don't really want to go until Willow is ready to find answers, because for some reason, I need answers. I don't feel like I'll be able to function out in the real world unless I can somehow make sense of everything that's happened in this house.

I take a seat across from Layla. "What do you think about staying a little longer?"

Her shoulders drop a little. "Seriously?"

"Yeah. I'm getting a lot of songwriting done. I can probably finish the album here if I have a little more time."

"I haven't heard the piano once."

"I haven't needed it. I've been writing lyrics," I lie.

She sighs and drops her phone to the table. "Not to be mean, but it's boring here, Leeds. I'm going stir crazy. And the boredom is making me tired. I feel exhausted every day. It's like all I do is sleep."

I know that exhaustion is my fault, but I still don't let up. "What if we compromise?"

She raises an eyebrow. "Depends on the compromise."

"I'll give you three hours today to pose me however you want for however many pictures you want to take. And you give me three more days to work on my album."

She seems attracted to that compromise. "I can even pose you in the rain?"

I nod.

A smile manages to break through her hangover. "Deal." She leans across the table and kisses me. "You won't regret this."

She's wrong. I already regret it. I've regretted almost every decision I've made at her expense since we got here.

Yet . . . I've done nothing to stop myself.

~

Layla *maybe* got four hours of sleep last night. Combine that with a three-hour photo shoot, a hangover, and very little food today, and I have no idea how she held out until eight o'clock before going upstairs to crash.

It's almost ten now, and there's been no sign of Willow. I've tried asking her if she's here, but she hasn't responded. Not even with the laptop.

I've spent the last hour working out new lyrics. If I'm going to lie to Layla and tell her music is what's keeping me in this house, I at least need to create said music.

I started writing a song about two weeks ago called "No Vacancy," so I've spent most of my time tonight reworking the lyrics.

It's been storming for four hours now. The forecast extended the rain to a third day, which concerns me. Layla seems content when she gets her pool days, but I don't know what mood three days of being stuck inside this house will put her in.

"What are you doing?"

I jump so violently my chair scoots back two feet. I grab at my chest and blow out a breath when I see Willow standing in the doorway. I didn't hear her walking down the stairs because of the thunder, so my reaction to her unexpected appearance makes her laugh.

"You look like you just saw a ghost," she says with a wink. She walks straight to the refrigerator. "Seriously, Leeds. Your girlfriend has an eating disorder. I'm worried about her." She grabs a plate of leftovers from the dinner I cooked earlier. Stuffed baked potatoes and Caesar salad. Layla only ate the salad, so I saved the baked potato for Willow.

I close out my document and then shut my laptop. Willow puts the plate in the microwave and then turns around to face me. "What was today all about? With the pictures, and the uncharacteristically vain photos?"

The entire time Layla was forcing me to pose today, I wondered where Willow was. If she was watching or not. I was hoping she wasn't.

"Nothing." I don't want to talk about the compromise I made with Layla, and I especially don't want to talk about the embarrassing fact that every time Layla posts a shirtless selfie of me, I get twice as many downloads on my music.

"Are you like a model or something?" Willow's voice is playful, but I still don't feel like talking about it. I'd almost rather her dive into Layla's thoughts just so I don't have to explain it to her.

"There's this thing . . . social media."

"I know what social media is," she says.

"Of course you do. Anyway. Layla is working to monetize my platform."

"So you're an influencer?"

I lean back in my seat, perplexed. "How do you even know what that is?"

"I watch TV. I know a lot of things. Are you famous?"

"No."

"But you want to be?" The microwave timer goes off. Willow grabs her plate and walks over to the table.

"Layla is hoping my music career takes off, so I humor her. Gives her something to focus on."

"What if she's right? What if you become famous?" Willow says.

"That's my fear."

She waves her fork in the air after taking a bite. "Is that how you can afford to stay here? Money from social media?"

"No. I only have three songs out. But I have money. An inheritance."

I expect her to make a comment about that, but Willow just eyes me curiously for a moment. "Are you just playing aloof, or do you really not want the music career to work out?"

"I'm undecided. I love writing music and I want people to hear it, but I don't know that I'm cut out for all that comes with it."

"You have the look."

"I definitely don't want to get famous because of how I look."

"What if you aren't as talented as you think you are, though? What if the only reason you have followers is because you're hot?"

I laugh at her bluntness. "You think I'm hot?"

She rolls her eyes. "You've seen a mirror before." She gestures toward my phone. "I want to hear one of your songs. Play the one you played for Layla at the piano the night you met her. I think it's called 'I Stopped.'"

"I thought you didn't look at her memories."

"I try not to. That one's hard to avoid, though. It's front and center in her head."

I like that Layla prefers that memory. It's one of my favorites too.

I open the music app and hit play on the song for Willow. But then I open my laptop and focus on it in an attempt to ignore the fact that she's listening to my music.

I hate listening to my own music. I try to busy myself with emails while she listens to each of the three songs intently. When they all finish playing, she scoots my phone back to me across the table.

"Your voice is haunting," she says.

"Is haunting good or bad coming from a ghost?"

She grins. "I guess it could be either." She's in a good mood. She's almost always in a good mood, even when she's upset with me for almost drugging my girlfriend or for continuously insisting she should find out why she's here. It's like whiplash, going from Layla, who feels so heavy, to Willow, who's like a gust of wind.

"Can you feel Layla's anxiety when you're inside of her?" I ask her.

"I don't feel it right now. That's probably because she isn't alert— nothing to be anxious about."

"But you can feel her love. And her sadness. You've said that before."

Willow nods. "Maybe her feelings for you are stronger than her anxiety. She does feel a lot for you."

That's good to know. "Does she think I'm going to propose to her?"

"Are you?"

"Probably."

Willow takes a sip of water. Swallows. She stares down at her plate for a moment in thought, and I can tell she's trying to sift through Layla's feelings. "She *hopes* you're going to propose, but I don't think she's expecting it this soon."

"What kind of ring does she want?"

"Does it matter? You already bought it. You keep it upstairs in your shoe like an idiot." *She knows about the engagement ring?* "Girls can sniff those things out like a bloodhound. She'll find it if you don't hide it better."

"So you've seen the ring? Do you think she'll like it?"

Willow smiles. "I have a feeling she'll like any ring you give her, even if it's plastic. She loves you more than . . ." Her voice fades before she finishes her sentence.

"More than what?"

Willow shakes her head, her eyes suddenly growing more serious. "Never mind. I shouldn't be sharing her thoughts with you. It feels wrong."

Willow finishes her food, but I can't help but wonder what the sudden change in her demeanor was about. *What was she about to say?*

She clears off the table and walks to the kitchen entry. She looks over her shoulder at me. "Come play me a song, Leeds."

I hesitate, because I don't know that I want to. I like the memory of playing a song for Layla in the Grand Room. I'm not sure I want to create that memory with anyone else. It feels like a betrayal.

Willow has already gone into the Grand Room. She's waiting in there for me. I hesitate for another few seconds, but then I ultimately leave the kitchen and walk across the hallway.

I pause in the doorway to the Grand Room because Willow is lowering the lid to the grand piano. Then she proceeds to climb up on top of it. She sprawls out across the piano on her stomach, stretching her arms out over it. She sees me eyeing her with perplexity. She smiles gently and says, "I want to feel the sound. I never get to feel things without a body. It's nice."

As much as I want to preserve my memory of this room with Layla, I feel equally bad not playing a song for Willow. She doesn't get to interact with people outside of me. That has to be lonely.

I reluctantly take a seat at the piano bench. "What do you want me to play?"

"Play the one you were writing earlier, on your laptop."

"I thought you weren't in there when I was on my laptop. I tried to talk to you."

She lifts her cheek off the piano. "I didn't want you to stop writing, so I pretended I wasn't there."

I thought she might have been in there. I don't know how. Sometimes it's like I can feel her in the room with me, but I don't know if that's because I know she's in this house or if she really does have a presence.

Willow lays her cheek against the varnished wood again, patiently waiting.

I look down at the piano keys and try to remember how the song begins. "I haven't finished writing it yet."

"Play what you have, then."

I start fingering the keys, and when I look back up at her, she's closed her eyes. "This one is called 'No Vacancy,'" I say quietly. Then I sing it for her.

I showed up rich while feeling poor
I didn't knock but they opened the door
Throwing stones, they pierce my eye
Leave tiny cracks all down my spine
We were royalty without a throne
Our castle didn't feel like home
Echoes of "I love you" in the halls
Our words absorbed into the walls
I checked us in so we couldn't leave
Thought maybe time would make me believe
If I took us back to the starting line
We'd never cross the finish line
My hands may not be red
But my heart, it feels the bleed
If my soul had a neon sign
It would read No Vacancy
If my soul had a neon sign
It would read No Vacancy

When I'm finished playing all the parts of the song I've written, I look up from the piano. Her eyes are still closed.

She remains pressed against the piano, like she doesn't want the feeling to end. She seems sad . . . sort of regretful. It makes me wonder if she'll miss this when we leave. She'll be alone with no one here to talk to at night, no one here to play music for her, no one here to give her something to do to pass her time while she just floats around in nothing.

She finally opens her eyes, but she doesn't move.

I feel my chest constrict when we make eye contact, because again, I just want to comfort her. But not because I'm mistaking this urge for some wandering remnant of how I feel for Layla—but because I want to comfort *her*.

Willow.

"I'm sorry you're so lonely," I whisper.

She smiles, but it's such a sad smile. "You're the one who wrote this song. I'm no lonelier than you."

Silence slowly descends over the room, wrapping us tightly in its grip.

But I don't say anything to break it. I soak it up. I soak her up. No one else ever will, and that makes me sad for her.

"She's really in love with you," Willow says.

I don't know why she says that. Does she sometimes feel Layla's urges to touch and kiss me, the same way I feel the urge to touch and kiss Layla? When she's inside of Layla, is it as confusing to her as it is to me?

"Her body is really tired tonight. I should let her sleep." Willow sits up on the piano. "You coming to bed?"

I want to.

Which is exactly why I shouldn't.

I swallow the *yes* that's stuck in my throat and look down at the piano keys. I place my fingers on them. "You go ahead."

She stares at me a moment, but I don't look at her. I begin playing the song over again, and when I do, she leaves the room. After she walks upstairs and I hear the bedroom door close, I stop the song. I lower my head to the piano.

What am I doing?

And why do I not want to stop?

CHAPTER FOURTEEN

I woke up determined to give Layla all my focus today. Maybe it was guilt. It wasn't hard to give her all my focus. She was by my side most of the day because the weather outside left us with little else to do.

It's almost midnight and Layla still hasn't fallen asleep.

That might be because of the storm. She doesn't like the idea of being in the middle of tornado alley during a thunderstorm, but I've been keeping an eye on the weather. There aren't any tornado warnings . . . just lots of lightning and rain. And thunder that makes her tense up every time it shakes the house.

I normally find this kind of weather relaxing, but right now I'm just irritated with it because it's keeping Layla awake.

She's lying on the couch with me in the Grand Room, scrolling through her social media posts. Her feet are in my lap. I'm trying to finish reading the book I started six months ago—the one about the game show host who claimed to be a spy—but my eyes are just scanning the screen. I'm not soaking up any of the words because I can't stop thinking about Willow. Layla did agree to give me a few more days in the house, but we'll still eventually have to leave.

Willow will be alone.

It's not like I can just come visit her—this place is in the middle of nowhere. It involves a flight, a rental car, hours of driving. It's an entire day of travel.

I'm going to have to put an offer in on the house if I want to help her find answers eventually. Even if Layla doesn't want to live here, I would hate for someone else to buy it. I could hire someone else to run the place—turn it back into a bed and breakfast so Willow wouldn't be lonely. There would be a constant revolving door of strangers. She might enjoy that more than sitting alone in an empty house.

And if I owned this place, it would give me an excuse to come back occasionally. To visit Willow without Layla growing suspicious.

Is that emotional cheating?

Willow is a ghost. It's not like she could come between me and Layla.

But I guess she has in a way.

Willow and I have grown comfortable with one another . . . to the point that I'm starting to prefer her company over Layla's. I'm not proud of that. Layla means so much to me, but I'm fascinated—*obsessed*, even—with the idea that this life isn't the only one that matters. One would think that would make me feel like this life matters even more, but I've felt myself growing distant from this world. I'm being pulled into Willow's, or maybe she's being pulled into mine. Either way, we don't belong in each other's worlds, but now that we've found an easy way to combine them, it makes me disinterested in everything else around me.

That's not Layla's fault. There's nothing Layla has done wrong. She's the victim in all of this. She was the victim six months ago, and she's the victim now, even though she's unaware of it. The only thing Layla did wrong is fall in love with me.

I thought this trip was going to make things better for her. Maybe that would have worked out had I not discovered Willow's existence in this house. Now I've done nothing but allow my fascination with whatever Willow is to drive an even bigger wedge between me and every other aspect of my life.

Layla seems unaware of any of it, though. She may think things are just fine between us. But that's only because she doesn't remember the details, and how great it was between us before I essentially became her caretaker.

Not that I would have made any other choice. But regardless of the love behind caring for her, or the good intentions—recovery still takes its toll, not only on the person recovering, but on everyone around them.

"What are you reading?" Layla asks.

I look over at her, and she's dropped her cell phone to her chest. Her head is tilted and her hair is spread out over the pillow beneath her. She's barely wearing anything—a silky see-through top that doesn't even cover her navel. A matching pair of cream-colored panties. I set my phone down on the arm of the couch and wrap my hand around Layla's ankle. I drag it slowly up to her knee. "Still trying to finish that same book."

"What book?"

"The one about the game show host who thinks he's an assassin."

She shakes her head a little. "Doesn't sound familiar."

I start to say, *"I told you about it,"* but then I remember that was one of the last conversations we had before she got shot. She has no memory of that entire day, or the week that followed. No memory of our conversations that day leading up to the moment she got shot. Sometimes I fill in the holes for her, but I don't want to talk about it right now. I'd feel bad for bringing up something that could trigger her anxiety.

"It's just some novel," I say, adjusting myself on the couch so that I'm lying next to her. She cuddles against me, pressing a kiss to my neck. I take in the scent of her shampoo. It's tropical—mangoes and bananas—and it reminds me of everywhere that isn't Lebanon, Kansas. Everywhere Layla would probably rather be than right here.

What will she think if I buy this house?

Should I even buy it?

Or should we just pack up and leave before every line I've already crossed becomes a wall so high we can't climb over?

~~~

"Leeds."

Layla's voice is a distant whisper, hanging in the air as I struggle with whether I want to leave my sleep and follow that voice.

"Leeds, wake up."

Her hand is on my cheek, and we're pressed together. We're still on the couch. It's not surprising we fell asleep, considering all the nights I spend awake with Willow. I've been getting just as little sleep as Layla gets.

I slip my hand inside the back of her silk shirt and run my palm up her skin. When I do this, she presses her hands so hard against my chest she propels herself off the couch and onto the floor. Her sudden movement, followed by the thud, forces my eyes wide open. I lean over the couch in search of her. She's on her back, staring up at me.

It's Willow. Not Layla.

"My bad," I say, scrambling to help her off the floor. "I thought you were Layla."

When she stands up, she looks down at herself—at the clothes Layla put on earlier. Or lack thereof.

My voice is rough when I say, "You should probably go change." I clear my throat and walk into the kitchen while she runs up the stairs.

I make us a pot of coffee because Willow feels Layla's exhaustion when she's inside of her. I certainly feel the exhaustion. It's late, and the last thing I need is coffee. The last thing I need is an excuse to stay up and chat with someone who isn't Layla. But when Willow comes back downstairs and enters the kitchen, I'm relieved to see her, and I instantly forget how wrong this is.

She threw on a T-shirt and a pair of Layla's pajama pants. She nudges her head toward the coffee. "Good idea."

When it's finished brewing, I fill two cups with coffee and slide one over to her. She's standing next to me at the counter. We're shoulder to shoulder as I pour cream into my cup and she stirs sugar into hers.

"Did you know in ancient Arab culture, a woman could only divorce her husband if he didn't like her coffee?" Willow asks.

I lean against the counter. "Is that true?"

She nods, leaning against the counter next to me, facing me. She sips slowly from her cup and then says, "I read it in one of those books in the Grand Room."

"How many have you read?"

"All of them."

"What other random facts have you learned?"

She sets her cup down and then pushes herself up onto the countertop. "The most expensive coffee in the world is made in Indonesia. It's expensive because the beans are eaten and digested by a cat before they're used to make the coffee."

I wasn't expecting a fact like that. I look down at my coffee and grimace. "What do they do? Dig the digested beans out of cat shit?"

She nods.

"People pay *more* money for coffee made from cat shit?"

Willow grins. "Rich people are weird. That could be you someday. Drinking cat shit coffee on your mega-yacht."

"I hope to hell not."

She presses both hands into the counter at her sides. She leans back a little, swinging her legs back and forth. "What's your mother like?"

That question throws me for a loop. "My mom?"

She nods. "I hear you on the phone with her sometimes."

There are so many times throughout the day I wonder where Willow is when she's not in Layla's body. Does she follow me around?

Does she just hang out in the Grand Room all day? Does she ever follow Layla around?

"She's a good person. I got lucky."

Willow releases a slow breath and then looks down at her swinging feet. She stops moving them. "I wonder what my mother was like."

It's the first time she's ever acknowledged that she might have had an actual human life prior to the one she's living. It makes me wonder if she's having a change of heart. If maybe she does want to try and research into her past.

"I'm thinking about putting in an offer on the house."

Willow perks up at that. "*This* house? You really are going to buy it?"

I nod.

"Does Layla want to live here?"

"Probably not. But I could pitch it to her as a business investment. It would give me a reason to visit you."

"Why doesn't she like it here? When I've looked back on her memories of this place, they all seem good."

"A lot has happened since we met. I don't know that it's this particular place she doesn't like. She just hasn't had a chance to settle since she was released from the hospital. I don't think anywhere will feel like home to her until we can pick out a place together, and I doubt she'll want a place this isolated."

"She lived in Chicago before, right? Do you think she wants to go back there?"

I stare at Willow, wondering if she knows that's what Layla wants, and she's just saying that as a hint. "I don't know. You tell me."

Willow shakes her head. "I don't want to dig around in her head anymore. Like I said before, her thoughts are chaotic."

"What do you mean by chaotic?"

"I'm not sure," Willow says with a shrug of her shoulders. "You say she's lost a lot of her memories, but to me, when I'm inside her head, there are too many for me to process. It's like they all overlap, so it's hard for me to really sift through them. But honestly, they aren't my thoughts to sift through, so I mostly just ignore them."

"That's probably the right thing to do."

She laughs half-heartedly. "I think we blurred the line between right and wrong a while ago."

Neither of us speaks for a moment after she says that. It's tough, because we both know this is wrong, but I think we're both hoping the other one doesn't put a stop to it. We obviously enjoy each other's company or we wouldn't be doing this night after night.

Willow looks at me thoughtfully. "What happened the night you and Layla were shot?"

I stand up straighter. Shuffle my weight to my other leg. "You can't just dig around in her head for that? It's not really something I like talking about."

Willow is silent for several seconds. "I could . . . but I want to hear your version."

I don't like talking about it. I swore to myself after I recounted every detail to the police that I'd never talk about it again unless Layla asked.

Willow is waiting for me to say something. I open my mouth to respond, just as thunder rolls across the sky and a streak of lightning hits nearby. Willow flinches, and the lights go out.

The kitchen lights didn't even flicker—they just immediately shut off, along with every other appliance in the house.

The sound of thunder is still rumbling through the house when Willow says, "Leeds?"

She sounds frightened.

I find her in the dark, and she's no longer sitting on the counter. She's standing in the middle of the kitchen. I rub my hands down her arms reassuringly. "It's okay. The power just went out. It'll probably kick back on in a second."

Willow steps back and says, "What's going on?" Her words come out quick and shaky. "Where are we?"

More lightning illuminates the kitchen, and I stare at her between flashes of darkness and bright light. Her eyes are full of fear. I can immediately tell I'm no longer looking at Willow. "Layla?"

"What the fuck is going on?" she says, her voice louder as she takes another step back. She grips the counter next to her, looking wildly around the kitchen. "Why am I in the kitchen?"

I immediately grab Layla and pull her against me. I press my hand against the back of her head. "It's okay," I say, trying to come up with an excuse as to why she's now standing in the middle of the kitchen with no memory as to how we ended up here. "The power went out. It woke us up."

"Why don't I remember that? How are we in the kitch—" She stops talking.

She releases a sigh.

I feel her relax, and I can immediately tell Willow has taken back over because she feels different in my arms. She pulls away from my chest.

"I'm sorry," Willow says. "The lightning startled me and I must have accidentally slipped out of her." There's a new concern in her eyes that wasn't there before. Willow brings her thumb up to her mouth and starts to chew on it. "She'll remember this tomorrow. She'll remember waking up down here."

I don't like seeing Willow worried just as much as I don't like seeing Layla worried. "Hey," I say, squeezing her hand. "It's okay. I'll pass it off like she had a nightmare, or she was half-asleep."

Willow nods, but I can still see the nervous energy in her expression. "Okay." She covers her face with her hands. "God, I'm so sorry."

"It's okay, Willow."

She nods again, but I can tell she doesn't feel reassured.

Neither do I.

THE INTERVIEW

"Did Layla remember the next day?"

I nod. "Yes. It was the first thing she asked about when she woke up. I played it off like she was half-asleep when the power went out, so I made her go to the kitchen with me, and she didn't fully wake up until the lightning struck."

"And she bought that?"

"Yeah. It was an easy sell. Anyone would believe they were in a daze or sleepwalking before their mind would automatically start questioning whether or not they were possessed by a ghost."

The man agrees with a nod. "Did Willow continue to use her body after that? Even after the slipup?"

I nod, but barely. It's not something I'm proud of, because no excuse is good enough for what we've done. Not even an excuse as worthy as ours.

"Did Layla ever grow to suspect anything?"

"She was concerned about why she was so tired all the time. Willow was using her body at night, so she wasn't getting as much sleep as she thought she was getting. She'd wake up confused as to why she slept in so late when she was going to bed so early. She started thinking it was related to her head injury."

"And you didn't tell her otherwise?"

I inhale and then slowly exhale before answering that question. "No. I went along with it. Made her an appointment to see the neurologist."

"What did the neurologist tell her?"

"The appointment isn't until next week."

"Are you going to take her?"

I shake my head. "No. I can't now. She's never going to forgive me for what I've done to her these last few days." I lean forward, pressing my palms to my forehead. "I've let this get out of hand and I'm not sure how to turn it around."

"Why didn't you just tell Willow to stop when you realized it began to affect Layla?"

"I didn't want her to stop."

"Because you were trying to help Willow?"

I wish I could say yes to that, but I shake my head. "We just fell into a routine, I think. It went on for days. Layla would fall asleep at night and Willow would take over. We'd watch movies. I'd cook for her. She'd read a book on the couch while I worked on music. There wasn't a good reason for us to do it . . . we still weren't using the time together to search for answers. We just enjoyed each other's company."

The man nods. "How does Willow feel about the part she plays in this?"

"She feels terrible. We both do."

"Yet you continue to do it?"

I'm growing frustrated with his questioning.

"Is it fair to assume this continued because you started to develop feelings for Willow?"

I can't even say yes out loud. Instead, I just nod.

CHAPTER FIFTEEN

We're supposed to check out in two days and head back to Tennessee. Layla has been cheerful about it.

I haven't been.

I'm sitting at the piano bench, trailing my fingers up and down the keys. I've been internally moping all day, like a child being forced to throw away his favorite toy.

I haven't spoken much to Willow since last night. We stayed up late watching another movie. I've noticed a recurring theme over the past several nights. We watch movies about ghosts, the afterlife, anything paranormal. Willow asks questions after the end of each movie, as if she's trying to figure out which version of this world she wants to believe in. Last night we watched *What Dreams May Come*. It made her cry.

She didn't ask a single question when it was over. She just rolled onto her side and looked at me sadly. I asked her what was wrong, and she said, *"I don't want to go back."*

"Back where?" I said.

"To nothing. I like being inside of Layla. I like spending time with you. It gets harder every time I have to leave her body."

I didn't know what to say because I felt the same way, so I just grabbed her hand and held it until we both fell asleep.

It's becoming difficult at night, watching her have to leave Layla, knowing she's just going back to a bare minimum of an existence in a huge and lonely house. And the closer we get to the day Layla and I are supposed to leave, the more sullen Willow and I have become when we spend time together.

I'm playing a low key on the piano—tapping it over and over with my finger—when one of the higher notes plays by itself. I immediately look around, but Layla is still upstairs.

Willow must be trying to get my attention.

I go to the kitchen to open my laptop, and she immediately begins typing.

I have bad news.

"What?"

Layla just found the ring.

My eyes immediately dart up toward the upstairs bedroom. "Is she digging through my things?"

Yes.

"What did she do when she found it?"

She gasped. Then she put it back and immediately texted Aspen and told her about it.

"Shit," I say with a heavy breath.

I wasn't ready for this. Not after I've spent the last two and a half weeks using Layla the way I've been using her. A proposal at this point would feel dishonest.

I sit down at the table and drop my head into my hands. Willow begins typing something into the document again.

She doesn't know which day you'll be proposing, so there's still an element of surprise there. You shouldn't let this upset you.

"It's not that," I say. "I just don't think I'm ready, but now it's all she's going to be thinking about."

If you aren't ready, why did you bring the ring with you?

"I brought it with me because this trip . . ." I lean back in my chair. "This trip was supposed to bring us closer together. But I feel even more distant than I did the day we arrived."

Is that my fault?

"No. I don't think what we're doing has helped, but it's not your fault."

I didn't know that's why you came here. Now I feel guilty for inserting myself into the narrative. I can stop. If you want to spend these last two days with Layla . . . I can disappear, and you won't even know I'm here.

My chest tightens at that thought. I don't want to spend these last two days here without Willow. "That's what I've been afraid you'll do, Willow. It isn't at all what I want." I close the laptop because I don't want to continue this conversation. Not over a laptop, anyway. I need to go talk to Layla. Gauge her mood. Maybe the ring freaked her out. Maybe she isn't ready either. Maybe this will prompt a long-overdue conversation between us.

I go upstairs and can hear the shower running. I walk into the bathroom, and Layla is brushing her teeth. She always does this. Turns on the shower to warm up the water and then stands at the sink for ten minutes to do her nighttime routine of brushing her teeth and washing her face and plucking her eyebrows. Then she barely has enough hot water left to actually make it through a full shower.

She grins as soon as I walk into the bathroom. She spits toothpaste into the sink and then rinses. Then she walks over to me and wraps her arms around me, pressing her mouth to mine. There's such a difference in her right now compared to the tired version of herself she's been dragging around during the daytime. She's definitely excited for the proposal. It's like it breathed new life into her.

"What are you doing?" she asks, her voice a disturbing level of cheerful.

"Working."

She slides her palms down my chest. "You should take a break. Shower with me."

I look over my shoulder like I have somewhere to be. "I took a shower this morning."

When I look back at her, she rolls her eyes and lowers her hands to my sweatpants. "Well then, *I'll* shower." She feathers her lips across my jaw as she reaches into my pants. "After I'm done with you."

Before I can stop her, she pushes me against the bathroom door and drops to her knees. We haven't had sex in three days. I don't know that I can come up with a good enough excuse to refuse a blow job without hurting her feelings.

She's on a high right now, assuming this trip is going to end with a proposal. She thinks we'll spend the rest of our lives together—me and Layla against the world.

And maybe we will. I don't even know. But she's not really in a position in which we can discuss it because she's taking me into her mouth, despite the fact that I'm not even hard yet. I look down at her, and even though I'm not immediately turned on by this because of the pandemonium in my head, I can't help but think of Willow when I look at Layla.

Sometimes, when I look at Layla, I *wish* she were Willow. At breakfast, I catch myself wishing I were chatting with a cheerful Willow over coffee, rather than Layla complaining about her headache. During the day when I'm chatting with Willow on the computer, I spend that time wishing she could take over Layla and I could talk to her face to face.

And now . . . as Layla slides her tongue up the length of me, I kind of wish it were Willow doing this to me.

I harden at that thought.

It's easy to pretend Layla is Willow because Layla's face is the only one I can attribute to Willow when I think about her. I wrap my hand in Layla's hair and watch her for a moment . . . wondering what this would feel like if it were Willow inside of Layla right now. Would Willow use her tongue like that? Would she make the same noises Layla makes?

She wraps her lips around me and takes me in as far as she can. My head falls back against the door and I groan, putting pressure on the back of her head, not wanting her to stop now.

One of her hands is moving up and down the length of me in rhythm with her mouth. Her other hand is sliding up my stomach. I grab it, squeeze it, press it to my chest as I think about Willow.

I imagine how Willow's kiss would feel. Would it feel the same as Layla's kiss?

Would sex with Willow feel different than sex with Layla?

Would she arch her back the same way Layla does when I push into her?

"Fuck." I release Layla's hand and grip the back of her head with both hands. "I'm about to finish," I say, warning her. She always stops when I say that so she can finish with her hand.

She pulls back, breathless, and whispers, "You can finish in my mouth this time."

There's a glimmer in her eye as she takes me back in her mouth—an excitement—and I know this is her way of thanking me for a proposal that has yet to happen. If I wasn't already on the brink of exploding, I'd probably put a stop to this, simply because I know where her head is at.

Everything about this moment is wrong. Layla thinks she's pleasuring her soon-to-be fiancé while I'm pretending she's the ghost I've been slowly falling for.

It's the strangest release I've ever had.

I don't even enjoy it.

My legs tremble as she keeps her mouth on me, swallowing every last bit of deception I've been handing her. I don't make a noise. I just close my eyes and wait for her to stop.

When she finally releases me, I can't even bring myself to look at her.

All I can think about are the words she said to me the first night we met, after I'd just told her she was the best sex I'd ever had. *"We always think that when we're in it. But then someone new comes along, and we forget how good we thought it was before, and the cycle starts all over again."*

Is that all Layla was to me? Part of an endless cycle of relationships?

I thought for sure she was the one. I felt it in my bones.

Now all I feel is remorse, because it wasn't until ten seconds ago that I realized I've already moved on to another cycle.

I've moved on to Willow.

It's Willow I want to talk to when I wake up. Willow I want to see before I close my eyes. Willow I want to spend all my time with during the day.

I prefer Willow over Layla now, in almost every way, and it's a heavy, appalling, shameful realization.

I hear the water running in the bathroom sink. I open my eyes and Layla is brushing her teeth again. She swishes the water around in her mouth and then spits it into the sink. She wipes the back of her hand across her mouth and smiles with pride. "Did I leave you speechless?" she says, laughing.

I have no idea what to say. *I'm sorry* wouldn't be appropriate.

"That was intense." It's not a lie. Intense isn't necessarily a good thing, and I don't want to lie to Layla anymore. It doesn't feel good.

She saunters back over to me and tucks me back into my sweat-pants. She leans in and kisses me gently on the cheek, leaving her mouth on my skin when she says, "Go back to work. You can return the favor tomorrow night." She backs away and takes off her shirt with a grin, and then finally gets in the shower.

The water has been running this whole time.

I walk into the bedroom and stare at our bed. The same bed I was on when I first began to fall in love with Layla.

Falling in love with her was weightless, like air was breezing through my bones.

Falling out of love is fucking heavy, like my lungs are carved from iron.

I walk over to the bed, and I drop down onto it. I don't go back downstairs. I can't face Willow tonight. I don't even want to face Layla.

I just want to sleep.

CHAPTER SIXTEEN

"Why do you think I'm able to touch things?"

Her voice rips me from the claws of a deep sleep. I open my eyes, and Willow is facing me, lying on her side. I don't know what time it is, but it's still dark outside.

I rub my eyes with the heels of my palms. "What do you mean?" My voice is still heavy with sleep.

"I can move things when I'm not in Layla's body," she says. "I can touch things. But you can't see me, and I can't even see myself, so I'm not made of matter. It doesn't make sense."

"Maybe you're made of energy. And you somehow channel that energy into something as dense as matter."

She sighs and rolls onto her back. She stares at the wooden beam over the bed. "You'd think if that were the case, I wouldn't be as strong as I am."

"What do you mean?"

"I can move big things too. I did it once. Moved every piece of furniture in the Grand Room around in the middle of the night."

"Because you were bored?" I ask.

"No. Because I hate Wallace Billings and I wanted to scare him."

She has my full attention now. I lift up onto my elbow. "Who is Wallace Billings?"

She cuts her eyes to mine, and there's a mischievous grin on her face. "He owns this place. I'm the reason he put it up for sale a few months ago."

She looks proud of whatever she did. There's a gleam in her eye, and I kind of find it fascinating. I've been wondering why this place was put up for sale.

She sits up, wrapping the bedsheet around her to cover herself. "You know how I can't remember how long I've been here?"

I nod.

"Well, I know Wallace inherited this place right before I showed up. Just based on conversations I've heard him have. His mother owned it, and it passed on to him when she died, but he wasn't sure what to do with it. If he should keep it open or sell it or move in. After a while, he started to lean toward moving his family here. And I know this is terrible, but I couldn't stand him. He was such an asshole to people. His wife, his kids, anyone he spoke to on the phone. I couldn't imagine sharing this place with him for however long I was going to end up being here."

"What did you do? Haunt him?"

"No," she says, shaking her head. But then she looks up and to the right. "Wait. I guess what I did *could* be defined as a haunting. I've just never really identified as a ghost, so to me, I was just pranking him."

"What'd you do?"

She tucks her chin against her chest a little, looking at me somewhat embarrassed. "Don't judge me."

"I'm not."

She relaxes a bit. "It was little things at first. I'd slam doors, turn off lights. Your typical ghostly encounters. It was fun watching him try to explain it all away. But the more I'd witness his asshole behavior, the bigger I went with the pranks. One night, after I decided I didn't want him in this house for another day, I moved all the furniture around in the Grand Room. I moved the couch against the opposite bookshelf.

I moved the piano to the other side of the room. I even moved books from one shelf to another."

"What was his reaction the next day when he saw everything had been moved?"

Willow presses her lips together tightly. She moves her head from side to side with a sheepish look on her face. "Well . . . that's the thing," she says. "I moved everything while he was still in the room."

I try to imagine what that must have been like for the guy—seeing an entire piano move across the room by itself.

"He put the house on the market that day, and he hasn't been back since."

"Holy shit," I say, laughing. "That explains the rush to sell."

She falls back onto her pillow, and she's smiling proudly. Her smile is infectious. I lie down on my own pillow, smiling right along with her.

The moment makes me think back to the few things that happened when I first arrived here. Willow saving me from burning down the kitchen. Her cleaning up the wine spill. That's hardly a haunting.

I roll my head until I'm facing her. "Why didn't you try to haunt me when I showed up?"

Willow loses her smile, gently facing me. "Because. You aren't an asshole. And I felt sorry for you."

"You felt sorry for me? Why?"

She shrugs. "You just seemed sad."

I seemed sad?

Am I sad?

I tear my gaze from hers and look up at the ceiling.

"Have you always been sad?" she asks.

"I'm not sure I know what you mean when you say sad. Give me an example."

"It's mostly when Layla leaves a room," Willow says. "You stare at the door for a long time with this distant look in your eyes. Sometimes you seem sad even when you're with her. I don't know. It's just a feeling I get. I'm probably wrong."

I shouldn't be shaking my head, but I am. "You aren't wrong."

She sits up again, holding the sheet up over her breasts. I tilt my head on the pillow and look at her.

"Do you not enjoy being with her?" she asks.

"I used to. But now it's . . . complicated," I keep my voice low because for whatever reason, it feels like less of an admission if I say it quietly. "A lot has changed between us since that night. Since the shooting. We aren't the same couple we were in the beginning. She's been through a lot, physically, emotionally, mentally. And of course I would never give up on her, but . . ." I don't know how to finish my sentence. I've never admitted any of this out loud.

"But what?" Willow asks.

I exhale. "Sometimes I wonder, if I would have met her today . . . how she is now . . . would I have fallen in love with her as easily as I fell in love with her in the beginning? I don't know. Part of me thinks maybe I wouldn't be able to fall in love with this version of her at all. And when I have those thoughts . . . it makes me feel like shit. Because *I'm* the reason she is the way she is. *I'm* the reason she's so unhappy now. Because I failed to protect her."

Willow's expression is sympathetic. Almost regretful—like she didn't mean to open up this can of worms. She inhales a soft breath and releases it into the silent room. "Maybe things will eventually go back to exactly how they were in the beginning between you two. If it's any consolation, you don't seem as sad now. Not like when you first showed up here."

I look at her pointedly. "That has nothing to do with Layla and everything to do with you," I admit.

Willow doesn't react to that with anything other than her eyes. They flicker a little, as if she wasn't expecting me to say it.

I shouldn't have said it. As soon as the words left my mouth, I felt the guilt. But I said it, and I said it because it's the truth. I look forward to these moments with Willow more than I look forward to time with Layla.

What does that say about me?

I sit up and slide my hands up my face, then into my hair. I'm gripping the back of my neck when I completely change the subject. "Are you hungry? Do you want me to make you something to eat?"

Willow stares at me, unmoving, as if my words are still sinking in. But then she nods and slips gracefully out of bed, leaving the sheet behind. She walks confidently to the closet and takes down one of Layla's shirts. She catches me watching her as she pulls it over her head. I can't even tear my eyes away this time.

"Nothing you haven't seen before," she says evenly. She walks out of the room, and I listen as her footsteps fade down the stairs.

I wait a couple of minutes before heading down myself. I'm shamefully aware that the sight of Willow naked had more of an effect on me than when Layla had my dick in her mouth. And that makes no fucking sense. It's Layla's body either way.

―――

I made grilled cheese. Layla only had a salad for dinner, and Willow said the hunger pains were intense tonight, so I made her two sandwiches.

I'm relieved Willow has been taking over Layla's body, even if just for the nutritional benefit. Not that grilled cheese is all that nutritional, but it's better on Layla's body than too few calories, and Layla certainly wouldn't willingly eat a grilled cheese.

Her obsession with dieting has been a concern of mine for a while now, but I haven't really made it a priority because so many other things with Layla have been my focus for the last six months. I thought the eating would work itself out.

It hasn't, but Willow at least makes it less of a concern for me.

She's on her second sandwich, and neither of us has spoken since I handed her the plate of food. I'm on my laptop, staring at the listing for the house. I'm still torn about what to do.

I don't want to leave Willow alone, but I know Layla doesn't want to stay here. I would ask Willow to come with us, but that's not really an option. I can't allow her to continue using Layla's body. It was only supposed to be a temporary fix—a way for Willow and me to communicate. But it's taking its toll on Layla.

It's taking a toll on me.

The only solution I can think of is to buy this place. If I do that, Layla and I can visit. Willow could still take over Layla's body the few times a year we come here. And in the meantime, we could work on finding answers for Willow. When she's ready for that, of course.

I email the Realtor and make an offer that's $10,000 over the asking price, but I let her know I'd like the option to continue to occupy the property during closing.

I don't know how Layla will feel about staying even longer, but Layla's concern doesn't seem to weigh on my decision. I've made it, and I'm prepared to deal with the fallout.

After I send the message to the Realtor, I check a few unopened messages in my in-box. One is from an address I don't recognize.

> Leeds,
>
> It's been a while since you've been in the forum. I apologize if reaching out to you beyond the forum makes you uncomfortable, but I do have a talent for separating the wheat from the chaff. I believe you, and I hope you can believe me in return.
>
> I can help your ghost.

There's no name attached to the email, but I recognize the title in the email address. UncoverInc.

How did he find me? I didn't even use my real name in the forum.

I immediately go to the forum to check my profile, wondering if it pulled my information from Facebook somehow. All the settings are private, though, but before I log back out, a chat message pops up.

Did you get my email?

I look across the table at Willow, but she's still eating, not paying attention to me. I shift in my chair and then hit respond.

Yes. How did you get my email address?

Never communicate with someone through a cell phone if you're hoping to stay anonymous. I, however, have no interest in you or who you are, so there's no need to be concerned. I'm interested in your ghost. Did you find anything out about her?

No.

Are you still at the bed & breakfast?

I lean back in my chair and stare at that message, unnerved. *He knows where we're staying?* My heart begins pumping wildly in my chest. The last time someone found out where we were staying—it didn't end well. I immediately push back from the table and walk to the front door to make sure it's locked.

I double-check the alarm system when I pass by it to make sure it's set. I check the other doors as well as every single window in the house. It takes me a while because this house is huge and there are a lot of windows, so by the time I make it back to the kitchen, I'm not surprised to see Willow is finished eating.

I *am* surprised to see that she's looking at my laptop. She points at the screen and looks up at me like I've betrayed her.

"What's this?"

I can't tell if she's upset or not. I shake my head and try to close the laptop, but she forces it back open. "Who is he?" she asks.

"I don't know."

"How does he know about me?"

"It's just someone I met in a forum. I thought it was anonymous, but he figured out how to contact me."

Willow's jaw hardens. She stands up and paces the kitchen. "Is that why you seemed anxious while I was eating?"

"I'm not anxious."

"You are. You checked all the windows and doors because whoever he is, he knows where we are."

"Don't worry. I'm overly cautious now. Everything's locked up."

Willow's shoulders are tense. It's only the second time I've seen her stressed while inside Layla. She pauses her pacing and says, "Why have you been talking to him? Do you want me out of this house?"

"No. I've been talking to him because when this first started, I thought I was going crazy."

"Why are you still talking to him?"

"He keeps contacting me. I'm not hiding anything, Willow. He's just adamant that he can help you, but I haven't taken him up on the offer because it isn't what you want right now."

She blows out a quick, frustrated breath. Then she walks to the freezer, opens it, and grabs a half gallon of ice cream. She retrieves a spoon and sticks it into the ice cream, then takes a big bite.

"We both know what answers mean for a ghost," she says, talking between bites of mint chocolate chip. "It means I'll be done here. Whatever the reason is for me being stuck here, if that man is right, I'll get unstuck. I won't be here anymore. You've seen all the movies. Patrick Swayze had to die twice in that movie. *Twice!*"

"They're just movies, Willow. Written by people in Hollywood who get paid to use their imagination. We don't know what actually happens next."

She waves her spoon at me while she paces, tucking the ice cream tub against her chest. "Maybe not, but it's a consensus. It's the theme in every ghost story. Every ghost is a ghost because something went wrong. They were either evil in a past life, or they have unfinished business, or they have to find forgiveness. Or *give* forgiveness." She plops down in a chair at the table. Her energy is all channeled into a frown. "What if I don't like what I find out? What if I don't like what's next?" She takes another bite with the spoon upside down, and then she just lets the spoon hang from her mouth while she leans forward, clasping her hands behind her head, digging her elbows into the table.

The spoon is just dangling from her mouth.

I never intended to upset her.

Before Layla and I showed up, Willow didn't have these concerns. She didn't even consider herself a ghost. She just existed in whatever realm she's in, and she was content with that until I came along. Nothing good has come from her crossing into this realm.

It's only caused Layla to stress about her fatigue.

It's turned me into a liar.

It's instilled a fear into Willow that wasn't there before.

"Willow," I say quietly. She looks up at me and pulls the spoon from her mouth. "Do you think what we're doing is wrong? Using Layla like we're doing?"

"Of *course* it's wrong. Just because we're able to do this doesn't mean we should be doing it."

As much as I don't want her to be right, I know she is. I've known all along, but the selfish side of me has been excusing it because I've been telling myself I'm helping Willow.

But before I got here, Willow didn't even want help. She took over Layla simply because she wanted to taste food. And even that might have been fine, but then I got way too involved. I became morbidly fascinated to the point that I've been putting Layla at risk. Maybe even Willow.

There may not be a handbook for how to deal with a ghost, but a person doesn't need it to be written down in order to know the difference between right and wrong.

Willow walks the ice cream back to the freezer. "You look tired," she says flatly.

"I am."

"You can go to bed," she says, waving toward the stairs. "I'm gonna watch a movie."

I don't want her to watch a movie. I'm not sure I want her using Layla's body anymore. "Layla's tired too. She needs to sleep."

Willow stiffens at my words. She can see in my resolute expression that I've reached my immoral threshold. She just stares at me, silently, sadly. "You want me to get out of her?" she whispers.

I nod, then turn and head upstairs because I don't want to see the look on Willow's face.

She isn't far behind me. She walks into the room a minute later, her eyes downcast. She doesn't look at me as she makes her way to Layla's side of the bed. She's still wearing the shirt she took out of Layla's closet earlier.

"Layla wasn't wearing clothes when she went to bed."

Willow pulls the shirt over her head and walks back to the closet to hang it. She doesn't bother covering herself on the walk back to the bed, but I'm not even looking at her body. I'm looking at the moon's reflection on her face, and the tears that rim her eyes.

She crawls into bed and pulls the covers up to her neck. Her back is to me, but I can hear her crying.

I hate that I've upset her. I don't want her to be upset, but I don't know how else to deal with this. She's a ghost who doesn't want help. I'm a guy who doesn't want to leave her. We're communicating through a girl we have no right to be using like we have been.

It feels like a breakup, and we aren't even intimate.

Her breaths are coming in short and shallow bursts, like she's trying her hardest to fight back her tears. The need to comfort her is overwhelming, especially because I'm the one who has made her feel this way. I move my head to her pillow and find her under the covers, then wrap my arm over her stomach.

She grips my arm with her hand and squeezes it supportively. It's her way of letting me know she understands my decision. But understanding it doesn't make it easier.

When Layla is sad, it's almost always fixable with whatever kind of medicine will cure her pain or ailment.

But with Willow, her sadness is unreachable, even from this proximity. I can't soothe the loneliness she feels in her world. I can't tell her it'll be okay, because I don't know that it will be. This is an unprecedented journey for both of us.

"I want you to message him back tomorrow," she says. "Ask him if he really thinks he can help me."

I close my eyes, relieved that she's finally willing to do something about this. The thought of her just living forever without purpose is depressing. I kiss the back of her head. "Okay," I whisper.

"Do you not want me to use Layla anymore?" she asks.

I don't answer that right away because it's not a simple yes or no. Of course I want her to use Layla because I like spending time with her. But I also want her to stop, because we've taken this way too far.

She takes my silence as confirmation that I don't want her to do it anymore.

I bury my face into her hair, but I still don't speak. Anything I say at this point feels like it'll just be a new item added to the list of ways I've betrayed Layla. Like the fact that I've put in an offer on the house. I haven't even told Willow. Now I'm not so sure she would even want me to buy it.

"I put in an offer on the house."

Willow rolls over. Her breast brushes against my arm, and I try to ignore it, but we're in a more intimate position than we've ever been in. It's hard to ignore when my face is just two inches from hers and she's looking up at me with hope shining through her tear-filled eyes.

"You did?"

I nod and lift my hand from her waist. I bring it to her forehead and move a piece of hair that's fallen over her eyes. "Yes. I wouldn't be here full-time, but I can come back and visit. I want to help you."

"What about Layla?" she asks.

I shrug, because I don't know what will happen with Layla. I don't know that she'll ever want to come back here. I don't know where we'll be when we leave here. Things with Layla feel different now that Willow has entered the picture.

But I also know that visits back to this place will just be another form of torture if we don't use Layla's body. Sure, we'll be able to communicate. But we'll have to do that without a way to look at each other, and that sounds like torment.

The room is quiet. So quiet I swear I can hear Willow's heart pounding in her chest. She's gazing up at me with a mixture of longing and sadness. I'm looking down at her much the same way.

Even buying this house wouldn't bring me reassurance. I'd still think about her every minute of the day when I'm not here.

I'll still pretend Layla is Willow every time I kiss her.

My eyes fall to Willow's lips, and I'm reminded of the crazy way my heart beat when I kissed Layla for the first time, only now it's an even smaller plink and a much bigger BOOM.

I never thought I'd feel more for someone than I felt that night. But right now . . . I'm feeling everything I can feel in this world, coupled with everything I could feel in Willow's world.

I run the back of my hand across her jaw, angling her face more toward mine. She keeps her eyes open as I slowly lower my head and rest my mouth against hers. There's a hesitation on both of our parts as our lips slide against each other with very little movement. It's as if we're both scared of what this will mean for our future.

Will crossing a physical line by kissing her make me crave her even more? Will it make me never want to leave? Will it weaken my resolve to the point that I let Willow take over Layla whenever she wants?

In this moment, I honestly don't care.

In this moment, the only thing I can care about is my selfish, insatiable need to kiss Willow. I wouldn't even care if this caused an upheaval to the entirety of *humanity*.

I slide my hands in her hair and slip my tongue into her mouth, and I don't do it gently. I kiss her with a need I didn't even know was buried inside me.

She moans into my mouth, and it fills me with even more urgency. I don't know why I'm kissing her like someone might steal this moment from us.

She responds in kind, threading her fingers through my hair, tilting her body more toward mine. She presses her breasts against my chest, and a sensational pull rolls through me. I want on top of her, inside of her. I want my mouth to cover every inch of her. I want to hear every single sound she's capable of making, and I want my hands and my tongue to be responsible for those sounds.

The kiss has only gone on for a matter of seconds, but it's long enough that an ache inside of me builds and builds to the point that the kiss becomes painful.

It becomes sad.

I've never had so many emotions run through me during a single kiss before, but I run through every feeling my body and mind are capable of until the one I want the least consumes me the most.

I ache everywhere, but it's the most prominent in my chest. It hurts so much I'm forced to pull away from her and suck in air because I feel like my heart is being strangled.

I roll onto my back and try to catch my breath, but there isn't enough air in this world to ease this feeling.

I find Willow's hand, and I hold it, but it's all I can do. I can't kiss her again. I can't go through that with her again, knowing she's not someone I get to keep for the rest of my life.

I shouldn't have done that. Now I don't want to leave. The only thing that feels important to me now is making sure Willow doesn't have to spend another day alone in this house.

I'm full of an immense need to find answers for why Willow is stuck in her world, because I desperately need her to get stuck in mine.

I tilt my head to look at her, and when I do, I wish I wouldn't have. It just makes it worse because she's looking back at me with a broken heart. She rolls toward me and tucks her head in the crook of my neck, curling herself around me. "Every time I have to leave her body, it feels like a punishment. Every night, over and over. It's torture."

I wrap my arms around her, wishing I could fix everything for her. But I can't.

I've just made it all so much worse.

CHAPTER SEVENTEEN

The bed is empty when I wake up. I touch Layla's pillow and run my hand over it, as if Willow is still lying there. *Maybe she is.*

I sit up to check the time, but I can't find my phone. I look on the floor. On the bed. It isn't in here.

Did Layla take it?

I rush downstairs to find her, my fear two steps ahead of me as I wonder why she took my phone and what she might be seeing on it. A conversation with Willow, the app for the security system. I rush into the kitchen, but Layla isn't there. I search the Grand Room, the downstairs bedrooms. I open the back door, but she isn't out by the pool.

I run to the front door and swing it open.

Layla is sitting on the porch steps, staring out over the front yard. There's a cigarette in her hand.

"What are you doing?"

She doesn't turn around to look at me, which makes me wonder what she found out. There are so many things. The cameras, the conversations on my laptop, the kiss last night.

I walk tentatively toward the steps and watch as Layla takes in a slow drag of the cigarette. "I wasn't aware you smoked," I say.

She blows the smoke out. "I don't. But I keep some hidden in my purse for when I'm stressed." She cuts her eyes at me, looking over her shoulder. I'm not sure what it is that caused that betrayal in her expression, but she definitely uncovered something.

I keep my voice steady when I say, "What's wrong, Layla?"

She looks away from me again. Her voice is flat when she says, "Why didn't you tell me you were buying this house?"

I lean my head back and blow out a silent breath of relief. I thought maybe she might have found the security footage. I wouldn't have been able to explain that.

But I expected her to be mad about this.

I'm even okay that she knows about it. I planned to tell her today anyway. "How did you find out?"

"The Realtor just stopped by." Layla jams her cigarette onto the wooden step next to her, and it feels like an insult. "The contract is on the kitchen counter. She'd like it back by the end of the day."

I've never seen her this angry. Her sentences are tight, and she won't look me in the eye. "Layla. It was supposed to be a surprise."

"The hell it was," she says. She stands up and brushes past me, then makes her way into the house and up the stairs.

I follow her, a little confused by her level of anger. I didn't expect her to be thrilled, but I also didn't expect her to be this incensed. "Layla," I say when I reach the top of the stairs. I get her name out, right as the bedroom door closes in my face. I open it and watch as she pulls an empty suitcase from beneath the bed. She tosses it on the bed, opens it, and then walks to the dresser. "Why are you so upset about this?"

She scoops up the entire contents of the dresser drawer and tosses them into the suitcase. "I don't want to live in the middle of *nowhere*. We're a couple. You should talk to me about things like this, but instead, you went behind my back." She walks to the closet now and grabs several of her shirts.

"I wasn't hiding it. It was a surprise. We fell in love here. I thought this place meant something to us."

Her face contorts into a mixture of confusion and anger. "My sister got married here. This place means more to her than it does to me. I don't even *like* Kansas. I've said it in all the ways I can possibly say it without being rude." She shoves the shirts in the suitcase, hangers still on them. "What is your ultimate goal, Leeds? To force me to live somewhere I don't want to live, or were you hoping I'd leave you and go back to Chicago?"

She's still packing, and I'm not sure I can convince her not to leave. But she can't leave. Not after last night. Not after that kiss with Willow. I have to convince her to stay, even if it's just for one last night. I need a chance to see Willow again. Even if it's just so I can tell her goodbye face to face.

I can't do that if Layla leaves.

I rush to the closet and dig inside my shoe. I frantically pull out the engagement ring. "I had a plan, Layla," I say, walking over to her.

She's staring at the ring in my hand.

"I was going to propose tonight and tell you about the house. I had it all planned out. You weren't supposed to find out this way."

Layla has stopped packing. She's staring at the box, and then she lifts her eyes to mine, but they're still filled with anger. "I already saw the ring. You realize you left the receipt inside the box, right?"

I don't know why that matters. I would have taken it out before I proposed anyway. "Why does that matter?"

"You bought the ring while I was in the hospital, Leeds. *Six months* ago. That means you've spent the last six months doubting whether you even want to be with me." She turns and zips up her suitcase. "If you don't want to leave, fine. Stay and close on your house. But I don't like it here, and I don't want to stay here. I'm taking the car."

Fuck.

Fuck.

If she leaves, I won't get to see Willow again.

I run through the bedroom, past Layla. I block the doorway and then kneel in front of her. She stops moving. "This isn't how I wanted this to happen," I say. "But I've known since the night I met you that I wanted to marry you. I bought this ring six months ago, knowing that once you recovered, we would come back here. I wanted to ask you to be my wife, but I wanted to do it here. Where we met. I love you, and I want to spend the rest of my life with you, Layla. Please don't go."

Layla doesn't move. She's staring at the ring now, less tense than she was a minute ago. Less angry.

"*Please*," I beg.

She hesitates, her expression still full of doubt. She releases the suitcase. "This is really confusing," she says. "I want to believe you. Why don't I believe you?"

Because you shouldn't, I want to say. Instead, I stand up and grab her hand. I look at her intently, and with what I hope looks like honesty. Because what I'm about to say is honest. "I knew I wanted to marry you the first night we met. I had never felt more connected to someone like I did to you." What I follow that up with is a lie, though. "I want to spend my life with you, Layla. Please. Marry me."

She believed that. I can see it in her expression. All her anger has turned to relief. "So you haven't been doubting us?"

Yes. For six months. "No. Not even for one second."

A tear spills out of her right eye, and then she shakes her head regretfully. "I ruined it. Leeds, I'm so sorry. I got angry and I ruined this whole thing."

I pull the ring out of the box. I slip it on her trembling finger. She's full on crying now. "It's not your fault. I should have planned this better."

She shakes her head and throws her arms around my neck. "No, it was perfect." She kisses me and then pulls back to look at the ring. "And yes. Yes, yes, yes, I'll marry you."

This was not the proposal I had imagined.

Far from it.

I try to keep a solid expression on my face, but the bigger her smile gets, the smaller I feel.

She kisses me again, and she tastes like cigarettes, and I have to force myself through the kiss.

I've done some pretty terrible things in the last year, but this may be the lowest I've ever sunk. I just proposed to a girl I'm not even sure I'm in love with anymore.

"I have to call Aspen," Layla says. She bounds out the bedroom door and down the stairs.

I just stand still in the bedroom, shaking my head. *What have I just done?*

I hear something behind me—a noise coming from the dresser. The bottom drawer slowly slides open by itself.

I walk over to the dresser and look inside the drawer. My laptop and my phone are tucked away inside. I pick up my phone and enter the pass code. I open the messages where Willow and I have most of our conversations. There's an unread message that reads, *I had to hide your phone and your laptop after the realtor left. Layla looked really angry and I didn't want her snooping.*

The message was sent an hour ago.

I sigh, walk over to the bed, and fall on top of it, face-first. "I'm sorry," I say out loud. "I had no other choice."

The room is silent. I lay my phone on the bed in case Willow wants to use it to respond to me.

She doesn't.

She doesn't speak to me at all.

CHAPTER EIGHTEEN

"You don't eat enough." My words come out harsher than I mean for them to. Layla looks up from the food she's been pretending to take bites of.

"I've eaten enough to gain three pounds since we got here."

"I'm not just talking about these past two weeks. You barely get eight hundred calories a day, tops. It worries me."

"My body is used to eight hundred calories. I function just fine on that."

"No, you don't. You're always hungry."

Layla laughs incredulously. "You say that like you know my body better than I do."

I'm making her angry. That isn't my intention. It's just that I've been angry all day and that's transferring onto Layla.

Willow hasn't spoken to me since I gave Layla the ring. I've tried talking to her every time Layla leaves the room, but she doesn't respond.

Yet another night I'll spend counting down the minutes until Layla falls asleep.

I take my plate to the sink and rinse it off. Layla can sense something is wrong with me. She pushes back from the table and walks over to me, sidling up next to me. "You okay?"

I realize I'm supposed to be on a high because I proposed to the *love of my life* today, but it is so fucking hard to fake a smile.

"Is it because of the house?" she asks. "Is it really that important to you?"

I don't hear any traces of anger in her voice. She seems genuinely curious, so I use her good mood to my advantage. I cup her chin in my hand. "This is where I met you, Layla. Of course it's important to me."

She smiles. "That's sweet." That doesn't mean she's okay with it, though.

"It would be a good investment." I don't even know if that's true. It could be a money pit. "You wouldn't have to live here. We could buy a house in Nashville and only visit this place when we need to check up on things."

She actually looks like she's contemplating everything I'm saying. "I wouldn't have to live here?"

"No. Think of it like a vacation home. But if I do buy it, we'll need to stay an extra week so I can close on it. Wrap some things up before we head back to Tennessee." I've never bought a piece of property before, but I'm pretty sure it takes more than a week to close. I don't want Layla to know that, though.

Layla drops her forehead to my chest. "A whole *week*," she says with a sigh. "Ugh. Fine. I trust you."

I take a step back. "Seriously?"

She nods. "Why not? It means a lot to you, and you'll be my husband soon. Besides, it might be cool to get married at the same place my sister got married."

I wrap my arms around her and I hug her. It's the first hug I've given her lately that hasn't felt forced, but I am so relieved. She's giving me an extra week here, which means I get to see Willow again.

And owning this place will give me more time to *help* Willow.

Maybe.

After my actions today, there's a chance Willow may never speak to me again.

⌒⌒

I proposed to Layla today, so it only made sense not to push her away when she wanted to make love tonight. She took off all her clothes and said she wanted me to make love to her while she only wore her engagement ring.

I had to think about Willow again in order to get through it. Then, when it was over and Layla wanted to cuddle, I pretended she was Willow while I gently ran my hand up and down her arm until she fell asleep.

That was half an hour ago, and we're still in the same position. She's asleep on my chest. I'm staring up at the ceiling—waiting for Willow to show up. *Hoping* she shows up.

I didn't call my mother to tell her I proposed to Layla. I'm not proud of it. I'm not proud of what it's going to do to Layla when I admit I'm not in love with her anymore.

She shifts against my chest and then sits up.

My whole body sighs with relief when I see it's Willow. I was beginning to think I'd made her angry enough not to take over Layla again.

She's staring down at Layla's ring. Then she slips it off her finger and sets it on the nightstand.

"I don't like how it feels," she says. She pulls the covers up over her bare chest and reaches across her body to scratch her shoulder. There's an elegance to Willow, and it's my favorite physical difference between them.

Attraction is strange. How can they use the same body, but my reaction to them is so different? How can sex with Layla earlier feel like a chore, but just looking at Willow feels like a reward?

"She's prettier when you're inside of her," I say.

Willow doesn't make eye contact. "That's not really a compliment to me. It's not my body." She gets up and walks confidently across the room. She goes to the bathroom and closes the door. A few seconds later, I hear the shower running.

She knows I had sex with Layla tonight. She's washing that away.

It has to be hard for Willow when I'm intimate with Layla. But I have to be physical with Layla to keep her here, or I won't get to see Willow.

It's the worst catch-22 imaginable. I can't break up with the girl I'm falling out of love with, or I won't get to spend time with the girl I'm falling in love with.

When Willow is finished showering, she walks back into the bedroom wearing a towel. She drops it to the floor and pulls on a T-shirt before crawling back into bed with me. She rolls onto her side, her back to me. She's hurting, and that's my fault.

"I don't want to marry her, Willow."

"Then you shouldn't have proposed," she says quickly.

"What was I supposed to do? Let her leave?"

Willow rolls over and sits up. "Yes." *She makes it sound so simple.*

"I didn't want her to take our last night together."

"What about *after* tonight?" she says. "What's going to happen if you buy this house? We'll have a scandalous affair whenever Layla is willing to come back here with you? I'll get to take over after I have to stand outside your door and listen to you have sex with her?"

I grab her hand and pull her against me, hating hearing that pain in her voice. She falls into my arms in a heap of defeat.

"This isn't fair to me," she says. "You get us both in your world, but I don't get you at all in mine."

I brush my hand gently over her hair. "If I knew how to do it any differently, I would. But I'm not in love with Layla anymore, if that helps at all."

"Yes, you are," Willow says quietly. "You're just confused. You showed up here in love with her, but I've made that complicated by using her body."

"It was complicated before I even got here. I thought this place could change that. Fix us somehow. But it just made it worse. You said yourself that I look sad when I'm with her."

Willow lifts off my chest and searches my eyes. "What if that's my fault, though? If I wasn't here, inserting myself into your life, you might have actually been able to reconnect with her."

I sigh, not wanting her to look at me when I say what I'm about to say. I'm scared it'll make her lose whatever respect she might have left for me. "It has nothing to do with you, Willow. I've seen Layla at her lowest points, and sometimes those low points are really, really low. At first, I blamed my fading feelings on the fact that our roles had changed so suddenly. I became her caretaker. I thought once she got better, things would change. But the further we got into her recovery, the more distant I started to feel. That isn't her fault. It isn't your fault. It's *my* fault." I drag my hands down my face with a huge exhale. "All of this is my fault. What we're doing to Layla now. What Sable did to her. What I did to *Sable*."

Willow sits up on the bed. She wraps her arms around her knees and is quiet for a moment. "I want to know what happened that night."

"Can't you just look at Layla's memories?"

"I want to hear your version."

"There's not much to tell. Sable shot Layla, then me when I entered the room. I ran for the gun."

Willow doesn't react to that with words, but I can see her whole body stiffen when I say that. "So . . . you shot her?" she asks in a whisper.

I nod. The memory of it all still feels surreal.

Willow rests her head on top of her knees and continues to stare at me. "Who was Sable to you?"

"I dated her for a few months. Last year, before I met Layla."

"But you broke up with her? Why?"

I swallow the thickness in my throat and sit up on the bed. Willow continues to observe me, but I can't look her in the eyes. I rest my elbows on my knees and focus my gaze on my hands. "I thought it would end up being a one-night stand at first, but she kept coming around. I didn't do anything about it because I didn't mind the company. But before I knew it, she was posting pictures of us online, calling me her boyfriend, coming to every show. Garrett and the guys in the band thought it was funny because they knew I was dragging it out because I felt sorry for her. I let it continue for several weeks longer than I should have because I didn't want to upset her. But then she started taking things a little too far, and it left me with no choice but to break things off."

"Taking things too far in what way?" Willow asks.

"She was upset that I wouldn't tell her I loved her back after only knowing her for a couple of weeks. She was upset that I hadn't posted a picture of us together on Instagram. She'd get irrationally angry when I would tell her I wasn't looking for anything serious, and then she'd try to tell me all the reasons she thought I was wrong. In my head, we were having fun. In her head, she was practically planning our wedding. When I finally did break up with her, she wouldn't stop calling me. Then she came to one of our shows, and she started screaming at me because I wouldn't take any of her calls. Garrett had to have her kicked out and wouldn't allow her at any future shows. I had to cut her off. Didn't know how else to deal with it. I thought she'd eventually get over it."

"Is that why she showed up at your house and did what she did? Because you had moved on with Layla?"

"I don't know, honestly. She was definitely upset by a picture I had posted with Layla. Upset enough to reach out to Layla on social media. But the police said she had a long list of diagnoses, some of which stemmed from childhood. Depression, bulimia, bipolar disorder, you name it. And she wasn't taking her medication for any of it. Maybe that's why she did what she did. Because she really was unstable."

"That had to be terrifying for Layla. And you."

I nod. "It was."

"Why does it seem like you feel guilty about it?" she asks. "It doesn't sound like you did anything wrong. People break up all the time."

I shrug. "I don't feel guilty for breaking up with her. I feel guilty for ending her life. I could have easily held her at gunpoint until the police arrived, but I didn't. I let my anger at what she'd done to Layla take over. I took her life, and I've regretted it since the moment I did it."

Willow's voice is quiet when she says, "You did what most people would do in that situation. She had an obsessive personality, and you were just a casualty of that. How were you supposed to know how deep it went, or that she had a fan club for you before you even met her?" She leans into me a little, urging me to make eye contact with her. "She forced you to take it as far as you did when she showed up to your house with a gun. That's not your fault."

I don't talk about this to anyone, so it's nice to hear her say those words. I'm about to tell her thank you.

But then my blood chills . . . *freezes* . . . shatters like tiny shards of glass exploding inside of me. The words that just came out of Willow's mouth are rushing through me, searching for a place to belong, but they *don't* belong.

Her words don't belong in Layla's head.

I never mentioned specifics about Sable to Layla. I never told Layla that Sable had a fan club.

I've certainly never told *Willow* that Sable ran a fan club.

How does Willow know anything at all about Sable? That's not something she should know.

I grab her wrist and I sit up, rolling her onto her back. I crawl out of the bed and stand next to it, staring down at her.

Her eyes are wide with confusion at my sudden movement.

I squeeze my jaw, silently trying to piece together a puzzle that has seemed so complicated, but really it's simple. It's a puzzle that only consists of three pieces.

Me.

Layla.

Sable.

Is that why Willow is here? Because she's Sable, in need of closure? If that's the case, why would she go by a different name?

"Why do you call yourself Willow?" I ask her.

My reaction is making her nervous. She rubs her hands up her arms. "You asked what my name was. I don't have one, so I just . . . made it up."

My words feel stuck in my throat. "You . . . *made it up?*"

"Yes. I already told you I don't have any memories. How would I know what my name was? I've never even spoken to anyone before you, so no one has ever asked me my name."

My mind begins to whirl in every possible direction. Why have I not considered this possibility? Sable is dead. *I'm* responsible for her death.

That's why she's here.

"Leeds?" Willow tosses the blanket aside as she watches me pace the room. "What's wrong?"

I stop walking, and then turn around and face her. I feel like the bottom has dropped out from under me and I'm about to free-fall straight through the house. "How did you know Sable had a fan club?"

Her eyes fill with something else now . . . something Willow's expression is never full of. *Guilt.*

For the first time since I arrived in this house, I'm finally having the reaction I should have had all along. Fear.

"Get out of Layla."

"Leeds . . ."

"Get. Out. Of. Layla!"

Willow scrambles to her feet. "Leeds, wait. You don't understand. It's confusing inside her head. Nothing makes sense. That's not my memory—it's one of Layla's." She's in front of me now, pleading.

I feel like a fucking fool. "I never *told* Layla that. She wouldn't have that memory. Only Sable would know that."

Willow's hands go up to the sides of her head like she can't come up with an excuse quick enough.

Willow is Sable, and I should have recognized that immediately. But I was too caught up in the idea of it all. Too enamored that something this huge was happening, and I was a part of it. I felt like I was part of something bigger than me or Layla, but all I've been a part of is destroying us even more than we've already been destroyed.

I want Willow out of Layla, and I don't even care if she does it while Layla isn't in the bed. I don't care if Layla is terrified when she opens her eyes and doesn't remember standing up. I plan on leaving with Layla tonight anyway. I need to get her as far away from Willow as possible.

I push past Willow and grab the suitcase Layla started packing earlier. I throw it on the bed, then grab our other suitcase. Willow doesn't say a word while I pack. Her eyes just follow me around the room as I gather our things.

I move to the bathroom and pack everything up; then I walk to the top of the staircase. I shove one of the suitcases forward and watch it topple down the stairs, and then I rush down the steps with the other one.

Willow is behind me, still inside of Layla.

I don't know why it took me so long to realize this. Willow is here for a reason. That reason is because she's the one who shot us. That reason has been staring me in the fucking face since I walked into this house. A house that went up for sale several months ago. A house that changed ownership not long before that.

Willow said she can't remember how long she's been in this house, but I remember her saying it wasn't long before ownership changed.

Which would mean . . . the timing coincides. Willow showed up here around the time I shot Sable.

I get to the kitchen and I grab my car keys and then turn to see Willow standing in the doorway. "We're leaving. I need you to get out of her."

She shakes her head, looking at me with imploring eyes. "Even if I was Sable in a past life, I'm not her now. I could never do what she did to you. What she did to Layla."

I'm squeezing my keys in my fist, full of even more fear now. Every time I've asked Willow to leave Layla before, she's done it.

What if she refuses to leave her now? What am I supposed to do?

"You said things were chaotic inside Layla's head. Are they chaotic because you have memories that aren't Layla's?"

Willow's chin is quivering. She nods.

"How many of Sable's memories do you have?"

She shrugs. "I don't know. I don't know what memories are Sable's, and I don't know what belongs to Layla. I have both when I'm inside of her. It's why I told you it was chaotic inside her head, because there are two versions of everything."

"Like what?"

Willow walks closer to me, and I take a step back. Her eyebrows draw apart in agony when I step away from her. She stifles a sob and then sits down at the table. She's covering her mouth with both hands now, as if she's trying to keep the sobs at bay while also trying to keep the truth at bay.

I reach behind me on the counter and grab a napkin. I hand it to her . . . wanting her to trust me as long as I'm still here. Long enough to let her explain herself, and then hopefully I can talk her into letting me leave with Layla. I repeat the question she's yet to answer, but I repeat it more gently.

"What memories do you have two versions of, Willow?"

She lifts her eyes to mine, wiping away tears with the napkin. "None of them when I'm not in Layla's body. But when I am inside of her . . . there are a lot."

I blow out an unsteady breath and turn away from her. *She's been lying to me this whole time.* "Do you remember the shooting?"

"Yes," she whispers.

"Do you remember doing it?"

There's a pause, and then . . .

"The memories all seem like mine when I'm inside Layla. So I don't know. It's there. But is it mine? I don't know."

I turn around and look at her. "Why else would you have access to Sable's memories?"

She looks away from me, covering her face with her hand, full of shame. "I don't know." She stands up, quickly, and rushes over to me. "If I was Sable, I'm not anymore, Leeds. I could never be capable of something like that."

I feel sick to my stomach. "Get out of Layla," I plead, knowing it's a hollow plea. There's no way she's going to let us leave now. Sable got to us once before, and now she's gotten to us again. And I fell for it, hook, line, and sinker.

Except this isn't some small mistake. It isn't even some huge betrayal.

This is far beyond anything I could even imagine. This is otherworldly.

Way beyond my comprehension.

Tears are spilling out of Willow's eyes. She just shakes her head, and with eyes full of sorrow, she says, "I'm so sorry."

And then she screams.

It's a bloodcurdling scream that makes my spine stiffen.

I can instantly tell Willow is no longer using Layla's body.

Layla looks around the kitchen and then grips the bar. She lowers herself, as if her knees are too weak to hold her up. "What is happening?"

Her voice is a shaky whisper. When she looks at me, her eyes are wide. "Leeds, what is happening to me?"

I grab Layla's hand and pull her up. "We need to leave. Now."

She's hysterical. She pushes away from me and says, "I need my medicine. I'm freaking out."

"I packed it."

She stops in the doorway and looks at me. "Why? I need it. Where is it?"

I walk to the foyer and grab our suitcases. "I'll get it for you in the car. We need to leave right now. Let's go."

She's unmoving. "Why are we leaving? Why am I downstairs?" She spins in a circle, looking up the stairs, and then into the kitchen. "I can't remember anything. I think something is wrong. Something is wrong with me."

"Nothing is wrong with you, Layla. It's this house. We need to get out of it."

She looks at me, and maybe it's the seriousness in my expression, but she finally nods in agreement. "Okay," she says, her voice full of nervousness. I open the door and push Layla out first. Then I pull the suitcases over the threshold.

"Hurry," I say, needing her to be faster before Willow takes over again.

We get halfway to the car when Layla stops. "Let's *go*, Layla."

She doesn't move.

I look at her but no longer see Layla standing next to me.

It's Willow again.

I just let go of the suitcases. I throw my hands up in defeat. The suitcases fall over, and I kick one. I kick it again. I kick it and I kick it and I kick it because she's not going to let us leave.

"Leeds, *stop*," Willow pleads.

I don't know how to get Layla out of her grasp now.

And even if she does slip out of Layla, is Willow going to follow us? How do I know she won't be in the car with us when we leave? I can't call the police. What the hell would I say? The ghost of the girl I killed is stalking me? *Again?*

How the fuck did I get myself into this mess?

"Listen to me," Willow says calmly. Her coolness is such a stark contrast to Layla's hysterics. "If I *was* Sable in a past life, I am not anymore. I'm Willow. And I could never do what Sable did to you and Layla. If you want to leave, I'm going to let you leave. But . . ."

I shake my head. "I don't even want to hear what you have to say. I want to leave."

She holds up a hand. "Please. Just let me say this." She takes two steps forward, slowly. "If I *was* Sable, then there's a reason I'm here. You've watched all the movies with me. You know all the theories. Why is Sable stuck here, Leeds? Maybe she needs your forgiveness. Or maybe you need hers? I don't know, but if you leave, we'll never figure that out. And you'll go the rest of your life knowing that ghosts exist, and you might be the reason one of them is stuck here. This is going to follow us forever. Both of us."

I shift my weight to my other leg. "I've been *trying* to help you figure this out since we started talking! You're the one who didn't want to know anything, Willow! *Now* you want my help? After I find out you've been lying to me for weeks?"

"I wasn't lying. I didn't know," she says. "I thought it was all just chaos inside Layla's head, because I don't have memories at all when I'm not in her head. I still don't know for sure. Your theory makes sense, but it doesn't feel right. There's something off about it." She steps closer again. I don't step back this time because part of me only sees Willow when I look at her, and that part of me still feels bad for her.

But not bad enough to stay.

I point at her. "You're the reason this happened, whether you remember it or not. You're the reason Layla almost died. I will not be the reason you ultimately kill her. *Get* out of her and *stay* out of her."

She's still calm, but now there are silent tears spilling down her cheeks. "I don't know why I'm here. But I'm here, and wherever this is, I don't feel like an evil person. I feel *good* and I feel *honest*. I am not whoever Sable was in her life. I feel like me. Like Willow. I'm the girl you've been watching movies with and eating leftovers with and spending time with. I'm the girl you kissed on that bed last night. *Me*. Not Sable. Not Layla. *Willow.*"

I clench my teeth. "Willow doesn't exist. It's a name you made up."

She closes the gap between us and takes my face in her hands, her eyes full of desperation. "I do exist. I'm right here. I'm standing right in front of you."

I can't look at her while she's crying like this. I spin around and rest my hands on my hips. I drop my head, unsure of what to do next. An entire minute goes by, and she just stands behind me, crying quietly.

I don't know what to do. I stare at the driveway, knowing that's the direction I should be going. But why is my internal compass pulling me in the opposite direction? Why am I even struggling with this decision? Why do I still feel drawn to stay here when she's the reason we're in this mess to begin with?

"Leeds?" she finally says. "Just . . . go."

I spin around, and Willow is looking at me, completely defeated. She waves toward the car. "Go. This isn't right. We shouldn't be doing this to Layla anyway. Go, get married, buy her a different house, have babies, be famous and shit. Be happy." She wipes the areas beneath her eyes with her fingers. "I want you to be happy. I promise I won't stop you when you leave with her this time, if that's what you want."

I study her for a moment, unsure what to believe.

And why the *hell* do I still feel bad for her?

I walk over and pick up one of the suitcases. Then the other. I walk them to the car and shut them in the trunk. She's standing at the driver's-side door.

I pause a few feet from her, watching her cautiously.

"Do me a favor?" she says. "Will you email that man and ask him to come here anyway? I need to figure this out now. I don't want to be here anymore."

Those words, and the agonizing way she said them, settle in my chest.

I don't want to be here anymore.

I clear my throat. "I'll email him tonight."

She smiles gently, and her lips are trembling when she whispers, "Thank you." Another tear falls out of her eye, and she looks up and to the right, her face pained. "I hope you have a good life."

And then she's gone.

Layla is hysterical again.

She spins in a circle, confused as to how she got outside.

I grab her hand and walk her to the passenger-side door. "Just get in the car," I say, trying to sound calm, but that's hard to do when she's screaming and scared and confused and sobbing. I buckle her in and walk around to the driver's-side door.

I place my hand on the door handle and pause for a moment. Layla is screaming for me to hurry. My head is pounding from the pressure of everything that's happened in the last hour. I just want to scream because I feel like I'm being torn in half right now.

I think about the night I met Layla. I think about what she said . . . about realms and how she believes we move from one realm, to the next, to the next. I think about how she said in the womb we don't remember existence *before* the womb. In life, we don't remember being in the womb. And how in the next realm, we may not remember *this* life.

What if Willow really doesn't remember being Sable?

What if who she is in this realm is different from who she was in her past realm?

She's right. No matter how far away from this place I get, I'll never stop thinking about this. I'll never stop needing answers.

I look back at the house . . . at the place that means the most to me in this world. *The heart of the country.*

If Willow . . . *Sable* . . . didn't need my help, why would she have come here?

There's a reason she's here. She knew I would show up here somehow. Maybe it was a cosmic force at play. Maybe it's something as simple as needing Layla's and my forgiveness.

Whatever it is, whether the reason is complicated or simple, this whole thing is bigger than Layla. This is bigger than me. This is so much bigger than the world I thought we existed in, and I'm trying to force it into a tiny little box and tuck it away like none of it is happening.

I feel the pull to help Willow in my gut, my bones, my heart. If I walk away, those feelings will stay here, in this house, with this ghost, and I'll leave feeling just as empty as I felt when I arrived.

I can't explain why, but walking away from this place out of fear feels so much worse than staying to help this girl find closure. If Layla and I are related to the reason she's stuck here, we're more than likely also her only way out.

"Leeds," Layla pleads. "Get in the car!"

I'll always feel a constant pull to this place, no matter where I am in life or how far I drive away from here.

And for the life of me . . . I can't figure out why. Why do I care what happens to Sable? Is she manipulating my thoughts somehow?

"Willow," I say into the air. "I have a question. Get back inside Layla again."

Layla is still yelling my name, begging me to hurry.

Then she stops.

She's suddenly calm as she unbuckles herself and opens her door. When she climbs out of the car and turns around, it's Willow looking back at me from over the top of the car.

"Have you ever gotten inside of me?" I ask her.

She immediately answers with a shake of her head. "No. Of course not."

The look on her face is a clear indicator that she isn't lying. "You said you only have memories when you're attached to a body," I say. "Is that right?"

She nods.

"If that man comes to help you, then you're going to need a body. You're going to need those memories."

It takes my words a few seconds to register, but when they do, Willow covers her mouth with her hand, trying to stifle her cry. Then she drops her hand to her chest, over her heart. "You're going to help me?"

I let go of a regretful sigh. "Yes. And I have no idea why. So please don't make me regret this. *Please.*"

Willow shakes her head adamantly. "I won't. But . . . Layla isn't going to stay here willingly. Not after tonight."

I walk back toward the house and away from the car. "I know."

This is the moment I truly question myself as a boyfriend, a caretaker, a human being. I don't know why I feel so strongly about staying, or why I feel so strongly about keeping Layla here with me. My behavior right now goes against every moral I have, but I've never felt this kind of certainty in my gut.

My gut is telling me this terrible decision will pay off when it's all said and done.

Which means this is the moment I'll likely regret the most.

THE INTERVIEW

"I'd like to speak to Willow now," the man says. He doesn't stop the tape recorder. He just stares at me expectantly, waiting for me to go upstairs and untie Layla.

When I make it up to the bedroom, I can tell Willow is already inside of her.

"He makes me nervous," she says.

"He seems harmless."

"He's just so ambiguous. It's been a one-sided conversation all night. He hasn't offered up anything."

I don't respond to that because I've known him just as long as Willow has, so I can't vouch for his character. But what's the worst that can happen? He doesn't have answers? We're already at that point, so it's not like he can make it any worse.

Willow is quiet as we descend the stairs. When we walk into the kitchen, he's leaning back in his chair, watching Willow intently. He's only been in her physical presence for a few seconds tonight, when she stopped Layla from opening the front door. He's looking at her like he's examining her from the inside out. Willow takes a seat across from him.

"Do you want something to drink?" I ask her.

She shakes her head, her eyes fixed on the man.

He rests his hand on the table, rapping against it with his fingertips. "What's your first memory of this place?"

Willow shrugs a little. "I don't have a specific first memory."

"You just feel like you've always been here?" he asks.

She nods. "Yes. I mean, I know I haven't. But I don't remember *not* being here, if that makes sense."

"Of course it makes sense," he says gently. "It's just like birth. Humans know they were born, but they don't remember it. This is no different."

Willow seems to relax a little with his comment.

The man leans forward, eyeing her closely. "Leeds tells me you have memories of your past life."

"I have memories that belong to both Layla and Sable, but only when I'm inside of her body."

"What memories do you have when you aren't inside Layla?"

"Just the memories I've made here."

The man nods in understanding, still studying her intently.

"But I have feelings," Willow adds. "Even when I'm not in a body."

"What kind of feelings?"

Willow's eyes cut to mine for a moment; then she looks down at her hands. "When Leeds first got here—I don't know, it's hard to explain. But it was like I was relieved to see him. It was the first time I remember feeling anything good."

"Do you think you were relieved to see *him* specifically, or just people in general? Could the feeling have been because you were lonely?"

Willow shakes her head. "No. I was relieved because I felt like . . . I'd *missed* him. I felt nothing for Layla. Only Leeds."

"And you felt this before you were in Layla's body for the first time?"

Willow nods.

I had no idea she felt anything at all when we first arrived. But it means very little. Sable thought she had feelings for me when she was alive, so it makes a little sense that those feelings would carry over into whatever place she's in right now.

Willow rubs the bandages on her wrists. I notice the man's eyes drop to Willow's hands. He stares at them. "How long have you been keeping Layla captive?" he asks.

"Captive is a strong term," I interject.

The man turns his attention to me. "What other term would you suggest?"

I try to think of an alternative, but I can't. He's right. We're holding Layla here against her will, and there's no soft way to describe that. "We tied her up shortly after I messaged you and asked for your help."

"Do you untie her when Willow takes over?" he asks me.

"Yes, but I don't think we can use her much longer. She's only slept a few hours over the last few days."

"What does Layla think is happening?" He looks at Willow. "Does she know about you yet?"

"Leeds tried to explain to her why she couldn't leave, but it still didn't calm her down. So . . . we thought the best way to get her to understand would be to show her."

The man turns to me this time. "And how did you do that?"

CHAPTER NINETEEN

I don't know what to call her now. Willow or Sable.

Sable seems like an insult. It's hard for the name to even pass through my head without it consuming me in a wave of negative emotions.

Even now, knowing what I know, the Sable I knew and the Willow I know still seem like two separate people. Maybe Willow is right, and in this realm, she's just Willow. She's not who she was in her past life.

I'm going to continue calling her Willow because I can't bring myself to refer to her as Sable.

When we walked back into the house earlier, I came straight to the laptop and opened up the messages in the forum. I typed: *We need your help.*

I didn't type anything else in the message. The man already somehow knows where we're staying, so if he's able to come, he'll come. And if he needs more information, he'll ask. I don't want to type too many details.

"She's going to be hysterical when she wakes up," Willow says. "You might want to get her medication out of the car in case she needs it."

"Good idea." I return to the car and grab both suitcases. When I shut the trunk, I look up at the house. I can see Willow through the huge bay windows in the kitchen. She's pacing back and forth, biting her thumbnail nervously. I watch her for a moment, wondering what's going to happen when Layla does wake up.

How am I going to explain this to her?

Do I tell her the truth?

I'm not sure I can convince her that everything that happened tonight was just a dream, and I'm not looking forward to telling her that I intend to stay in this house even longer. I'll just figure it out as I go along. That's all I can do at this point. I can't just call up people I know and ask for advice on how to properly hold your girlfriend against her will so your ghost friend can use her body.

This is definitely a play-it-by-ear situation.

When I'm back inside the house with the suitcases, I turn on the security system. Then Willow follows me upstairs. We unpack the suitcases and try to replace everything just the way it was before I packed them. If I'm going to try to convince Layla that she dreamt everything that happened earlier, it'll need to appear like we never packed up to leave in the first place.

Willow is sitting on the bed when I return from putting Layla's toiletries on the bathroom counter. She's hugging her knees, her back against the headboard.

"What are you going to say to her when she wakes up?" Willow asks.

"I don't know yet."

She nods, folding her lips together tightly. I walk over to the bed and take a seat. She lays her head on her knees and stares at me. She looks so small right now, curled up into herself. So vulnerable.

Maybe it's why I chose to stay and help her, because she's never felt like a threat to me. Not in this house anyway. Even still, after knowing what I know, I can't bring myself to hate her. I can't even bring myself to regret any of this. I've enjoyed my time with her here, no matter who she used to be. I still feel drawn to her presence now.

I still want Willow here over Layla, and I realize that's fucked up, but I can't help how I feel, no matter how much I wish I didn't feel it.

"Should I stay awake while you sleep?" I ask her.

"I don't think you need to. It'll be better if you try to get some sleep too."

"What if she wakes up while I'm asleep?"

"I won't sleep, even if Layla does. If she wakes up, I'll let you know. I'll slip into her again if I need to, but only if I have to."

We both lie down and pull the blanket over us.

I want to wrap my arms around her because she looks scared. But there's too much between us now for that. No matter how much I still feel an irrational pull toward her, I can't kiss her like I did last night, knowing what I know now.

Willow doesn't even seem like she expects me to. She closes her eyes. "Good night, Leeds," she whispers.

＊

I wake up to a violent shake, like my entire body is being jostled around inside a dryer. I feel hands on my shoulders. Someone is pulling on my shirt. My eyes are so heavy I feel like I might have to use my fingers to pry them open.

"Leeds!" When she says my name, my eyes finally flick open. I immediately sit up on the bed. Layla has turned the lamp on and is standing next to me. She's pulling on my hand now. "Something is *wrong*," she whispers . . . her voice panicked.

She attempts to pull me out of bed, but I don't move. She finally releases my hand and goes to the dresser. She pulls out a pair of blue jeans and steps into them. "Something is wrong with me, Leeds. We need to leave. I don't want to be here."

I try to keep my voice steady when I say, "You had a bad dream, Layla. Come back to bed."

She looks at me like I've insulted her. She takes two quick steps forward and says, "I'm not *dreaming*!" She hisses the word *dreaming* in a feverish way, but then she looks away as if she's embarrassed by her own outburst. "I'm not dreaming," she mutters.

I get out of the bed and meet her near the dresser. "It's okay, Layla. I'm here." I try to hug her, but she pushes against me, jamming a finger into my chest.

"You *know* it's not okay! You were there earlier! You were trying to leave too!" She grips her forehead with one of her hands and spins in a circle, looking frantically around the room until her gaze is fixed on mine again. "What is happening? Am I going crazy?"

Guilt knots in my stomach because of the direction her thoughts are going, but I say nothing to disprove those thoughts. Maybe it's better if she assumes she's going crazy. The truth would be too hard for her to accept.

But is it right to let her think she's losing her sanity?

Layla stares at me for several very long, worrisome seconds, as if she knows I'm holding back. Distrust slips between us. It's just a flash—a second of darkness in her eyes—as if she's questioning whether or not I'm on her side. Before I can even answer that silent question, she darts for the bedroom door and runs toward the stairs.

She's trying to leave.

She can't leave.

I chase her. I pass her. I get to the front door before she does, and I press my back to it, stretching my arms out across it. "I can't let you leave like this. You're upset."

She shakes her head, small fast jerks, and her eyes brim with tears and fear. Then she rushes into the kitchen. I follow behind her and watch as she takes a knife out of the butcher block and spins around, waving it wildly at me. "Let. Me. Leave." Her voice is low and threatening, but it's also trembling.

"Put the knife down," I plead.

"I'll put it down when I'm in the car."

I shake my head. "I can't let you leave, Layla."

"You can't make me *stay*!" she screams. "*Why* are you trying to make me *stay*?" She covers her mouth with her hand to stifle a sob, but she keeps the knife up, pointed in my direction. "Something is happening to us, Leeds. You're going crazy. Or maybe it's me, I don't know, but it's this house and we need to get out. *Please.*"

I grip the back of my neck as I try to think of what to say. How to calm her down. I don't know what excuse I can use to get her to stay, but I don't want her to leave in such a hysterical state. And then it hits me. "The car won't start."

Her eyes narrow.

"I tried to start it earlier. It's dead. We can't leave until the battery I ordered gets here."

She points the knife at me like it's her index finger. "You're *lying*!"

"I'm not lying."

"Then let me try to start it." She begins to walk toward the exit to the kitchen, but I block it.

That's when it really hits her. Until this moment, she was just confused and a little bit scared, but she gets it now. She realizes I'm not entirely on her side.

I want to be on her side, but there's something preventing me from choosing. It's like my conscience is torn in half, or possibly even missing altogether.

She lunges forward, but the knife in her hand comes loose from her grip and flies across the kitchen. It hits the window and then falls to the floor with a clatter. She's staring at the knife, wide eyed. She looks at me, and then looks back down at the knife. I'm several feet from her, so she knows I didn't knock it out of her hand.

She screams.

As suddenly as her screaming begins, it stops.

Willow has taken over.

"You're going to have to lock her in the bedroom," she says.

I walk out of the kitchen because I need more room to think. I pace the foyer, my hands clasped together behind my head. "She'll try to climb out the window."

"Lock her in a different bedroom."

"They all have windows," I say.

"Is there a basement?"

"I can't do that to her. No one wants to be locked in a basement."

"No one wants to be locked up *any*where, Leeds."

I spin around and face Willow. "Can't you just stay inside of her until the man gets here?"

She shakes her head. "Her body is too exhausted at this point. I can't keep her awake, no matter how hard I try."

I'd rather Layla not be in and out of consciousness like this. It's driving her mad, but I'm not sure I can let her go at this point. She'd go straight to the police.

I'm in it now.

There's no going back.

"I'm going to have to tie her to the bed."

Willow nods. "Okay, but then what happens? When this is over? She's not going to just let you walk away from this. She thinks you're holding her against her will."

"I mean, I am. But I'll cross that bridge when I get to it."

"You can't take the fall for this. Tell her you tried to leave, but I wouldn't let you. Make her think you're a victim in this too. She needs to feel like someone is on her side."

"You want me to tell her about you?"

Willow nods. "Maybe not everything. You can give her just enough information to let her know this isn't your fault and that there's something bigger at play. Maybe that will calm her down toward you. I don't really care how she feels toward me, or this house. I just don't want her to blame you."

It might work. I can convince her it's out of our control, that there's some other force keeping us here. It won't calm her down by any means, because the idea of that will be hard to wrap her mind around, but in the end, she might not blame me. That's all I can hope for as a result. Not to end up spending the rest of this life in prison.

"We need to find rope."

CHAPTER TWENTY

I open my camera app, set my phone on the dresser, and point it at Willow. She's sitting calmly on the bed, her legs crossed, her back against the headboard. Her hands are tied to the bedpost near her head.

I hit record, and then I go sit on the bed next to her.

I squeeze her hand reassuringly because she looks nervous. Then I look into the camera of my phone. "Layla, I know this is confusing. I know it's scary. But I need you to listen to me." I blow out a breath. "There's someone in this house. Someone we can't see. It's bigger than me and you. She's stronger than me and you. And until I help her, we can't leave."

I look at Willow. "What's your name?"

"Willow," she says.

"Are you a danger to Layla?"

"No."

"Am I a danger to Layla?"

Willow shakes her head. "No."

"Am I holding Layla against her will?"

"No," she says. "But I am. Just for another day." Willow looks at the camera. "Then it'll be over, Layla. Please don't be upset with Leeds for this. It's out of his control."

"What will happen if Layla tries to escape?" I ask her.

She's still looking at the camera when she says, "You can't escape, Layla. It's better to just wait this out as calmly as you can."

With that, I walk over to my phone and stop the recording.

"She's going to be scared when she sees that," Willow says.

"She's already scared." I turn out the light, but the room isn't pitch black because the sun is probably about to rise. We've been up all night. I close the bedroom curtain. "Try to get some sleep. I'll deal with her when she wakes up."

Willow nods and then leans her head against her arms, which are dangling from the rope. "I'll try," she whispers.

⟳

She fell asleep about half an hour ago. I moved the security camera from the Grand Room into our bedroom. That way I can keep an eye on Layla if I need to go downstairs.

I've been sitting in a chair next to the bed since Willow fell asleep, but it's been a challenge just keeping my eyes open. I want to be by Layla's side when she wakes up. She's going to be scared. Terrified.

My eyelids are falling shut when my phone pings with a notification. I jerk in the chair and look over at Layla. It didn't wake her.

I have a new notification from the forum. I frantically move my fingers over the screen to unlock my phone, and then I click on the notification and read his message.

I'm on my way.

That's all his message says. He didn't even ask questions. I'm relieved, but I also have no idea what to expect. *Who* to expect. When to expect him.

I close my eyes and press my phone against my forehead, releasing a rush of air from what seem like concrete lungs. I feel the weight of all that's happened since I came into her life. Every ounce of it, as if every bad decision I've made were compressed into the shape of a cinder block, and that cinder block is pressing down on my chest.

Layla gasps before she screams.

The weight on my chest doubles when I see the panic set in.

Her eyes are flittering around the room wildly. Then she screams again when she sees she's tied to the bed. She rubs her wrists together in an attempt to slide out of the rope, but the rope doesn't budge.

I press a calming hand to the side of her head to try and get her to look at me, but she's in fight-or-flight mode now. She's digging her heels into the mattress, trying to get away from me, but she has nowhere to go.

"It's okay, it's okay," I say quietly. "Don't be scared."

She's taking in huge gasps of air like there isn't enough of it in the room. She's crying again. Every tear that falls down her cheek feels like a knife jamming into my heart.

I may not have the same feelings for her that I used to have, but I still love her. And despite what it might seem like right now, I don't want any harm to come to her.

There's such a morbid irony to this moment. Sable caused a lot of grief and pain to Layla's life. And now, in order to help Sable, Layla is suffering yet again.

It isn't worth it. No part of me should want or even care to help Sable, but to me, I'm not helping Sable. I'm helping Willow.

None of it makes sense, but it's like I'm not entirely in control of my choices. I can't be, or I wouldn't be making such a shitty one right now.

I crawl onto the bed with Layla and I hold her, because no matter how scared she is right now, I know there's still a part of her that needs to be comforted. Or maybe it's just me who needs to comfort her. Either way, I wrap my arms around her, and I hold her through her hysterics. I hold her until the screams and pleas and cries begin to exhaust her, and she's finally still long enough for me to speak to her without her interrupting me.

"I need to show you something. After I show it to you, you'll understand why you're tied to the bed."

She doesn't even look at me. She's still sobbing, but it's a desperate cry, as if I've lost my mind and there's nothing she can do about it. I open the video on my phone and put it in front of her. She jerks her eyes away in defiance.

I hit play on the video, and she doesn't look down at the screen. I make sure the volume is all the way up so she can hear my words through her tears. She's staring up at the ceiling, and she continues to do so until she hears herself speak.

When she hears her own voice utter the name *Willow*, her eyes fall to my screen. She witnesses a memory of herself she can't remember, and she watches in silent horror.

And then she screams. It's a scream like nothing I've ever heard.

The sound of it rips my heart in half.

CHAPTER
TWENTY-ONE

After I played the video, Layla was terrified and confused and became even more combative toward me. It's been a day and a half since I showed her the video, and she's still upstairs screaming. Her voice is hoarse now. She'll go through small bursts of hysterics, then she'll be angry, then she's too exhausted to feel anything at all. Every hour, she moves through the entire spectrum of emotions.

Willow took over her body long enough to make sure Layla was getting food, but we aren't sure when the man is going to show up. He indicated he was on his way, but from where? It's almost dark out now, and I've received no messages from him since the one he sent yesterday. Every minute that passes is another minute I feel terrible for torturing Layla the way that I am.

I walk upstairs to go keep her company. I've been sitting with her periodically, trying to reassure her. I feel like if she can see that I'm calm, then maybe it'll help her to not feel so afraid. When I showed her the video yesterday, she just kept saying, *"That's not me, that's not me, that's not me."*

I didn't want to put her through more agony, so I didn't force her to watch it again. It took me days to become open to the possibility of Willow. I can't expect Layla to accept it immediately, especially while being tied to a bed and held against her will.

When I open the door, she stops yelling. She keeps her eyes trained on me as I walk to the bed. She flinches as if I'm going to do something to her. I sit down in the chair next to the bed and brush the hair from her eyes. "I am *not* going to hurt you. I'm trying to help you."

Her eyes are swollen from the toll the crying has taken on her. "If that's true, then let's leave," she pleads.

"We will."

"When?"

"Willow doesn't want us to leave until I help her talk to a guy about her situation. I'm hoping he'll be here tonight."

"*Willow* wants to talk to him?"

I nod.

Layla laughs, but it's kind of a frightening sound considering the situation. "Willow," she whispers. "*Willow.* I called myself Willow in that video." She cuts her eyes to mine. "Did you drug me?"

"No. Willow is a spirit trapped in this house who sometimes uses your body to communicate."

"A *spirit*." She says it flatly, as if I've lost my mind.

"You saw the video, Layla. There's no other way to explain what you saw."

"I saw a video in which you drugged me and forced me to say things I don't remember saying."

I sigh and lean back in the chair. "I wouldn't do that to you." I say that, but at this point, I'm not sure it's something that's beyond my integrity. I'm not sure I even have a shred of integrity left, to be honest.

"If you let me go, I won't tell anyone," she says. "I promise. I won't go to the police. I just want to leave. I won't even use the car, I'll walk."

"I'm not going to keep you tied up forever. As soon as the man gets here and does what he needs to do, I'll let you go."

Her face hardens, and she looks away from me.

A light shines across the wall, pulling both of our attentions toward the bedroom window. The curtain is closed, so I walk to the window and push it aside.

There's a man climbing out of a white pickup truck. He's a large man . . . tall, not wide, with a bushy beard. There's a hat on his head—some sort of cap that seems to match the logo on his work truck. He tosses the cap into the pickup before running a hand through his hair and looking up at the house. He sees me in the window.

He nods once, then starts heading for the front door.

"Help!" Layla's voice is desperate and loud. *So loud.*

"Please be quiet." I rush over to the bed and cover her mouth with my hand. "The quieter you are, the faster he can help. I need you to promise me you'll be quiet."

She's still screaming against my hand. I look around the room for the tape I brought up with the rope yesterday. I didn't want to do this, but I'm going to have to. I can't have a conversation with this man downstairs while Layla is screaming her head off upstairs. I tear off two pieces of tape and cover her mouth with both pieces.

I hold her face gently in my hands. "I am *so* sorry, Layla." I kiss her on her forehead and then leave the room.

The doorbell rings just as I reach the bottom of the stairwell.

I open the door, not sure what I was expecting, but it certainly wasn't this guy. He's in his late thirties, early forties. He's wearing a Jiffy Lube shirt, and he smells like motor oil.

"Sorry about the smell," he says, waving at himself. "It's the only body I could find when I got into town."

It's the only . . . *what?*

He pushes the door open and squeezes between me and the door. He chuckles at the expression on my face. "You thought I was like you?"

He looks around the foyer and into the Grand Room. "Nice place. I can see the appeal."

I close the door and lock it. "You're like Willow?"

The man turns to me and nods, but then his attention is pulled to the top of the stairs. Layla is beating the headboard against the wall. There's no denying her muffled screams. We can hear them clearly, even from down here. "Who is that?"

"My girlfriend. Layla."

"Why is she making all that noise?"

"I had to tie her to the bed."

The man raises an eyebrow. "Is she gonna be an issue?"

I shake my head. "No. She's just upset with me, but I don't need you to help with her. I need you to help with Willow."

"Where is Willow?"

"She's here. Layla needs to rest, though. I don't want to use her yet, so I'll answer whatever questions I can until you need to ask Willow specific questions."

The man walks to the kitchen table and sets a briefcase down. He opens it and pulls out a tape recorder.

I wasn't aware everything I would be telling him would be recorded.

I have my girlfriend tied to a bed upstairs, and the only thing I know about this man is that his username is UncoverInc. Now he's about to record everything I'm about to admit to?

"How do I know I can trust you?" I ask him, eyeing the recorder.

The man glances up at me. "You don't have any other choice, do you?"

CHAPTER
TWENTY-TWO

I've caught him up with everything I can think of, all the way up to the second he sat down at this table. "So . . . that's where we are," I say. "What's your advice? How do we help Sable find closure?"

"You sound so sure that Sable has anything at all to do with this." The man turns his attention to Willow. "Have you ever taken over Leeds?"

"No," Willow says. "Only Layla."

"I think you should try it. I'd like to see how your memories compare while inside his head."

Willow looks at me with concern. She even looks somewhat uncomfortable with the idea of this. "I won't do it if you don't want me to."

"I'm fine with it." I *am* fine with it. I'm fine with anything he thinks might help us out of this situation. And to be honest, I've been curious what it's like. What Layla feels when it happens to her.

Willow stands up. "I won't be inside Layla if I move into Leeds. We'll need to tie her up again."

There's a nervous energy between us as we ascend the stairs to the bedroom, because we're about to do something we've never done before. Something we've never even thought to do.

Willow sits on the bed and looks up at me as I reach for the rope still tied around the bedpost. "Are you sure about this?"

"I have nothing to hide, Willow. It's fine. It might even help." I wrap the rope around her wrists and begin to tie them.

"How could it help?"

I shrug. "I don't know. But he's like you. He isn't like me. He knows more than both of us put together, so we just have to trust him. It's all we have left."

She inhales, and when she exhales, she leaves Layla's body.

Layla just slumps against the headboard. "Not *again*," she says, her voice full of defeat. "Why is this happening?" The expression on her face is an agonizing one. I force myself to look away.

"I don't know," I say quietly. "But I'm sorry it's happening." I walk to the door, and Layla is calling after me, but I can't stay to listen to her pleas. I lock the door behind me and head back downstairs.

"Where should I sit?" I ask the man.

He motions to the chair I've been sitting in this whole time. "Right there will be fine." He reaches out his hand. "Give me your phone. I'll record our interaction while she's inside of you and play it back for you when it's over."

I slide my phone to him, and he props it up using his briefcase. He points the camera at me and presses record. I suck in a nervous rush of air. I'm staring at the phone when I say, "I'm ready, Willow."

I only feel it for a second.

A whoosh, like a rush of wind moving through my head. It's as quick as the fluttering of an eyelid, but I know time has passed, because when I open my eyes, I'm still looking at my phone, but the minutes on the recording have changed. It went from just a few seconds to over three minutes. It's like being under anesthesia for a surgery. You're awake, and then you're awake again, with no memory of the in-between.

"Did it already happen?" I ask, looking at the man.

He's staring at me with narrowed eyes, as if he's working through a difficult equation. He reaches over and hits stop on the cell phone recording.

I bring my hands up to a point against my chin, overwhelmed by the simplicity of what just happened, but also overwhelmed by the magnitude of it. It was a strange sensation, but also not entirely unfamiliar. Someone might pass it off as a dizzy spell.

I think back to all the times Willow has done this to Layla. How terrifying it must have been for Layla to be in the middle of a bite of food, and then one blink later and her plate is suddenly empty.

One second she was upstairs; the next second she was outside.

I run my palms down my face, flooded with guilt for what this has done to Layla's mental stability. I knew this was affecting her, but now that I've put myself in her shoes, I feel even worse.

Not to mention, I still have her tied up like she means nothing to me. I can't believe I've been letting Willow do this to Layla.

"What did Willow say?" I ask him. "I want to watch the video."

He picks up my phone, but before he hands it to me, he says, "Do you have access to Layla's medical records?"

I have access because I've been to every appointment she's had since I've been with her, but I don't know why he'd need them. "Why?"

"I'd like to see them."

"Why?" I say again.

"Because I'd like to see them," he repeats.

This man has given me absolutely nothing tonight. Just question after question and not a single answer. I sigh, frustrated, and then pull my laptop in front of me. It takes me a couple of minutes to log in to Layla's medical records, and then I slide the laptop over to him. "You think you're ever going to give us an explanation, or is this one-sided interview going to go on all night?"

The man stares intently at the computer screen as he responds. "Go get Layla for Willow so I can show you both the video."

I gladly push back from the table. I walk up the stairs, wondering what the video is going to show. And why does he need Willow in Layla's body to play it back to me?

I think Willow needs to stay out of Layla from this point forward. There's not really a reason to take over anymore. We've told the man everything. Layla has been through enough.

Part of me wants to untie her and let her leave so she'll be put out of her misery, but the room is quiet when I open the door. Willow has already taken over Layla again.

It's probably for the best. I feel too guilty to face Layla right now.

"It isn't right—what we've been doing to Layla," I say. I untie the knots and loosen the rope.

Willow just nods in agreement. When I've released her hands, she wipes at her eyes, and I notice for the first time she's crying.

"What's wrong? What did you find out?"

"I don't know what any of it meant," she whispers, her voice catching in her throat.

Then she's off the bed and past me and out the bedroom door. She's walking with urgency in her steps. I rush down the stairs behind her, and when I get to the kitchen, she grabs my phone from the man. She shoves it into my hands like she doesn't want another second to pass without me seeing the video.

My hand is shaking, so I lay my phone on the table as the video begins to play.

I see myself on the screen, and right when I say, *"I'm ready, Willow,"* on camera, there's an instant change in me. My posture stiffens. My eyes open. I look down at my shirt and then hear the man's voice when he says, "Willow?"

242

My head nods up and down.

It's so strange . . . seeing myself do things I don't remember doing.

I turn the volume all the way up on my phone so I can hear the conversation he had with Willow while she was inside my head.

"What do you feel?" the man asks Willow.

"Worried."

"Don't be," the man says. "I just want to clear up a few things. I need you to try and see everything from Leeds's point of view right now. Can you see his thoughts? His memories?"

Willow nods.

"I want you to go back to the day Leeds and Layla were shot. Do you have that memory?"

"Yes."

"You can see that day from his point of view?"

"This feels wrong," Willow says. "I shouldn't be in him. It feels different. I only want to use Layla."

"Give it one more minute. I just have a few questions," the man says. "What did Leeds feel when he heard the gun?"

"He was . . . scared."

"And what did Sable feel?"

Willow doesn't speak through me for several seconds. She's silent. Then, "I don't know. I can't find that memory."

"Do you have another memory of that moment?"

"No. Just the memory Leeds has. I remember what happened before he heard the gunshot, but not during."

"What happened before?"

"He was in his bedroom with Layla, packing for a trip."

"What about after that? What's the next memory you have that doesn't belong to Leeds?"

"There isn't one after that. All these memories belong to Leeds."

"Okay," the man says. "Almost done. Let's back up. Go back to the night Leeds and Layla met here."

"Okay," Willow says. "I have that memory."

"What did Leeds feel the first time he looked at Layla?"

She blows out a steady breath. Then she laughs. "He thought I was a terrible dancer."

"Okay. Good. You can leave him now," the man says.

In the video, my eyes flick open and I'm staring directly at the camera again. Then the video ends.

I lock the screen on my phone and fall back into my seat. "You asked like three questions," I say, waving my hand toward my phone. "How did that even help?"

The man is still staring at my laptop. Willow is pacing the kitchen behind me, biting her fingernails again.

This entire thing seems pointless. I'm ready to call it quits and get Layla out of here when the man looks up at Willow and says, "Why did you say he thought you were a terrible dancer?"

She looks from him to me. "Because that's what he felt in that moment."

"But you didn't say *Layla* was a terrible dancer," he says. "You specifically said, 'He thought *I* was a terrible dancer.' You referred to yourself as Layla when you were in Leeds's head."

"Oh," she says, her voice a faint whisper. "I don't know. I can't explain that."

The man motions toward her chair. "Sit down."

Willow sits.

"According to Layla's medical records, they had to resuscitate her after she was shot. Once before paramedics got her into the ambulance. And again at the hospital."

"That's right," I say. "Like I told you, it was touch and go for an entire week."

"So she flatlined?"

I nod.

The man shoots me an inquisitive look. "You said Layla has been different since the attack. Memory loss, personality changes . . . can you think of anything else about her that's different now than from before the injury?"

"Everything," I say. "It affected her a lot."

"Are there things about Willow that remind you of Layla?"

I look at Willow, then look back at the man. "Of course. She's in Layla's body when we communicate, so there are lots of similarities."

He directs his attention toward Willow. "How did it feel taking over Leeds's body?"

"Strange," she says.

"Does it feel strange when you possess Layla's body?"

She nods. "Yes, but . . . in a different way."

"How are they different?" he asks.

"It's hard to explain," she says. "I didn't feel like I belonged in Leeds's body. It felt foreign. Hard to control. Hard to remain in his head."

"But you don't feel that way when you're in Layla's body?"

"No."

"You feel like it's easier to possess Layla's body?"

Willow nods. The man leans toward her. "Does it feel . . . *familiar*?"

Willow's eyes cut to mine for a brief moment; then she looks back at the man and nods. "Yes. That's a good way to describe it."

The man shakes his head with a look of complete disbelief on his face. "I've never seen anything like this before."

"Anything like what?" I ask. I'm confused by his line of questioning.

"Your situation is very unique."

"How so?"

"I knew it was possible, but I've never actually seen it myself."

I want to strangle the words out of him. "Can you please just tell us what's going on?"

He nods. "Yes. Yes, of course." It's the most expressive he's been tonight. He stands up and walks around to the side of the kitchen table, leaning against it, looking at both of us intently. "Death from bullet wounds is usually the result of excessive blood loss, so it probably took Sable several minutes to die after you shot her. And in that same time frame, Layla *also* flatlined. There were two souls in the same room that left two bodies at the same time. Which means when Layla's body was revived by paramedics, there's a strong possibility that the wrong soul entered that body."

I stare at him in disbelief. "Are you kidding me?" I ask. "That's the best you can come up with?"

"Bear with me," he says. He nudges his head toward Willow. "When Willow is inside of Layla, she can remember things from both Sable's and Layla's points of view. But when she was inside you, she could only remember things from yours and *Layla's* points of view. Sable's memories didn't move with her into your body." He pushes away from the table and begins pacing the kitchen. "The reason it's hard for your girlfriend to remember things isn't because of memory loss. It's because they aren't her memories. She has to search for them, and even then, she can only pull up a memory when it's prompted. The only logical explanation for this would be that the soul who has been walking around inside Layla's body since the night of the shooting is *not* Layla."

Logical? He thinks telling me that Layla isn't really Layla is a *logical* explanation?

It was a feat for me to come to terms with there being an afterlife. But this is beyond the capabilities of my imagination. *This is absurd.* Ridiculous. Unfathomable. "If Sable is Layla, then where is Layla?" I ask.

He points at Willow. "She's right there."

I look at Willow, too confused—or maybe too scared—to accept what this delusional man is trying to spoon-feed us. I rest my elbows on the table and press my palms against my forehead. I try to slow down my thoughts.

"What would make this possible?" I ask. "Why would Sable's soul choose Layla's body rather than her own?"

The man shrugs, and I'm not sure I like that shrug. I would much prefer him to be absolute in his responses. "Maybe it's not so much where her soul belonged in that moment, but where it *wished* it belonged. Sable obviously wanted what Layla had, or she wouldn't have done what she did. Perhaps what we desire can sometimes be so strong it overpowers our fate."

I press my palms against the sides of my head in an attempt to extract every ounce of rationality from the depths of my brain. I need every last drop if I want to be able to digest this absurdity.

This is a concept I can't immediately grasp, but if I've learned anything since coming here, it's that entertaining the unfathomable often leads to believing the unfathomable.

I press my palms onto the table and lean back in my chair. "If this is true, wouldn't Willow have memories when she isn't inside someone else's head? Willow doesn't remember anything at all."

"Memories fade quickly in the afterlife, especially when you don't have a body and a brain to attach them to. You just have feelings, but you can't connect them to anything. It's why they're called *lost* souls."

Willow says nothing during all of this. She just listens, which isn't hard to do because the man keeps talking, filling my head with way more information than I can keep up with.

"We call them spares," he says. "They're like souls who no longer have a body, but the soul isn't quite dead, so they aren't considered traditional ghosts. It's very rare that the circumstances are right for something like this to occur, but it's not unheard of. Two souls leave two bodies at once in the same room. Only one of the bodies is revived.

The wrong soul attaches to the revived body, and the right soul becomes stuck, with nowhere to go."

Willow places her palms on the table. She speaks for the first time with a curious tilt of her head. "If this is true . . . and I'm Layla . . . how and why did I end up stuck here in this house?"

"When a soul leaves a body, but refuses to move on, it usually ends up in a place that meant something to them during life. This place has no meaning to Sable. But it has a lot of meaning to you. That's why your soul came here after it was displaced, because it's the only place you knew Leeds might find you."

He thinks Layla's soul got *displaced*? It's such a simple term to explain something so monumental. But no matter how simple or monumental this may be, I've never wanted to believe something more, while also hoping to hell it's not true. "You're wrong," I say firmly. "I would have known if Layla wasn't Layla."

"You *did* know," the man says adamantly. "It's why you started falling out of love with Layla after her surgery. Because she wasn't the Layla you fell in love with when you met her."

I push back from the table. I walk across the kitchen, wanting to punch something. Throw something. I've been through enough already. I don't need someone showing up here and fucking with my head even more.

"This is ridiculous," I mutter. "What are the chances that souls could be switched?" I don't know if I'm asking Willow, the man, or myself.

"Stranger things have happened. You said yourself you didn't believe in ghosts before you returned here, but look at you now," the man says.

"Ghosts are one thing. But *this*? This is something you'd see in a movie."

"Leeds," Willow says. Her voice is calm. Quiet.

I spin around and look at her.

Really look at her.

Part of me wants to believe this guy because that would explain this inexplicable pull I feel toward Willow. Even when I thought she might be Sable.

It would also explain why Layla has seemed like a completely different person since the accident.

But if he's right, and Willow is Layla, that means . . .

I shake my head.

It would mean Layla is dead.

It would mean it's *Layla* who has been stuck in this house alone.

I grip the counter, my knees weak. I try to think of a way to disprove his theory. Or prove it. I don't even know which theory I want to be true at this point.

"I need more proof," I say to him.

The man motions toward my seat, so I walk across the kitchen and return to the table. I take a sip of water, my pulse pounding in my throat.

"Do you know the full extent of Layla's memory loss since the accident?" the man asks.

I try to think back to what she could remember, but I don't have a lot to go on. She doesn't like to talk about that night, and I avoid talking too much about the past because I don't like to remind her of her loss of memory. I shake my head. "No. I've never quizzed her about it because I feel bad. But there have been things I've noticed that she forgot. Like on the flight here when I mentioned the name of the bed and breakfast, it was like she had no memory of it until I reminded her."

"If Sable's soul took over Layla's body, she would have difficulty accessing Layla's memories right away, because they aren't hers. They're there—in her brain—but they wouldn't be so easy to get to when her spirit didn't actually experience those memories."

Willow speaks up. "But wouldn't Layla know she was Sable? Sable's memories are also there, in her head. When she woke up from surgery, she would have known she was in the wrong body, right?"

"Not necessarily," he says. "Like you said, when you were in her head, her memories were confusing. That could be because when a person dies, they don't normally take their entire identities with them."

I'm watching Willow as she takes in what he's saying. She looks just as confused and as skeptical as I feel.

"There's a possibility that when she woke up from surgery, she might have felt displaced. Confused. Even looking in the mirror might be confusing for her, because maybe she doesn't feel attached to the reflection looking back at her. All of this confusion, which was blamed on amnesia, is probably what's been fueling her anxiety and panic attacks." The man taps his fingers on the table in thought for a moment. I stare at his fingers, waiting for him to offer up more proof. He pauses his hand and locks eyes with Willow. "If you are Layla, you would have memories of the two of you that Sable wouldn't be able to access right away." He turns to me this time. "Are there other memories you've noticed Layla struggle with besides the name of this bed and breakfast?"

I think back on everything that could be a clue. Things that have been missing from Layla's memory over the last six months that I blamed on her memory loss. I pull up recent things that are fresh in my mind.

I turn and look at Willow. "What's the deadliest time of day?"

"Eleven in the morning," Willow says instantly.

I stiffen at that answer.

Last week when I brought that up, Layla acted like she had no idea what I was talking about. But Willow also could have heard that conversation in the kitchen, so it doesn't really help prove much.

"Fuck." I squeeze my eyes shut, trying to think of something else that seemed to have escaped Layla's memory recently. Something Willow wouldn't have heard.

I think about a conversation that happened in the Grand Room last week. I mentioned a book I had been reading, but Layla had no idea what I was talking about. Then I changed the subject and never mentioned the title of the book, so Willow shouldn't know it. "What . . . what book was I reading the night I was supposed to leave for—"

Willow cuts me off. "*Confessions of a Dangerous Mind.* It was about a game show host who claimed he was an assassin." Layla couldn't remember either of those things last week. "You told me you read e-books because paperbacks take up too much space in your luggage."

I immediately turn and look at Willow after she says that.

All the pieces of the puzzle feel like they're beginning to lock into place, and I don't know if I want to fall to the floor in agony or wrap my arms around her. But before I do either . . . I have one more question.

"If you're Layla . . . you would know this." My voice is fearful. Hopeful. "What was your first impression of me?"

She blows out a shaky breath. "You looked like you were dying inside."

I can't move. This is too much. "Holy shit."

She leans forward and grips her forehead. "Leeds. All these memories of you and Layla meeting here. The kiss in the pool, the song you played for her . . . is that *me*? Are these *my* memories?"

I can't say anything. I just watch her as she grapples with the same realization I'm grappling with.

I think back on the last several months of my life, and how I felt like so much changed in Layla. It's like she became a different person after that surgery.

She did.

She was a completely different person. Her entire personality changed; the way I felt about her changed. And now that I'm looking back on it, there are even similarities between the Layla who woke up from the surgery and the Sable I dated. Sable had bulimia. Layla became obsessed with her weight after surgery. Sable was obsessed with social media, and . . . me. Layla became obsessed with building my platform. Sable suffered from a number of mental illnesses, and the more days that passed after Layla's surgery, it seemed like *Layla* was starting to suffer from those same mental illnesses. And the day we arrived here, I knew it was Layla who punched that mirror. I didn't understand why she'd do it, but I *knew* she did it.

When Layla woke up from that surgery, she was not the same girl I fell in love with.

But all the things I loved about Layla in those first couple of months of knowing her are the exact same ones I started to notice in Willow. Her personality, her mood, her playfulness, the familiarity in the way she kissed, her strange and random facts. I used to tell Layla she was like a morbid version of Wikipedia.

That's also one of the things I recognized and liked about Willow.

That triggers another memory that should have been an obvious clue.

"On the bed, upstairs," I say to Willow. "The night you were watching *Ghost*. I said, *'You are so strange.'* But I also said that to you when I first met you. Because . . . I was fascinated by you and enamored with you, and then when I met Willow, she felt so familiar, and . . ."

I can't finish my sentence because it feels like the cinder block that has been weighing down on my chest has just lifted.

I no longer feel like I'm falling out of love with Layla, because I've been falling in love with her this whole time in Willow.

Layla is Willow, and now that I'm looking at her, I have no idea how I didn't see it before tonight.

I take her face in my hands. "It *is* you. This whole time I've been falling back in love with *you*. The same girl I fell in love with the moment I saw you dancing like an idiot on the grass in the backyard."

She laughs at the memory—a memory she owns. A memory we share together. A memory that doesn't belong to Sable.

A tear rolls down her cheek, and I wipe it away and pull her to me. She wraps her arms around me. I had no idea how much I missed her until this very second. But I've missed her so much. I missed what we shared in the first two months we were together. I've missed her since the night she was shot.

I've had this constant hollow feeling inside me since that night, and for so long I've felt guilty for feeling that way. For feeling like I lost her when she was still right in front of me. I even felt guilty for the way Willow reminded me of her.

That guilt is gone now. I feel justified. Every choice I made . . . every feeling Willow filled me with . . . it was all justified, because my soul was already in love with hers. It's why I felt an inexplicable pull to this place. To Willow. Even when I thought Willow was Sable, I still felt that pull, and it confused me.

It all makes sense now.

I press my lips to hers and I kiss her. I kiss *Layla*. As soon as she kisses me back, I feel everything I used to feel when I would kiss her. Everything I thought I'd lost. It's right here. It's been here all along.

I keep touching her face between kisses, amazed to finally see it. It's why there was such a huge difference every time Willow would take over Layla. It's why Willow seemed more comfortable and confident in Layla's body. It's because it was hers all along. It never belonged to Sable. Sable has seemed uncomfortable in it since the day she woke up from surgery.

Willow is smiling through her tears when she says, "This explains why I was so relieved when you showed up here, Leeds. It was because I missed you, even though I couldn't remember you." She kisses me again, and I never want to let go of her.

But something tears us apart anyway. The sound of the front door slamming shut.

I look over my shoulder, and the man is no longer standing in the kitchen.

We both rush out of the kitchen and to the front door.

"Wait!" I say, running after him. He's climbing into his truck by the time I reach him. "Where are you going?"

"You don't really need me anymore. You found your answer."

I shake my head. "No. No, we didn't. You have to fix it now. Sable is still in the wrong body. Layla is still stuck in nothing." I wave my hand toward Layla. "Switch them out."

The man looks at me pityingly. "I find answers, but that doesn't always mean there are solutions."

I try to remain calm, but I want to strangle him for that response. "Are you kidding me? What are we supposed to do? There has to be a way to fix this!"

He starts the truck and closes his door. He rolls down the window and leans out of it. "Only one soul can lay claim to a body. Sure, Layla is able to slip into her old body, but it's only temporary. Like a possession. You'll never be able to get Sable out of Layla's body. Not until she dies, at least. But when that happens, they'll both be dead." He starts to roll up his window, but I frantically beat on the glass. He rolls it halfway down. "Look. I'm sorry this happened to you guys. I really am. But I'm afraid you'll just have to figure out a way to live like this until the three of you move on for good."

I take a step back. "*That's* your advice? To leave Sable tied to a bed for the rest of our lives?"

He shrugs. "Well, Sable kind of brought it on herself, if you ask me." He puts the truck in reverse. "Maybe you should let Sable leave, and you can stay here with Layla's spirit."

I'm so angry at that advice I kick the door of his truck, leaving a dent. I kick it again. I want to scream.

The man rolls his window all the way down and leans over the door. He sees the dent. "Now, don't do that to Randall's truck. He'll be confused enough when he wakes up at work and can't remember what happened to half his night." He puts his cap back on and slowly begins to back out of the driveway. "A human dies every second, and they don't always die the right way. I have a lot more people to help." He raises a hand in the air. "I'll keep in touch online. Sure would like to see how you two work this one out."

He turns his truck around in the driveway.

We watch him in silence until he's gone. Until it's just the two of us.

He really was just here to give us answers. Nothing more and nothing less.

I'm full of a frustration that can't be settled, but at the same time, I feel like I've been given clarity. It's like the strand of hair that's been strangling my heart finally broke loose and it's beating that out-of-control, irregular beat again that only Layla's presence can create.

A plink and a BOOM.

"Layla?" I whisper.

"Yeah?"

I turn to her. "Nothing. I just wanted to say your name." I pull her to me. I hold Layla for several minutes as we stand in silence in the front yard. I'm not holding Sable or Willow or a false version of Layla.

I hold *Layla*.

I may not have a solution. I don't know how I'm going to keep her in my arms forever, but for right now, I have her. And I'm making damn sure she never spends another night alone in this house again.

CHAPTER TWENTY-THREE

The mood in the house has shifted drastically in the last hour. We spent the first ten minutes kissing, hugging, reveling in the knowledge that our love somehow transcended realms.

We now have answers as to why Layla's soul ended up here. But those answers are accompanied by a million more questions and a lot of unexpected grief.

I don't even know how to properly mourn the idea that Layla essentially died . . . because she's here with me. But she isn't.

It feels like she's been returned to me, but in a horrific way. I feel further away from her than I've ever been, even though we're standing in the bedroom and I'm holding her in my arms.

I feel helpless.

Her face is pressed against my chest, and we have no idea what to do next. I don't want to come face to face with Sable, and if Layla goes to sleep, that will happen. I'm too angry to do that right now.

"Do you think Sable knows?" Layla asks, pulling back to look up at me.

I shake my head. "No. I think she's probably just as confused as you are. She has these memories that she can't explain. That don't belong inside the head she lives in."

"That has to be scary for her," Layla says. "Waking up in the hospital with conflicting memories. Recognizing Aspen and my mother but not quite being able to place them, then being told they're her family."

I grip Layla's cheeks with both hands. "Do not feel sorry for her," I say. "She did this. None of this would have happened to either of you if she hadn't shown up to my house with intentions of hurting us."

Layla nods. "Are you going to tell her what happened? That she's Sable?"

"Probably. She deserves an explanation as to why she's been tied up."

"When are you telling her?"

I shrug. "I feel like the sooner we let her know, the faster we can hopefully come up with a solution."

"What if she demands to leave?"

"She will. I have no doubt about that."

"Are you going to let her leave?"

I shake my head. "No."

Layla's eyebrows draw apart in worry. "We can't keep her here against her will. If someone finds out, you could get in legal trouble."

"She's not leaving here in your body. It's yours."

"Tell that to the police," Layla says.

"No one has to know. But she is not leaving here until we figure out how to fix this."

Layla grips the back of her neck and pulls away from me. "You heard that man. He said there's no way to fix this."

"He also said this is rare. Maybe it doesn't happen enough for anyone to have figured out a solution yet. We'll be patient. We'll do our research. We'll figure this out, Layla."

I wrap my arms around her again, hoping to ease her nerves. But that's hard to do when I know she can feel my rapid heartbeat against her chest.

I'm just as worried as she is. If not more.

"I think you should tell her now," Layla says. "Maybe if she realizes what she's done, she'll stop fighting you. Maybe she'll help us figure this out."

Layla has always seen the best in people.

The problem with that is I'm not sure there's enough good in Sable that would make her want to help us. She is, after all, the reason we're here right now.

"Okay," I say. "But I have to tie you up first."

Layla crawls onto the bed. After I tie her up, she says, "I know you're angry at her right now. But don't be mean to her."

I nod, but it isn't a promise.

Angry is an understatement.

Layla closes her eyes and takes a breath. When her eyes open and I can tell it's not Layla looking back at me, I feel nothing but resentment. I don't feel remorse when she starts to quietly cry. I don't feel guilt when she starts to plead with me to untie her. I sit on the edge of the bed next to her feet, and I just stare at her.

At least she's not hysterical or screaming this time. We might actually be able to have a conversation about this.

"Are you going to let me leave now?" she asks.

"I want to ask you some questions first."

"And then you'll let me go?"

"Yes."

She nods. "Okay, but . . . can you please untie me first? I'm sore. I've been in this position for hours."

She's been tied up for one minute. She doesn't realize she walks around freely most of the time. "I'll untie you after you answer my questions."

She adjusts herself on the bed so that she's sitting a little farther away from me. She pulls her knees in and looks at me nervously. "You look angry," she says quietly. "Why are you angry?"

"What do you remember about the night you were shot?"

"I don't like talking about that. You know that."

"Why? Because you don't remember it like I do?"

She shakes her head. "No. It's because I don't remember it at all."

"That's not entirely true," I say. "I think you just remember it in a way that's confusing to you."

She shakes her head. "I don't want to talk about it."

I continue to speak, despite her pleas for me to stop. "I know what's going on inside your head. You say you have amnesia, but I'm not so sure you do. It's just harder for you to access Layla's memories because they're mixed in with other memories. It's why . . . sometimes . . . when I bring up something from the past, you don't have that memory right away. It's like you have to sift through them. Dig them up."

I can see her breath catch.

I lean forward and look her directly in the eye. "Do you sometimes feel like you have too many memories? Memories that don't even belong to you?"

Her bottom lip begins to tremble slightly. She's scared, but she's trying to hide it.

"Do you remember opening the door when Sable knocked on it that night?"

She nods. "Yes."

"But you also remember being the person who *knocked* on the door."

Her eyes widen. "Why would you say that?" she says immediately.

"Because . . . you're Sable."

She stares at me for several long seconds. "Are you crazy?"

"Your memories are confusing because you're in the wrong body."

Her stare becomes threatening. "You better let me go right now, or I will have you arrested so fast, Leeds. I will. Don't think I'm going to forgive you for this."

"Have you known this whole time that you might be Sable?"

"Fuck you," she hisses. "Let me go."

"Why did you punch the bathroom mirror when we got here? Do you see Sable's face sometimes when you look in the mirror?"

"Of *course* I see her face sometimes! She *shot* me, Leeds! I have PTSD!"

She didn't deny punching the mirror. "You don't have PTSD. It's an actual memory."

"You sound like a lunatic."

I keep my voice steady when I say, "You shot me. And you shot Layla. And I know you remember doing it."

She shakes her head. "I shot *Layla*? I AM Layla!"

I shake my head. "I know it's confusing. But you aren't Layla. You're only able to access some of her memories, because you're inside Layla's head and you have access to them. But when I shot you, you died. And when you shot Layla, *she* died. But only for a few seconds. Long enough for your soul to end up in the wrong body. And Layla's soul ended up stuck here, in this house."

She's crying now. "You're scaring me." Her voice is timid. "You aren't making any sense. I *am* Layla. How could you possibly think I'm not Layla?"

I would begin to list all the proof, but there's too much. Instead, I try to think of a question only Layla would be able to answer right away. One Layla has already answered, but that Sable would struggle to remember.

"What song did I sing to you the first night we met here?"

She says, "I . . . that was a long time ago."

"Which song did I sing for you? You have three seconds to answer me."

"'Remember Me'?" She says the name of the song like it's a question.

"No. I sang 'I Stopped.' Layla remembers."

"Stop talking about me like I'm not Layla. This is *insane.*" She's crawled more toward the head of the bed, like she's trying to get away from me.

I don't blame her for being scared of me. If someone had tried to explain this to me a month ago, I wouldn't have been able to believe it. I attempt to come off as levelheaded as I can because I know she thinks the opposite of me right now. "I can't expect you to accept this any easier than I did, but it's true. It's just going to take time, and maybe proof, before you fully comprehend what's happening. For that, I'm sorry, but I can't let you leave now. Not until I figure out how to fix this for Layla."

"But I *am* Layla," she whispers, still trying to convince herself that this isn't happening.

I look behind me. "Layla, take over."

I wait a few seconds until I see the change.

Layla opens her eyes. She relaxes her legs, but her expression doesn't relax. She looks like she's about to cry, and I don't know if it's because there isn't a doubt left in her as to whether she's Layla, or if she feels bad for the situation Sable is in now.

I lean forward and untie her hands. When her wrists are free, she lunges forward and wraps her arms tightly around me. She starts to cry.

It becomes real in this moment. Knowing that Sable struggles to access memories I made with Layla—memories that are front and center in Layla's mind—has eliminated any shred of doubt that still hung between us.

Layla grips the back of my head and presses her cheek against mine. Her voice is full of fear. "Please help me find a way back."

I close my eyes. "I won't stop fighting for you until we figure this out. I promise."

CHAPTER
TWENTY-FOUR

I'm washing Layla's hair in the shower. It's an eerie duplication of the morning after we met, standing together in this shower. Only this time we're quiet. I'm not asking her questions because I feel like my need for answers has brought us nothing but gloom. It makes me wonder if she regrets me having shown up here. Had I not shown up, she wouldn't be aware of just how much she doesn't belong in her realm. She wouldn't know how unfair it is.

She wouldn't know she might not be able to get back.

We didn't sleep at all last night. We spent hours searching for solutions online and skimming paranormal books in the Grand Room. We've found nothing so far, even though we searched until two hours after the sun rose.

Today is a new day. After we get some much-needed sleep, we'll start it all over again. I refuse to allow Layla to feel hopeless about this situation.

When I'm finished rinsing her hair, I press a kiss against the top of her head. She relaxes into me with a sigh, her back to my chest, and we just let the hot water beat down on us as we stand together in silence. It's not romantic. It's not sexy.

We're just sad.

"Her body is exhausted," Layla says.

"It's not her body. It's yours."

She turns around and looks up at me. Her eyes are hollow and tired. She needs to sleep, but now that she knows she belongs more in this body than she does in the spiritual realm, she doesn't like the idea of going back to nothing. She told me earlier that it scares her now.

That gutted me.

I don't want her to let Sable take over again, but it's inevitable. It's the only way her body can recuperate.

"Take two sleeping pills," I say. "Maybe she won't wake up for a while."

Layla nods.

We get out of the shower, and I grab two pills for her. Layla takes them with a sip of water and then climbs into the bed. I close the blackout curtains to shut out the sun. I crawl in bed with her, but this time I don't hesitate to pull her against me. It finally feels normal again—having her in this bed with me.

As normal as our situation can feel.

I keep expecting to wake up from this nightmare. I don't like thinking back on the last several months, and all the signs that were right in front of me. It makes me feel ignorant—like my closed-mindedness hindered us in some way. I never believed in ghosts or spirits, but if I did, would I have noticed Layla wasn't actually Layla?

Are there other people in this world who—like Sable—assume they're suffering from some form of amnesia that makes memories hard to sift through, when in reality, they just don't belong in the body they're inhabiting? They're merely a spirit trapped in the wrong body.

"Leeds." Layla whispers my name, but even through her whisper, I can feel the weight of it.

"What is it?"

She tucks her head against my shoulder. "I think there's only one way to fix this."

"How?"

She sucks in a heavy breath. And then, as she exhales, she says, "You're going to have to kill me. And then hope to hell that you can bring me right back." I squeeze my eyes shut, trying to push her words away from me. I don't even want to hear them, but she continues talking. "If I can flatline long enough for Sable's soul to leave my body, then maybe my soul could take back over before you bring me back."

"Stop," I say immediately. "It's too risky. So much could go wrong."

"We can't live like this forever."

"But we can."

She pulls away from my shoulder and looks up at me. Her eyes are full of tears. "It's exhausting. I can't live like this, day after day. And do you really want to hold a girl captive upstairs in this house for the rest of your life?"

I don't. It's agonizing, but it's better than the thought of Layla possibly dying. "This isn't the solution."

"And living this way *is*? She won't sleep unless we drug her, and then I'm left with the side effects. I'm tired. *You're* tired. If this is the only way I can exist with you . . . then I'd rather not exist at all," she says. She's crying now, and I can't take it. I don't want to see her upset, but the selfish part of me would rather see her upset than not see her at all.

"If we did it and it went wrong, I would never forgive myself. I can't live without you, Layla."

"You can. You have for the past seven months."

I look at her pointedly. "And I've been fucking miserable."

She stares at me solemnly. Then, as if she somehow feels sympathy for me, she places her hand on my cheek and kisses me. Her kiss is sweet, but it's also desolate. I don't know what to do with it.

It's torture, kissing her through her pain, because I know what's going on in her mind right now. She thinks death is the answer.

I'm afraid death will be the end.

"I don't want to talk about this anymore," I say.

"We're going to have to do something about this. And soon, while I still have the energy."

"I'm not going to agree to it."

Layla's fingers trail down my arm until she finds my hand. She slips her fingers through mine. "It can work, Leeds. If we plan it out just right, it'll work."

"How can you be so sure?"

"Because," she says. She presses a kiss against my jaw. "I love you more than Sable does. I'll *make* it work."

I want to believe her. But what happens if it doesn't work? What if I can't bring her back? If her body dies for good, her spirit will likely die right along with it.

And then what would I do? How would I explain her death to the police? To her family? To Aspen?

Layla reaches up a hand to smooth out my furrowed brow. "Relax," she says. "We can worry about the details after we wake up."

I nod, wanting nothing more than to put these thoughts away. I just want to think about Layla.

I trace my fingers delicately over her lips, and she's gazing up at me with the same expression she was looking at me with when we were lying in the grass the first night we met. Right before I asked her why she was so pretty.

I trail my fingers over the freckles spilled over the bridge of her nose. "Why are you so pretty?" I whisper.

That memory makes her smile.

This is what I've been missing. These moments with Layla. The unspoken memories we share together . . . the looks we give each other. We had an immediate connection the night we met. A connection so strong it brought me back here to her when I didn't even know I was searching for her. A connection that *kept* me here, even when I was convinced Willow was Sable.

Layla kisses me again, only this time our kiss doesn't stop. It lasts for so long my lips feel swollen by the time I push into her.

She wraps herself tightly around me as we make love. I keep my eyes open the whole time because I'm amazed by how different it is now that I have her back. It's exactly like it used to be. Intense and perfect and full of meaning.

When it's over and she's wrapped in my arms, I realize she might be right.

We found each other once—when we met.

Then we found each other again—after she died.

That makes me believe in us enough to think we could do it a third time.

CHAPTER TWENTY-FIVE

Layla has spent the last two days meticulously planning out her death.

I've spent the last two days trying to find alternative solutions.

Sadly, I've found nothing.

She's growing weaker. The longer she continues to take over Sable, the less sleep Sable gets. And when Layla does leave her body long enough for Sable to sleep, Sable sleeps very little. Only when the meds kick in, and even then, not for long.

Sable continues to try to escape, which has resulted in her wrists suffering even more damage. The marks are too prominent to hide. I keep them bandaged up, but I worry because Aspen and Chad are due to show back up today and we aren't sure how to hide Layla's wrists from them. Right now, she's wearing one of my long-sleeved shirts because there wasn't anything with sleeves long enough to cover her wrists in her wardrobe.

Hopefully Aspen doesn't notice the bandages.

Hopefully Aspen doesn't notice *anything*.

Layla's legs are across my lap, and we're mindlessly watching TV when we hear their car pull into the drive. We're not actually paying attention to the TV. We're just attempting to appear normal, which we'll be attempting to do for the next twenty-four hours while Aspen and Chad are here.

Layla stands up and pulls the sleeves of her shirt down. She tucks them beneath her thumbs and heads toward the door. I follow her.

Aspen is already peeking her head inside when we make it to the foyer. I open the door all the way and take Aspen's bag. Layla hugs her as soon as she walks through the door.

The hug catches me off guard. It isn't a casual greeting. She hugs her tightly, like she's missed her. I guess she has. Layla was confused the last time Aspen was here. She thought all her feelings belonged to someone else, so she probably didn't acknowledge that the pull she felt toward Aspen was real.

"Well, hello," Aspen says, laughing at Layla's affection. Layla releases her, and Aspen tilts her head, looking at her curiously. "You look exhausted."

Layla shrugs it off. "I've been sick for a few days. Feel much better now, though," she lies, smiling brightly.

Chad nods his head toward me and grabs Aspen's bag. "Please tell me you have beer. I've been driving twelve hours, and I need beer." He walks toward the stairs to take their bags up to their usual bedroom, but Layla stretches her arm out, ushering Chad toward the hallway instead.

"Y'all get the downstairs bedroom this time," Layla says. "The upstairs bathroom is broken."

She's lying, and I'm not sure why, but I help Chad take their things to the downstairs bedroom. Then the four of us congregate in the kitchen as Chad searches for something to drink.

"What's for dinner?" he asks. "It smells good."

Layla and I threw a casserole together about an hour ago. In the wake of everything happening, it was a nice reprieve. We've had a few moments over the last couple of days that I've somehow managed to enjoy, despite our circumstances. It's hard not to let the reality of our situation remain front and center in our minds, but in the few times we've been preoccupied with something else, it was a welcome reminder of how things used to be between us. Before Sable.

"There's a casserole in the oven," Layla says. "It's almost ready." She looks at Aspen. "How was the trip to Colorado?"

Aspen smiles, but it's obviously forced. She and Chad exchange a look. "Interesting," Aspen says. "Two flat tires, one broken taillight, six hours wasted while we were stuck in a ditch."

"Those six hours were not wasted," Chad says to her, raising an eyebrow.

Aspen grins, and that's enough of that conversation.

⁓

"She seems different."

I spin around at the sound of Aspen's voice. I thought I was alone in the kitchen.

"What do you mean?" I ask cautiously.

"Better," she says. "It's like I finally have my sister back. Good call bringing her here. I think it's helped her."

I blow out a subtle release of air. "Yeah. Yeah, she's definitely much better."

"She looks tired, though. And she's lost weight."

I nod. "I'm keeping an eye on her. Like she said, she had the flu last week."

"The flu?" Aspen asks with a tilt of her head. "She just told me it was food poisoning."

Shit.

Layla and I need to make sure our lies align in the future.

I nod once. "Yeah. That too. Shitty week." I grab my cell phone and Aspen follows me as I head outside, where Layla and Chad are.

Layla is seated at the patio table, next to a heating lamp I turned on after dinner. Chad is sitting at the edge of the pool with his feet in the water. I heated the pool yesterday when we realized they were coming.

I walk over to Layla and press a kiss to the top of her head before sitting down next to her. She grabs my hand and smiles at me.

We spend the next half hour pretending our worlds are right side up. We laugh at Aspen's and Chad's jokes. We force ourselves to appear relaxed. We even make plans to go on a road trip with them in two months.

A road trip we know can't happen if we don't figure out a way to solve this.

It hits me as I'm sitting here—why Layla is willing to risk her life in order to get her life back.

It's because she doesn't have a life at all while she's stuck in this house at Sable's mercy.

We can't risk leaving this place when Layla is merely a temporary possessor of her own body. And what would life be like for Layla if I forced her to remain in our current setup? She'd be a visitor to this world . . . at Sable's mercy. We'll never be able to leave. We won't even be able to take the trip we just planned to take with Aspen and Chad in two months.

This is it. This will be her life. Exhausted and imprisoned.

I'm pulled out of my own thoughts when Layla laughs loudly.

I catch myself staring too hard at her every now and then, but I'm fascinated watching her just be herself, even if she is forcing it. But there are moments—a split second here and there—when I forget this isn't our normal.

But it's not our normal. Hanging out with her sister can never be normal. It'll have to be meticulously planned. She'll never get to leave this place with Aspen.

Even their visits here can never be normal. When Chad and Aspen go to bed tonight, Layla is either going to have to figure out how to stay awake all night in order to prevent Sable from taking back over, or I'm going to have to figure out how to keep Sable quiet if she wakes up while Chad and Aspen are still in this house.

Maybe that's why Layla put Chad and Aspen in the downstairs bedroom. That way, if Sable were to take over momentarily while they're here, they might not hear any commotion from Sable before Layla can slip back into her.

"Layla told me you put in an offer on this place?" Aspen asks, looking at me. I must have been tuned out of their conversation, because I'm not sure what led to this question.

I nod. "Yeah, last week. Should be closing soon."

"I hope you know we're going to be here all the time. Wichita isn't that far away, and I miss this place." She looks at Layla. "I even miss you," she says teasingly.

Layla smiles and reaches out, squeezing Aspen's hand. "You have no idea how much I've missed you too. I can't wait for everything to go back to normal." Her words are sweet, but Aspen has no idea how much double meaning lies behind them.

Layla's back is to the pool, so she doesn't notice when Chad gets out of the water and makes his way to the deep end. He backs up until he's about ten feet from the pool. Then he takes off his shirt and starts sprinting toward the water. He jumps, wrapping his arms around his knees, and yells right before he makes a huge splash.

Layla's whole body jerks from the unexpected commotion behind her.

Almost immediately, I see the change. It's like I can tell the exact moment when Layla slips out of her body now.

I freeze when I recognize Sable has taken over. The unexpected splash in the pool must have startled Layla, like the night the lightning scared her.

Sable's eyes widen, and she looks over her shoulder, sitting straight up in her chair. She stands up suddenly, knocking her chair backward. "What the . . . ?" She looks down at her arms, then up at the house. "How did I get outside?"

I stand up immediately and try to slip between her and Aspen, but Sable takes a quick step back. "Don't you dare come near me!" she screams at me.

Shit.

Aspen stands now. "Layla? What's wrong?"

Sable continues to back away from me. She points at me while looking frantically at Aspen. "He's drugging me! He won't let me leave!" I shake my head, ready to defend myself, but before I can open my mouth, Sable pulls one of her shirtsleeves up, revealing the bandage on one of her wrists. "He keeps me tied up!"

I lunge toward her to stop her, but before I reach her, her arm falls to her side and her eyes close. I stand in front of her, gripping her shoulders, trying to shield her from Aspen's view. Layla inhales a slow breath, and then she calmly opens her eyes. I see the fear pool in her face.

"What is wrong?" Aspen says, her voice louder and full of panic. "What do you mean he's drugging you?" Aspen pushes herself between me and Layla, breaking us apart.

Aspen is holding Layla's face in her hands, trying to get her to look at her and not me.

I grip the sides of my head and take a step back. I have no idea how she's going to explain this slipup.

Layla's eyes are wide, as if she's struggling to figure out a way out of this. I have no idea what to say. Aspen looks over her shoulder and glares at me as if I'm a monster.

"Just . . . kidding?" Layla says, completely unconvincing.

"Wh . . . *what*?" Aspen says.

Chad is sloshing over to us now, his jeans leaving puddles of water behind him. "What's going on?"

Aspen points at Layla. "She . . . she just said Leeds is drugging her. And keeping her tied up."

"I was kidding," Layla says, looking back and forth between them, attempting to explain away the outburst. She's forcing a smile, but everything is so tense now.

"That's a weird thing to joke about," Chad says.

"I don't think it's a joke," Aspen says. "Show me your wrist again."

Layla tucks her sleeve beneath her thumb and pulls her hand away. "It was an inside joke," she says. She looks at me. "Tell her, Leeds."

I don't know what to tell her. At this point, there's no way Aspen will believe a word that comes out of my mouth. But I nod anyway and move closer to Layla as I wrap a hand around her waist. "She's right. It's a weird inside joke. It's only funny to us."

Aspen stares at Layla in disbelief. Then she brings her hands to her forehead as if she doesn't know what to make of the last minute of her life. She shakes her head, confused. Unconvinced. "Come inside the house with me, Layla," she says, reaching a hand out to her sister.

Layla just stares at it. Then she shakes her head. "Aspen, I know that was weird. I'm sorry. I do things I can't explain sometimes . . . because of the brain injury. I thought it would be a funny joke. It fell flat."

Aspen studies her sister's face . . . looking for a sign. A silent plea for help, maybe. "This is seriously fucked up," she says. Then she pushes past us and heads to the house.

Chad watches Aspen disappear into the house. Then he downs the rest of his beer. He wipes his mouth with the back of his hand. "You guys are strange," he says, right before he follows after Aspen.

It's just Layla and me outside now.

Layla covers her face with her hands. "I can't believe that just happened."

I pull her in for a hug. "They'll get over it."

Layla shakes her head adamantly. "Aspen won't. I saw the look on her face. She doesn't trust you now." She presses her face against my chest. "We can't keep doing this, Leeds. I want it to stop."

I nod, but only because I want her to relax. I'll momentarily agree with anything if it puts her mind at ease.

"Tonight. I want to do it tonight."

I shake my head. "Please, no."

"We're doing it tonight." Her voice is resolute. Her words final.

I feel like I've sunk to the bottom of the pool. My lungs feel dense with water. I clear my throat. "How are we supposed to do this tonight? Your sister is here."

As if she's been thinking about it the whole time, she answers immediately. "I think drowning would be the easiest way. We'd have to time it perfectly. You'd have to be sure my heart stops before you start to resuscitate me."

I separate myself from her and begin to pace the concrete surrounding the pool. "I don't know that I feel comfortable with that. I don't even know how to do CPR."

"Aspen is a nurse."

"Aspen won't go along with this," I say.

Layla closes any space between us and lowers her voice. "She doesn't have to. We'll play it off like it isn't planned. Like it's an accident. As soon as my heart stops beating, you'll yell for her. I made sure one of their bedroom windows is open, so she'll hear you. And if she doesn't, just run to the window and wake her up."

That's why she put them downstairs. "You already had this planned out?"

Layla's eyes are firm. "Don't judge me. You have no idea what it's like for me."

There's a world of pain in her expression like I've never seen. I don't even know how to argue against that pain.

She's right. I don't know what it's like for her. I won't even pretend to know. All I can do at this point is love her enough to attempt to find trust in her instincts.

"What if I can't bring you back right away? What happens if the ambulance takes your body away before you're able to slip back into it?"

"Don't let them. Make sure Aspen brings me back."

"How do you know Aspen will know what to do?"

"She's a nurse. She saves lives every day."

I don't like this. "What if it works and we bring your body back? How do we know Sable won't come back instead of you?"

"I won't let her, Leeds." Layla says that with such conviction I can't help but trust her. I pull her to me and rest my chin on top of her head. For the first time since finding out ghosts are real . . . I'm terrified.

"I love you."

Her words are muffled against my chest when she says, "I love you too. So much. That's how I know this is going to work."

CHAPTER
TWENTY-SIX

It's been two hours since we came upstairs to prepare for Layla's drowning.

Two hours since it started to feel like my world might be coming to an end.

She has everything planned out. She even wrote down instructions and is making me study them like this is some kind of fucking college exit exam.

1. Hold me under until I'm no longer struggling for air.
2. Check my pulse. When it stops, call 911 immediately.
3. Wake up Aspen.
4. Start resuscitation.
5. You only have five minutes to save my life.

I let the paper fall to the bed. *Five minutes.* I can't read it again.

"Do you need more time to look it over?" she asks me.

"I'm going to need years before I'm ready to do this."

She lifts a hand and touches the side of my head. "I know you're scared. I'm scared too. But the longer we let this go on, the weaker I'm going to be. We need to do it now before we have more slipups. Before Aspen becomes even more suspicious." She grabs the sheet of paper and folds it up. Then she walks to the bathroom and flushes it in the toilet. On her way back into the bedroom, she grabs my laptop and sets it on her side of the bed. She clears her throat and then says, "I typed up a suicide note. I think it's important to have, just in case."

I cover my face with my hand. "A suicide note?" I can't keep my voice down. "How are you so calm about this? You just wrote a *suicide* note, Layla."

"I don't want you to take the fall if this doesn't work. I scheduled it to send as an email for four hours from now. You know the login to my email. If I don't make it . . . allow the email to send. But if I do make it . . . delete it. Because it's going to everyone, Leeds. You, Aspen, my mother . . ." Her voice is even—mechanical, almost—as if she's completely detached from the reality of what we're about to do.

She grabs my hand, wanting me to stand up. Wanting me to follow her.

The next several minutes feel surreal. I follow her out of the bedroom, down the stairs, and to the backyard.

She walks calmly into the pool, and so much of this moment is wrapped in the night we met. The first time we spoke was in this pool. Our first kiss was in this pool.

Why does it feel like our final goodbye might happen in the pool?

My pulse is frantic. I can't catch a breath. The reality of what we're about to do may not be absorbing into her, but it has taken over every part of me.

She's standing in the middle of the pool, in the same spot where I found her floating on her back that first night we met. And by some miracle, she has the same expression on her face. Serene. "I need you in the water with me, Leeds." I realize she's remaining as calm as she is because she knows if she doesn't, I'll talk her out of this. I'll talk *myself* out of this.

But she's right. We need to do it now, before she becomes even weaker from lack of sleep.

I'm reluctant as I make my way toward the pool. The water is warm when I step into it, and it hits me that she had me turn on the pool heater yesterday—not so we could swim but for this very purpose.

We keep our eyes locked together as I make my way to her.

When I meet her in the middle, I have to close my eyes, because I finally see a trace of fear in her expression. She snakes her arms around my waist and presses her face against my chest. "I know you don't want this, Leeds. But I want my life back. I need it back." Her voice is shaking. "Every time I have to leave my own body, it's like a brand-new heartbreak."

I kiss her on top of her head, but I say nothing. I couldn't speak if I wanted to. The fear is too thick in my throat.

"Listen to me," she says, guiding my gaze to hers. "I'm going to have to let Sable take over. It'll be better if she's scared and confused when her heart stops. Because I'll be alert and ready."

She's right. Layla will have the advantage if she's waiting by the sidelines.

"As soon as I slip out of her in a minute, Sable is going to panic when she wakes up and sees that she's in this pool with you. That's when you do it. You shove her under, and you hold her down and you don't let her up for air, no matter how scared you are or how guilty you feel."

I imagine what that will be like for Sable. Being drowned with no knowledge of why. She's going to be terrified. She's going to fight back. And I'm somehow going to have to look past the fact that it'll be Layla's body I'm drowning as I kill Sable for a second time.

"Hey," Layla says, her voice sympathetic and gentle. She's looking at me like she knows exactly what I'm thinking. She always does. She understands my thoughts as if they're whispered into her head as soon as I have them. "You won't be ending Sable's life, Leeds. You'll be saving mine. You can do this."

That's the perspective I needed to move forward. This is about what's deserved. It isn't about what's moral. "Okay. You're right. I can do this. *We* can do this."

"Good. Okay." She sucks in a rush of air, but it's a fragile intake, marred by fear. "Are you ready?"

I shake my head adamantly because who could be ready for something like this? I take her face in my hands, and we lock eyes. She's scared. Her lips are quivering. When her hands rest against my chest, I can feel her fingers trembling.

I owe this to her. She's been forced to spend so much time here alone, waiting for someone she couldn't remember. I press my forehead to hers, and we close our eyes. When I'm this close to her, I can feel an unfrayed connection not even death could break. We're bound together for eternity, and if I don't get this right—if I lose her—that tether will feel like a noose tightening around my heart until it stops.

I kiss her. I kiss her hard, and I don't want to stop, because what if this is the last time I ever get to kiss her?

I kiss her until I taste tears. Both of ours.

I kiss her until she makes me stop.

She presses her forehead against my chest, and I can feel the sadness in her sigh. "I love you," she says.

I wrap my arms tightly around her and press my cheek against the top of her head. "I love *you*, Layla."

"Thank you for finding me," she whispers.

And then she's gone.

It's no longer Layla I'm holding, but Sable. I can feel the change in the way she jerks against me and then lifts her head from my chest, wide eyed.

I have my hand over her mouth before she can even scream.

And maybe it's the part of me that resents her that finds strength, or maybe it's the part of me that wants Layla back more than I want air, but I do it. I shove her under. In order to hold her there, I have to use every part of me. I cage her body between my legs. I wrap my fingers in her hair for leverage.

She thrashes in the water . . . claws at my arms and my chest. She tries everything to escape—to take in a breath, but she's screaming just under the surface, her lungs swiftly taking in water.

I stare up at the sky because if I look down at her, I'll stop. I wouldn't be able to look at Layla's face and continue to do what I'm doing. And even though I know it's Sable behind Layla's eyes right now, if I looked into them, I'm afraid all I would see is a terrified Layla. I squeeze my eyes shut and tighten my hold.

I wait and I wait and I wait for her to stop struggling. It feels like it'll never end. I count as I hold her under. I get all the way to one hundred and eighteen seconds before she finally stops fighting.

And even then, when I think it might be over, she claws at me again, her fingers seeking out a savior.

She grips my left wrist, and she squeezes it with very little strength.

Then . . . I feel nothing.

The underwater screams have ceased for several seconds. Her hair begins to slip through my fingers. I keep my eyes closed and hold my breath until I'm certain there isn't any air left in her lungs. Then I slowly drop my gaze.

Her hair is covering her face, so I brush it out of the way. Her eyes are open, but they aren't looking up at me. They aren't looking at anything. There's no focus to them. No *life*.

That's when I start to panic.

I pull her up until her head is out of the water, and it's obvious Sable is no longer inside this body. But neither is Layla.

A wail escapes my throat when I see Layla's lifeless eyes. Her arms are limp at her sides. I hook my hands under her and start dragging her toward the steps at the shallow end.

"Aspen!" I scream. "Help!"

It's almost impossible to move her as fast as I imagined I would move her. The backs of her legs are dragging against the pool steps, then the concrete. When I finally have Layla on her back at the side of the pool, I grab for my cell phone. I dial 911.

"Aspen!" I scream. I start administering CPR the exact way Layla showed me how to do it, but I feel like I'm doing everything wrong.

The phone is by my side. When an operator picks up, I just start screaming the address into the phone while I try to resuscitate Layla.

Five minutes.

That's all we have.

"Five minutes," I whisper. Her lips are blue. Nothing about her feels alive. I need Aspen because I don't know if I'm doing this right.

But I don't want to leave Layla's side.

"Aspen!" I scream again.

Before I'm even finished saying her name, Aspen is on her knees next to me. "Move!" she yells, pushing me out of her way. I fall backward and watch as Aspen leans Layla onto her side to clear her airway; then she pushes her onto her back again and begins chest compressions.

Chad is here too. He grabs my cell phone and begins speaking with the 911 operator. I move around Aspen, toward Layla's head, and I lean forward, cradling her head.

"You can do it, Layla," I beg her. "Please, come back. Please. I can't do this without you. Come back, come back, come back."

She doesn't. She's just as lifeless as when I was dragging her out of the pool.

I'm crying. Aspen is crying.

But Aspen doesn't stop trying to save her. She does everything she can. I try to help, but I'm useless.

It feels like it's been longer than five minutes.

It feels like it's been a fucking eternity.

I once had the thought that minutes seemed to matter more when I spent them with Layla, but they've never mattered more than right now as we're trying to save her life.

Aspen is growing more hysterical, which makes me think she knows it's too late. Too much time has passed. Did I hold her under for too long?

Did I do this?

I feel like I'm sinking lower . . . somehow melting into the concrete. I'm on my knees and my elbows, my hands clasped tightly behind my head, and I have never physically been in so much pain.

Why did I let her talk me into this? We could have found a way to live like this. I'd rather live a miserable existence with her than not exist with her at all.

"Layla." I whisper her name. Can she hear me? If she's not in her body right now, is she still here? Is she watching this? Is she watching me?

I hear a gurgling sound.

Aspen immediately turns Layla's head to the side again. I watch as water spills out of Layla's mouth and onto the concrete.

"Layla!" I scream her name. "Layla!"

But her eyes don't open. She's still unresponsive.

"They're eight minutes away," Chad says, lowering the phone.

"That's not soon enough," Aspen mutters. She resumes the chest compressions. And once again, Layla begins to choke.

"Layla, come back, come back," I plead.

Aspen grabs her wrist to check for a pulse. It's like all the sounds of the world are automatically put on mute while I wait for her response.

"She has a pulse. Barely."

"You only have five minutes to save my life."

I immediately slip my hands under Layla's arms and start to pull her up.

"What are you doing?" Aspen asks, her voice panicked.

"We need to meet the ambulance!" I yell. "Let's go!"

Chad helps me carry Layla to the front yard. We slip her into the back seat of my car, and Aspen and Chad both climb into the back with her. Aspen keeps her hand on Layla's wrist to make sure she maintains a pulse as I peel out of the driveway.

"Faster," Aspen says.

I can't go any faster. The gas pedal is touching the floor.

I drive for what seems like miles, but in actuality is probably only two, before we meet the ambulance. As soon as I see their lights coming over the hill, I start flashing mine. I bring the car to a stop in the middle of the highway so the ambulance will be forced to stop for us.

I help Chad and Aspen drag Layla out of the back seat. She's still lifeless.

The paramedics meet us with a gurney. They pull her onto the ambulance, but when I start to climb in after her, Aspen grabs me and pulls me back. She pushes her way in front of me and climbs into the ambulance. When my eyes meet hers, she's looking at me like I'm a monster. "Stay the fuck away from my sister."

The doors close.

The ambulance speeds away.

I drop to my knees.

CHAPTER TWENTY-SEVEN

It's been thirty-eight minutes since I pulled her out of the water.

I'm pacing the waiting room.

Chad is several feet away on his phone, probably trying to call Aspen. We haven't seen her since we walked into the emergency room. Chad had to pull me out of the road and drive the car here. I was too upset.

No one is able to tell us anything.

Thirty-*nine* minutes pass.

Forty.

Chad hangs up the phone. I rush over to him, hoping he got word from Aspen. He just shakes his head. "She's not answering. I think she left her phone at the house."

I nod and resume pacing. I'm watching my feet move over the floor, but it feels like I'm floating. Like I'm not actually moving. This all feels like a dream.

A nightmare.

"What was she doing in the pool?"

I spin around at the sound of Aspen's voice. She's standing behind me now, her eyes narrowed at me. Her cheeks are mottled and tearstained.

"Is she okay?" I ask her.

Aspen shakes her head, and my heart feels like it melts and leaks down into my rib cage. "I don't know anything. They won't let me in the room," she says. "Why was she in the water, Leeds?" Her eyes are accusing.

Chad walks up to her and wraps his arm around her shoulders. He tries to usher her to a chair, but she shakes him off and turns her attention back to me. "Why the *fuck* was she in the *water*, Leeds?"

Her scream gets the attention of everyone in the room. She's hysterical. Angry. She thinks I did this to her sister.

"I don't know," I lie. "But I did not do this to her."

Aspen's eyes fall, and when they do, they freeze on my arms. She just stares at my arms, and the way she's looking at them forces me to follow her focus. When I look down at myself, I see that my arms are covered in scratch marks. Fingernail scrapes that have drawn blood. *Fresh* blood.

I look back up at Aspen just as she starts to cry hysterically. Chad is forced to hold her up. He carries her to a chair, but the whole time he's backing her away from me, she's screaming at me. "Why? Why did you do this to my sister?"

There's nothing I can say or do to take that assumption away from Aspen. Too much has happened tonight to make her believe I'm innocent.

And if Layla doesn't make it . . . neither do I. Because no one will ever accept the truth. If this were last month—I wouldn't have believed the truth either.

But the idea that Aspen will never trust me again, even if Layla makes it, is still not an outcome I'm okay with.

Chad is doing his best to calm Aspen, but she's hysterical. I walk over to them and kneel in front of her. "Aspen," I say, my voice firm and low. "She had a seizure in the water. I was trying to help her, but I couldn't do it on my own. I couldn't keep her above water. That's when I called you. I didn't do this to her."

She doesn't believe me. I can see the distrust in her eyes.

"Why did Layla say you were keeping her tied up earlier?" Aspen asks. "Why would she say that?"

I open my mouth in an attempt to explain, but I have no answer. I clamp it shut and my jaw hardens.

"Leeds?"

The voice comes from behind me.

I stand up and spin around at the same time Aspen jumps up out of the chair. A doctor is standing at the entrance to the waiting room. "Leeds Gabriel?" he says.

I can't help but feel relief that this man is sparing me from an explanation I wasn't able to give Aspen, but I'm terrified he's here to deliver news I'm not prepared for. I step forward. "Is she okay?"

The doctor pushes open the door behind him. "She's asking for you."

I don't know how I have the strength to even take a step, because those words knock the breath out of me. But somehow, I make it across the floor, to the door, down the hallway, and into a room where Layla is on a bed, covered in a blanket, her hair still wet and piled over her shoulder.

I pause when I enter the room, because I don't know exactly what I'm walking into. It's hard to tell just by looking at her.

Is she Layla?

Aspen pushes past me and rushes to her bedside. Aspen is crying. Hugging her.

But Layla isn't looking at Aspen. She's looking straight at me.

There's no emotion on her face. No way to tell if I'm staring at Layla right now or if I'm staring at Sable. I want to believe it's Layla, because I *feel* like it's Layla. I'm just too scared to trust my instinct right now.

I need her to say something.

"Layla?" My voice is a whisper. A question.

A single tear falls out of her eye and rolls down her cheek. She nods . . . barely. "Leeds," she says. "Do you know what you look like right now?"

I shake my head.

Her mouth curls into a smile. "You look like you're dying inside."

That statement becomes the only proof I need. I rush to her, slipping between Aspen and the bed. I lower the rail and I crawl into bed with her and I hold her while she clings to me. I kiss her over and over, all over her face, her hands, the top of her head. She's crying, but she's also laughing.

"We did it," she says.

I sigh, pressing my cheek to hers. "We did it, Layla." I wipe tears from her cheeks.

"Say that again. Say my name again."

"Layla," I whisper. "Layla, Layla, Layla."

She kisses me.

Layla kisses me.

Layla.

EPILOGUE

Layla and I came out of this experience knowing one thing for certain, and that is the simple fact that we now know *nothing* for certain.

This life and whatever comes after it are more than we can comprehend, so we don't even try. All we can do is appreciate that we figured out how to get a second chance together. And with that second chance, we're doing everything we can to make sure we don't need a third.

We don't know if Sable moved on to another realm or if her spirit is now stuck somewhere that could be tied to a memory of me, so Layla and I decided the best course of action would be to start over. Completely.

We never went back to the bed and breakfast in Lebanon, Kansas. We never even went back to our temporary apartment in Tennessee. When Layla was released from the hospital, we drove straight to the airport and asked where the next available flight was heading.

That's how we ended up here in Montana.

Neither of us has ever been here before, and that gives us a sense of comfort. We stayed in a hotel for a few weeks until we closed on a house. We made sure we purchased a new construction. We figured it would be better if there was no history tied to the home we bought. There would be less chance of us encountering an entity that isn't of this realm.

The house is probably more than we need, but as soon as Layla laid eyes on it for the first time, I could tell by the way she gasped that this would be our home. The house sits on ten acres of rolling hills with unobstructed views of the Beartooth Mountains from our backyard.

It's a unique and modern home, unlike any other house in the area. So much so the house feels a little out of place in the midst of all the nature surrounding us. I think we were drawn to it because it's reminiscent of how Layla and I feel in the world now. It's like we don't quite fit in because we're living with this huge secret we can't share with anyone.

How would we even begin to tell someone what happened to us? People would think we're crazy. Layla doesn't even feel she can explain her experience to Aspen. She's afraid it would make Aspen believe Layla's head injury is worse than we initially thought.

It's going to take time to win Aspen over. She doesn't trust me after everything that happened, and now that I've whisked Layla away to a secluded home in Montana, it's only heightened Aspen's concern for her sister. I'll win Aspen's favor back eventually. I'm confident of that. Layla is my soul mate in every realm of life.

Layla and I have spent the last few days getting settled into our home. Because we didn't bring anything with us, this move mainly consisted of shopping for furniture and everything else the house needed that we didn't have.

We're both exhausted. As soon as the sun began to set earlier, we collapsed into a new patio chair together and have been sitting here quietly for the last half hour, listening to music playing through the Alexa device.

Layla is tucked against my side with her arm draped over my stomach and her head against my shoulder. My hand is in her hair, twisting its way through her curls, when one of the songs I wrote begins to play.

This must be a playlist of Layla's.

She immediately perks up and flashes a smile. "My favorite," she says. And she means it. She listens to my songs so often I'm starting to get sick of my own voice.

Layla slides out of the chair and begins swaying flirtatiously to the music. She spins around, lifting her arms in the air as she dances in front of me. "Alexa," she says. "Volume max."

The song gets louder, and Layla closes her eyes and continues dancing. She's out of sync and not at all graceful.

She's still a terrible dancer. It was the first thing I noticed about her . . . and it's the absolute last thing I would ever want to change.

ACKNOWLEDGMENTS

I had so much fun exploring a genre I've never dabbled in before, even though I spooked myself a few times. Thanks to those of you who gave it a chance, especially if paranormal isn't your thing. It was a huge stretch of the imagination for me, but that's what I love about writing.

A huge thank-you to my agent, Jane Dystel, and everyone at Dystel, Goderich & Bourret literary agency. You all work hard to get my books in the hands of readers, and I appreciate each of you so much.

Thank you to the entire team at Montlake Publishing. You all have been a dream to work with, and I look forward to many more books to come.

I'd also like to thank the entire Goodreads staff. We authors are so lucky to have a platform dedicated to books and you guys have always been so responsive and pleasant to work with.

Thank you to my early readers, Tasara Richardson, Maria Blalock, Melinda Knight, Anjanette Guerrero, Vannoy Fite, Lin Reynolds, Brooke Howard, Karen Lawson, and Susan Rossman. You always get the worst versions yet somehow still ask for those versions. I appreciate all you do for these books.

To Stephanie and Erica, my two main gals. Without you both, I'd not be living my dream. We have the best job ever.

Thank you to everyone who works or volunteers for the Bookworm Box and Book Bonanza. I am so grateful for all you do to make these charities a success.

A HUGE thank-you to every member of CoHorts, and the wonderful admins, Pamela Carrion, Chelle Lagoski Northcutt, Kristin Phillips, Laurie Darter, Murphy Rae, and Stephanie Cohen.

Thank you to my wonderful family. My mother, my husband, my sisters, my boys.

But most of all, thank you to you, the reader, for reading this book. This year has proven to be a challenging one for the world, so thank you for continuing to turn to art for comfort.